Take
the Honey
and Run

Also available by Jennie Marts

Page Turners

What to Do About Wednesday
A Halloween Hookup
A Cowboy for Christmas
Tangled Up in Tuesday
Just Another Maniac Monday
Easy Like Sunday Mourning
Another Saturday Night and I Ain't Got No Body

Hearts of Montana

Stolen Away
Hidden Away
Tucked Away

Bannister Brothers

Skirting the Ice
Worth the Shot
Icing on the Date

Cotton Creek

Catching the Cowgirl
Hooked on Love
Romancing the Ranger

Cowboys of Creedence

Wish Upon a Cowboy
It Started with a Cowboy
You Had Me at Cowboy
Caught Up in a Cowboy

Creedence Horse Rescue

Every Bit a Cowboy
Never Enough Cowboy
How to Cowboy
When a Cowboy Loves a Woman
A Cowboy State of Mind

Hallmark Publishing

Cowboy Ever After
Rescuing Harmony Ranch

Take the Honey and Run

A BEE KEEPING MYSTERY

Jennie Marts

CROOKED
LANE

NEW YORK

Published in the United States by Crooked Lane Books, an imprint of The Quick Brown Fox & Company LLC.

Crooked Lane Books and its logo are trademarks of The Quick Brown Fox & Company LLC.

Library of Congress Catalog-in-Publication data available upon request.

ISBN (hardcover): 978-1-63910-307-2
ISBN (ebook): 978-1-63910-311-9

Cover design by Ben Perini

Printed in the United States.

www.crookedlanebooks.com

Crooked Lane Books
34 West 27th St., 10th Floor
New York, NY 10001

First Edition: July 2023

10 9 8 7 6 5 4 3 2 1

This book is dedicated to

My mom, Lee

For inspiring my love of reading,
writing, and a great mystery

Thanks for everything, Mom

As a successful mystery author, Bailey Briggs writes about murder, but nothing prepares her for actually discovering the dead body of the founder of her hometown of Humble Hills, Colorado—especially when her eccentric bee-keeping grandmother's hot spiced honey turns out to "bee" the murder weapon and her granny is now the prime suspect.

Chapter One

The speedometer ticked up another notch, matching Bailey Briggs's pulse as she and her daughter drove down the two-lane highway heading toward her hometown of Humble Hills, Colorado. Cooper, their golden retriever, leaned forward and gave her ear a quick lick, as if he could sense the tension in her shoulders. She let out her breath, but the closer they got to Honeybuzz Mountain Ranch, the place where she'd grown up, the more the memories washed over her, most of them good, but a few cut through her heart like a warm knife slicing butter.

"Geez, Mom, what's the rush?" Daisy, her twelve-year-old daughter, asked. "You don't usually speed like this."

"I know, but it's two fifty-five, and you know how Granny Bee is about being late for high tea at three."

"Yes." Daisy rolled her eyes, a regrettable new habit Bailey had been noticing in her normally easygoing daughter. "I know how she is, but I don't understand why it's such a big deal."

"I don't either, but it's important to her. Ever since she declared herself the queen bee of Honeybuzz Mountain, she's insisted on a high tea every Friday at three, like we're some kind of royalty."

"I didn't realize Colorado had declared a monarchy."

"Oh, honey, haven't you realized by now, in our world, it only matters what Granny Bee declares, and this is one of her sacred decrees."

Daisy shrugged. "And if we're late, what will she do? Chop off our heads? Send us to the gallows?"

"Worse, she'll put the *sting*-eye on me. You think Italian grandmas who use the stink-eye are bad, bee-keeping grannies who use the sting-eye are worse."

Daisy smiled as she shook her head. "She's not that bad. Besides, it's been two years since we've been back to the ranch. I think she'll just be glad to see us. Even if we are a few minutes late."

Bailey slowed to a crawl as they pulled up behind an old green tractor putzing its way down the blacktop. She let out a frustrated growl as she gestured to the cowboy leaning casually back in the seat. "We could make it if this guy would get out of the way."

"Oh no," Daisy said, smacking a hand to her forehead. "I can't believe a *tractor* is the thing standing in our way. You already have *tractor trauma*. Just the mention of one usually gets that weird vein pulsing in the side of your forehead."

"I do not have *tractor trauma*. Or a weird vein in my fore-head." She rubbed at a spot above her eyebrow. "And it's not like the stupid things come up that often in our conversations."

"Oh no." Daisy threw in another eye roll. "You've only told me a *gazillion* times about the night when you were a senior in high school and you and your boyfriend stole a tractor and acci-dentally drove it into a pond."

Bailey frowned. "I don't think I've mentioned it a *gazillion* times."

"Then how do I know the whole story about Sawyer Dunn, the bad-boy cowboy and love of your life, who took the fall for the tractor incident and got sent away to his uncle's in Montana, never to be heard from again?"

Bailey lifted one shoulder in a shrug. "That's a bit of an abbreviated version of the story." Although her daughter had actually summed the facts up pretty well. If she were honest, thoughts of Sawyer had been creeping into her mind ever since they'd hit the county line. So, *of course*, a tractor would be thing impeding them making it to Granny Bee's on time.

She glanced at the speedometer before leaning sideways to see around the tractor. "Why is he going so slow? We're not even going five miles an hour." Not seeing another vehicle coming from the opposite direction, she eased the car into the other lane to pass the puttering cowboy.

She'd barely stepped on the gas when he turned to look at her, and her breath caught in her throat. The driver was about her age and wore jeans, a faded blue T-shirt, and a straw cowboy hat. He had on a pair of dark aviator sunglasses—*who wears aviators with a cowboy hat anyway?*—but even behind the dark shades, Bailey would recognize him anywhere.

His sandy blond hair had darkened to a chestnut brown, but he still had the same broad shoulders, the same square jaw that appeared to be chiseled from the marble of the gods.

No, it couldn't be. She was just imagining it was him because he'd been on her mind.

Her throat tightened as her focus returned to the road. She slowed to get back in behind him, but not before Cooper caught sight of the two Black Angus cows plodding down the blacktop in front of the tractor and let out a round of excited barks.

The dog's barking must have spooked one of the cows, because it bucked up, then charged across the road.

"Mom! Watch out!"

Bailey jerked the wheel to avoid the cow now heading straight toward her car. The overcorrection combined with the loose gravel on the road sent the car skidding toward the opposite side. She wrenched the wheel back again, but it was too late.

The tires hit the soft shoulder and then, as if in slow motion, the whole right side of the car slid into the ditch.

Bailey shot her arm out in front of her daughter's chest, the universal mom version of an extra seat belt. "You okay, honey?" she asked her daughter, ignoring the jolt of pain in her chest where she'd smashed into her own seat belt.

"I'm fine," Daisy said, twisting in her seat to check on Cooper. "You okay, boy?"

The dog tried to scramble over the console, pushing between the seats to alternately lick Daisy's chin, then Bailey's cheek. The car was leaning to the side, but thankfully they hadn't been going fast enough or hit the ditch hard enough to deploy the airbags. She ruffled the dog's ears then pressed a hand to her chest. "Oh my gosh. I'm so sorry. I didn't even see those cows in the road."

"It's okay, Mom," Daisy assured her. "It could have been way worse. We could have hit one."

The man driving the tractor pulled to the side and cut the engine before hopping off and hurrying toward them. He yanked the driver's door open. "You all okay?"

Bailey couldn't breathe, couldn't speak. But her paralysis had nothing to do with the accident and everything to do with the cowboy currently leaning into her car—so close she could smell the laundry detergent on his shirt and the woodsy scent of his aftershave, a scent she knew as well as her own. "S-Sawyer?" she finally managed to sputter. "What are you doing here? I can't believe it."

He had her wrist in his hand as if feeling for her pulse. "Did either of you hit your head? Anything feel broken?" he asked, his tone serious as his gaze raked over both of them, which was a pretty impressive feat considering he was also letting the dog lick slobbery kisses across his cheek.

"We're okay," Bailey said, blinking as if he were a mirage and might disappear any second. "Except I might have just had a heart attack from the shock of seeing you. Or maybe I passed out and you're not actually real." She tentatively stretched her hand out and touched his cheek. He felt real, the scruff of his whiskers tickling the pads of her fingertips.

He reached up and squeezed her hand in his, just for a moment before letting it go. "I can assure you, Bailey, that I am very real. And so is that cow you almost took out."

Cow? What cow? She couldn't seem to focus on anything other than the crystal blue color of his eyes and the lingering warmth of his touch.

"*Sawyer?*" Daisy asked, squinting at the man. "This guy is Sawyer Dunn? The hot bad-boy cowboy you stole a tractor with?" She peered around Bailey's shoulder. "Is that the tractor?"

Sawyer raised an eyebrow as his gaze returned to Bailey's, and one side of his lips tugged up in a grin. "*Bad boy?* I haven't been called that in a long time."

Bailey shook her head. That roguish grin of his had her considering all sorts of things. And none of them were things she should be thinking about while her daughter was sitting next to her in a car halfway buried in a ditch. "What are you doing here?" she asked him again.

"Before you almost ran me off the highway, I was herding these cows back to your grandma's ranch. I recognized her brand when I found them on the road by a downed tree that had taken out a section of her fence. I repaired the fence and figured I'd just drive these guys back to Granny Bee's. Easier than her sending someone out to get them."

"*You* fixed the fence?"

"Sure, I've got my own ranch now. I spend the majority of my days fixing things." His eyes narrowed in a smoldering gaze that had her breath catching in her chest. "And you know I've always been good with my hands."

Oh yeah, she remembered. Oh crud, here came a few more of those dang considerations again. She swallowed, pushing away the wanton thoughts as she tried to get her brain back on track. "I just didn't know your skills included barbed wire and fixin' fence."

"I know a lot more than I used to. People do change, you know." He offered Daisy a reassuring smile. "My bad-boy days are long behind me. I'm a regular Boy Scout now."

Bailey let out a laugh, accompanied by a snort, earning her a sideways glance from both her daughter and the dog. "I'm sure you are, Sawyer."

He held out his hand. "Let's get you all out of there. I'll give you a ride to Honeybuzz. Your car's not going anywhere for the moment, and Granny Bee's probably already fuming that you're late for high tea."

The bank was just steep enough to make it awkward to climb out of the car. Sawyer leaned in and curled an arm around her waist, hauling her out as the dog jumped over the seat and clambered across her. This was certainly not the way she'd imagined seeing Sawyer Dunn again—and she had imagined a million scenarios involving running into him someday—but in her musings, she'd always been ten pounds lighter and dressed to the nines, with her hair perfectly coiffed. Never in jeans and her old cowboy boots, with her hair pulled up in a messy bun and dog slobber across her chest.

She turned around, trying to focus on her daughter, and *not* the ten pounds she most certainly had not lost, as they both tried to help Daisy, who was nimbly crawling over the console and out the door.

Bailey pulled her into a hug, then did another cursory check in case she'd missed a head injury or broken bone in her earlier assessment. "You sure you're okay, honey?"

"I'm fine, Mom."

"*Mom?*" The word was soft on Sawyer's lips as his gaze slid to Bailey's hand, no doubt noting the absence of a wedding ring.

Bailey kept one arm around her daughter's shoulder, maybe more for her support than Daisy's. "Sawyer Dunn, this is my daughter, Daisy."

He nodded. "Good to meet you."

"You too," Daisy said, thrusting her hand out to shake his. "I've heard *allll* about you."

That grin tugged at Sawyer's lips again. "Don't believe everything you hear, kid."

Not wanting to get anywhere near that conversation, Bailey walked around to the front of the car, giving a forlorn look at her tire embedded in the ditch. "Dang. We're really stuck."

"I'll call the garage to come tow you out. But for now, we'd better get you to Granny's ranch. Another ten minutes and she'll be calling out the state patrol." He nodded to the tractor. "Hop on. I'll run you down there."

Bailey shook her head. "Forget it. The way you were driving, we can get there faster if we walk."

He chuckled and gestured to the cows, both now munching at the tall grass in the opposite ditch. "Looks like they'll be fine for a few minutes. I can kick it up a gear to get you there *close* to on time, then come back and get them."

Daisy looked from her mom to the cowboy, then shrugged her small shoulders. "Come on, Mom. You said this trip to Granny Bee's would be an adventure. What better way to start an adventure than arriving on a tractor?"

Her daughter had a point. And Granny Bee *did* love a grand entrance. "Fine." She eyed the tractor skeptically. "I don't suppose there's a seat belt on that thing."

Sawyer chuckled. "No. But I promise to drive carefully." He held out his hand to help Daisy up to the wide bench seat.

She ignored it, easily scrambling up the side. "Carefully is fine, but please tell me you're going to go faster than when you were following those cows."

He pulled back like she'd socked him in the chest. "Geez, everybody's a critic." He offered the seat to Bailey. "I'm happy to let you drive instead of me."

She shook her head. "My tractor-driving days are long past. I'm fine taking the sidestep."

"Suit yourself," he said, hauling himself into the seat, then reaching back down to give her a hand up.

She swore her fingertips tingled as she placed her hand in his. Reaching for the grab handle with her free hand, she let him pull her up and tried to gain her balance on the small sidestep. His hand was warm, his palm slightly callused, but the sensation of having his fingers wrapped around hers again had Bailey's heart thumping against her chest like a manic jackhammer. She couldn't speak, as it was taking all her concentration not to fall off the sidestep in a heady swoon.

Sawyer had been ridiculously cute as a teenager, tall and lean, with shaggy, sun-streaked hair that always looked like it was in need of a cut. His hair was still a tad long, and he was still fit, but this Sawyer was even taller and had the muscular build of a man. He'd grown into his looks, and *handsome* didn't seem adequate to describe the hot cowboy holding her hand and making her pulse pound like she was sixteen again.

"At least the dog isn't giving me a hard time," he said with a grin that had Bailey's insides doing a funny scramble. "Will he be okay running alongside the tractor? I'll keep an eye out for him."

"He'll be fine," Bailey assured him, finally finding her voice. At least one of them would be. Her brain seemed to be scrambled as well, as his arm brushed the side of her leg.

"He loves to run," Daisy said. "I do too. I'm on the track team at my school."

"Yeah? What events?"

"Hurdles, high jump, and long distance."

"I did track in school too," he told her. "I don't know that I was any good, but I still like to run."

"I don't know that I'm any good either, but I'm tall for my age so those are the best events for me."

"How old are you?" he asked as he reached to release the emergency brake.

"Twelve."

His hand stilled on the brake, his expression quizzical as he stole a quick glance at Daisy. It only lasted a second, but Bailey saw it, and it was long enough for her to catch a sweet flash of tenderness in his eyes that stole the breath from her lungs before he blinked and it was gone.

She swallowed back the threat of emotion suddenly clogging her throat. Seeing Sawyer *and* coming home to Honeybuzz Mountain was enough for her today, she couldn't go *there* as well. Time to change the subject. "Nice tractor," she told him. "Did you steal this one too?"

"Maybe," he said with a shrug, his easy smile back as he fired up the engine and dropped it into gear.

The ride only lasted five minutes, but Bailey was aware of every rut and bump they hit that had her leg or shoulder colliding with Sawyer's until they rounded the last curve and Honeybuzz Mountain Ranch came into view.

The gorgeous landscape tugged at her heart, the breeze on her face whispering only one word. *Home.*

As they rumbled into the driveway, Bailey noted the new touches to the ranch. Granny Bee had told her they'd replaced the chicken coop, the boards had been old and rotting, and one of her favorite pigs had passed over the rainbow bridge. Ellis Dunn, Bailey's favorite ranch hand, and the closest thing she had to a father figure in her life, had retired that winter, and Granny had hired a new man to manage the farm. Bailey had always wondered if a romance had been blooming in Blossom Briggs's life with Ellis, but if there had been, her grandmother had never let on.

Everything else about the ranch felt the same, like Honey-buzz Mountain had been suspended in time. The large, rambling, two-story farmhouse still sported a cheery shade of yellow paint, the wide porch still encased in white rails. The porch swing and rocking chairs still formed a cozy circle, the spot on the porch the best for Granny Bee to oversee her vast domain—cattle grazing in the green pastures, horses in the corral next to the barn, the bunkhouse, and neat rows of white bee boxes stark against the colorful flower-filled meadow. The house was nestled against the mountain range, vying for attention with the huge white barn, the Honeybuzz Mountain logo emblazoned on its front.

They passed a small sign welcoming visitors to HONEYBUZZ MOUNTAIN RANCH, THE LAND OF MILK AND HONEY. Granny Bee only had one milk cow compared to the several hundred head of cattle she raised, but she always thought *milk* and honey sounded better than land of *beef* and honey.

As if the chugging engine of the tractor weren't loud enough, Cooper announced their arrival with several barks. The front screen door banged open as they pulled up, and Bailey expected to see Granny Bee strolling out, her arms spread wide in a flourish of welcome.

But instead, an older man came stumbling out backward, his arms waving animatedly as a red-faced Granny Bee stomped toward him. Well, more like limp-stomped, since her right foot was encased in a blue medical boot. Granny was obviously riled up, but Bailey's first thought was that she was glad she didn't have to use crutches. Maybe the break wasn't as bad as Gran had originally made it sound, although that was the main reason she'd used to talk Bailey into coming home.

Bailey couldn't hear the words coming out of her grand-mother's mouth, but she recognized the angry expression and the intent of the long, bony finger pointed at the man's chest.

It had been a long time since Bailey had seen him, but she recognized the man as Werner Humble, the town's founder; she'd seen him enough times at parades and town functions. But she'd never seen him like this, with the thick shock of white hair falling haphazardly across his forehead, the tail of his shirt untucked, and one side of his cheek flaming red as if from a recent slap.

The members of The Hive came spilling out onto the porch, her grandmother's book club and posse encircling their leader, heeding the call for backup. Despite the altercation happening with her grandmother and the town founder, Bailey's heart warmed at the sight of her two great-aunts, Aster and Marigold, both brandishing weapons of their own sort. Her Aunt Marigold came ready for business as she whacked a rolling pin into her palm, her lip sneering as if she were ready to rumble. Her Aunt Aster, the shorter and plumper of the two women, but no less feisty, brandished a rolled-up newspaper as if she were going to swat a naughty dog.

Bailey's best friend's grandmother, Rosa Delgado, leaned against the side of the porch, slowly sipping her tea from a china cup, but the steely look she used to glare at Werner held almost as much malice as the rolling pin.

Bringing up the rear was Dorothy Duffield—Dot to her friends—who was the newest member of The Hive, having only been in the group the last eight or ten years, compared to the several decades of the other women. Dot's hands were empty as she wrung them together at her waist, but her pinched expression conveyed a combination of anger and bewilderment.

Another older man, this one wearing jeans, boots, and a gray Stetson, came out of the barn and hurried toward the porch. Bailey could only guess he was the newly hired farm manager.

Sawyer killed the engine just in time for them all to hear her grandmother's raised voice yell, "Werner Humble, you need to get the hell off my property! You set foot on my land again, and I swear on my bees, I *will* kill you."

Chapter Two

B ailey risked a quick questioning glance at Sawyer. *What the heck is going on?* But he just shrugged.

She hopped down and hurried toward her grandmother, ignoring the muttering town founder as he walked past her. Taking the porch steps two at a time, she raced up and enfolded her grandmother in her arms.

"Hello, love," Granny Bee said into her ear as she hugged her back. "I'm so glad to see you. Even though you *are* late for high tea."

Bailey took just a moment to breathe in her grandmother— the comforting scents of fabric softener, lavender, and the floral perfume she'd worn for years. In age and size, Granny Bee was in the middle of her sisters, just a scooch under five seven and the evidence of a few too many biscuits slathered in butter and honey around her middle. She called herself pleasantly plump, but she was also active enough, walking all over the ranch and caring for the bees and the cattle, so her body was strong and in great health for a woman approaching seventy. And though she wasn't necessarily tall, her personality was big enough to make her seem that way.

"Are you okay?" Bailey asked, feeling the slightest tremble in her grandmother's arms.

"I'm fine." Granny brushed her concerns away as she turned and opened her arms to Daisy. "Get over here, Granddaughter, and give your great-granny some sugar."

Daisy laughed as she hugged Granny Bee. "Sorry we're late. We had a little trouble with our car. But Sawyer gave us a ride."

Granny glanced from Bailey to Sawyer to the tractor, then back to her granddaughter again. "Everybody okay?"

Bailey nodded, knowing there was a lot more to that question than just about the car. "We're fine. I just didn't see some cows in the road and slid into the ditch."

"I already texted the garage. They're going to tow it here," Sawyer said, tipping his hat first to Granny then to the women of The Hive. "So, you want to tell me what that was all about?"

Aster stepped forward, then must have realized she was still holding the rolled-up newspaper and dropped it into one of the rockers. She fluffed her chin-length silvery bob. "Oh, Sawyer. Sorry you had to hear that. You know how Bee overreacts. Obviously, she's not going to *kill* Werner," Aster assured him.

"I wouldn't put it past her," Marigold quipped.

"You don't need to speak for me, Aster," Granny said, a hint of scolding in her voice. "I meant what I said. If that man sets foot on my property again, I'll run him over with my truck."

Unless she'd gotten a new rig, Granny drove an old beat-up Ford pickup that shouldn't still be running, but the beast never seemed to die. And depending on her mood, Gran either ambled along the road, enjoying the scenery, or barreled down the highway like a cat with its tail on fire.

"Blossom Briggs, you stop that talk right now. You're not going to run anyone over. At least not on purpose," Aster scolded back, and Bailey knew it was serious, because hardly anyone, beyond her great aunts, ever used her grandmother's given name. Although Bailey wasn't sure why Aster kept tipping her head toward Sawyer as she admonished Granny.

"What was he doing here?" Bailey asked, trying to get the subject off her grandmother's murderous intentions. "Did he come out to buy some honey?"

"Heavens, no," Granny said. "The man is deathly allergic to bees, pollen, and honey. I swear he holds up his EpiPen whenever I mention the bees, like it's a wooden stake and I'm a vampire he's warding off."

"Then what was he doing here?"

"Making an inappropriate pass at me, that's what," Granny answered with a huff. "And in my own kitchen, no less."

Dot gasped. "That snake," she muttered, not quite under her breath.

Dot seemed miffed, but her aunt Aster had gone positively pale.

Bailey put an arm out to steady her. "You okay, Auntie?"

"What?" Aster asked absently, pressing a hand to her chest. "Oh yes, I'm fine. Thank you, honey. Just goes to show, you can never really know a person."

Bailey tilted her head. "Oh? Do you know Werner well?"

Aster gave a little snort. "Apparently not as well as I thought I did."

Before her aunt could say more, the sound of an engine roaring down the driveway had Bailey turning to see a sporty red Mustang convertible screech to a stop in the cloud of dust. Her face broke into a grin as a tall, gorgeous woman in a form-fitting wrap dress two shades darker than the car climbed out and practically ran toward the porch and up the steps. Which was quite a feat in four-inch wedge heels and a dress that fit her curvaceous figure so snugly it should have been illegal.

Evie Delgado Espinoza was as sweet as she was beautiful. She was also funny, gutsy, ornery as all get out, and the best friend Bailey had ever had. She threw her arms around her friend, hugging her tightly.

"Dang, girl," Evie said, squeezing her once more before letting go. "It's so good to see you. I've missed you like crazy."

"I know. I'm sorry. I've had back-to-back deadlines with the last three books, and you know how I get when I'm buried in the writing cave or dug into a story."

"Yes, I know. That's why I sent you that . . ."

"I know. And I loved it, of course."

"I knew you would. I got one for myself too."

"I used it to help with my . . ."

Evie let out a hearty laugh. "Me too."

They spoke in that way that two friends who had grown up together did—finishing sentences was unnecessary. Since Bailey had been an only child and Evie the only girl of her siblings, the two women were more like sisters than friends, sharing secrets, clothes, and sleeping over at each other's houses often enough to feel like they had two families.

"Life has just been crazy lately." Bailey wrapped an arm around Daisy's shoulder. "Plus, I've got to feed and clothe and keep this wild child out of trouble."

Evie pulled Daisy into a hug. "She can't be that much trouble."

"I'm kidding. She's a good kid." *Most of the time.* When she wasn't rolling her eyes at her mother, like she was currently doing.

Daisy let out an accompanying sigh to go with her expression. "She's also standing right here, you know."

Evie laughed and squeezed her tighter. "I've been dying for you to get here so I could spoil the heck out of you."

Bailey raised a warning eyebrow at her daughter. "If your Aunt Evie starts any sentence with the words 'You know what would be fun?' just turn around and walk away."

"Why?" Daisy protested. "I like fun."

"Yeah, Bailes," Evie chimed in, planting a hand on her hip. "She likes fun."

"No way. This is the kind of fun that could land you in jail." She ought to know. Although she *might* have been to blame for that one time. *Still.* She pointed at Daisy. "Just tell her your mom won't let you and walk, no . . . *run* away."

"You maybe should have followed your own advice a time or two," Sawyer muttered. He stood with his arms crossed over his chest and his back to the wall, as if keeping an eye on the ranch and the motley crew of women assembled on the porch.

Evie offered the cowboy a knowing grin, and Bailey suddenly felt like her best friend was enjoying their reunion a little too much. "Hey, Sawyer."

He tipped his hat the slightest bit. "Evie."

"Pretty great having our girl home, isn't it?" She put her arm around Bailey and kept talking, not giving him a chance to answer, as she pointed to her friend's feet. "Although you look more like a cowgirl in those boots than a famous mystery writer." She smiled warmly at Bailey as if they shared a secret. "I've still got mine too."

She'd slipped on her old pink and brown Ropers that morning, forgetting how comfortable the cowboy boots were. Having them on her feet brought back a breath of comfort and familiarity as well as a rush of memories. She and Evie had picked them out together, Evie getting a black and teal pair while Bailey had picked the pink and brown. They'd worn them everywhere, with jeans, and shorts, and cute dresses like they'd worn to the concert that night at the county fair, the first night she'd danced with Sawyer.

"We need to get Daisy a new pair," Bailey told her. "She's been growing like a weed this summer, and the pair Granny Bee sent for her last birthday are already two sizes too small."

Sawyer pushed off from the wall. "Well, on that note, I think I'll take off. Not that I don't enjoy a good conversation about shoe shopping … ." He tipped his hat toward the older women. "Ladies. You take care now, Granny Bee, and let me know if you have any more trouble with Werner Humble. As it stands, I think he and I might already be having a conversation about the way to treat a lady."

Granny waved a hand his direction. "Oh, you don't have to do that, honey. I can take care of myself. And that old coot doesn't scare me a bit." She nodded to the group of women who began filing back into the house. "Besides, I've got The Hive to watch my back, if I ever need anything."

"I'm sure," Sawyer muttered, as he sauntered down the porch steps. He turned back to offer another nod. "Bailey. Daisy. Good to see you. Or meet you."

"We'll be seeing you around, I'm sure," Evie said, her voice taking on a tone that dripped with pure sugar.

Bailey nudged her in the ribs.

"I'm sure," Sawyer said, pausing to give a lingering glance at Evie's Mustang. "Car still looks good."

"I can't believe you're still driving that thing," Bailey said, trying to tear her eyes away from Sawyer as he continued toward the tractor. "Gosh, we had some great times in that car."

"Of course I am. You know I've always loved it. And it's like a family heirloom. My dad would come back to haunt me if I tried to sell it." It had been her father's car, and he had given it to her for her sixteenth birthday, the year before he died. "I think my brother's rebuilt the engine three times now, but it still runs great."

"I'm sure," she said, knowing exactly which of her four brothers she was talking about. "He still have the garage on Fourth and Main?"

Evie nodded. "Yep. And by the way, I passed him on the way here. He was pulling your car out of the ditch."

Bailey's pulse raced a little at the thought of seeing Evie's brother, Mateo. Like Sawyer, he was also good with his hands. He could fix anything—anything except the broken heart of an abandoned teenage girl. Although not for lack of trying.

"You girls better get in here and get some tea and biscuits before everything gets too cold," Granny Bee instructed.

Cooper had made his way around to greet all the women, then the golden retriever had stretched out in a patch of sunlight. Daisy had already gone inside and brought him out a bowl of water, and Bailey instructed him to *stay*.

Evie caught her toe on a loose board in the porch as they turned to go back in and swore as she grabbed for Bailey's arm. "Brother trucker."

Bailey arched an eyebrow at her friend as she righted herself and smoothed down her dress.

"Abuela has been bugging me to stop swearing so much," Evie explained with a sheepish shrug.

"How's that going?"

"She's failing miserably," Rosa answered, wrapping Bailey in a warm hug of soft cotton and scents of starch and saffron. "How are you, *chiquita querida*? You look good. I like your hair longer like this."

"I'm good. And glad to be home. I've missed you, Abuelita." She narrowed her eyes, then swept her glance over Rosa, Evie, and Granny Bee. "Although I can't believe *none* of you told me that Sawyer was back in town."

Granny Bee offered her an offhand shrug as she went through the screen door. "You would've known if you'd come home more often."

"She has a point," Rosa said, following her inside.

Bailey leveled her best friend with a steely glare. "What's your excuse?"

Evie's eyes flashed with amusement. "It was just so much more fun this way."

Bailey swatted at her friend as they walked into the house.

The big, rambling farmhouse hadn't changed much, except for the addition of even more bee décor. From the foyer, polished hardwood floors led to a spacious, sunny, yellow kitchen on the left, loaded with lots of kitschy bee decorations, and a large living area sat to the right. The same chintz-covered sofas and wingback chairs in pale pink and green florals sat clustered in a conversation circle, with the high tea setup in the middle. Small saucers of cucumber sandwiches, scones, and raspberry-filled cookies covered the antique coffee table. Teacups and saucers of fine china circled the outside of the table. Three teapots sat in the center—a delicate matching one, a tall pink one, and a chunkier pastel blue one in a knitted pink cozy.

Granny Bee held up the fanciest one as Bailey plopped down onto the sofa next to her. "Tea, dear?"

"Yes, please. My throat is as dry as the Colorado sand dunes." She picked up her grandmother's cup, not one of the fine delicate set, but a bright yellow mug with a picture of a bee wearing a tiny tiara, and took a sip. She almost spit it back out. "Granny Bee," she admonished. "This isn't tea. It's *beer*."

Granny let out a miffed huff as she carried the teapot toward the kitchen. "It most certainly is *not* beer." She said the word as if it left a bad taste in her mouth. "It's a microbrew."

"But a microbrew is—"

"Delicious," her Aunt Marigold cut her off. "This one is called Beehive."

Aster lowered her voice as she leaned toward Bailey. "We tried for years to get your grandmother to let us have alcohol at high tea. We even told her beer had the word *bee* in it, but she swore beer was too gauche."

"Then Marigold found this Beehive Honey Wheat microbrew, and suddenly she allowed it. It's even brewed here in Colorado," Rosa explained, raising a teacup as if in a toast.

Bailey balked. "What? Not you too, Abuelita."

"Friday afternoon high tea has gotten a lot more interesting," Rosa said with a wink.

Dot leaned in, keeping her voice a whisper, even though Granny was now in the kitchen. "We also found a Bumble Bee Wine, for those of us who are a little more refined."

"Refined, my behind," Aunt Marigold muttered as she lifted her cup and took a sip.

Aster poked at her leg. "You're just crabby because you're the designated driver this week and couldn't have any."

Bailey shook her head. "Wine *and* beer? I mean microbrew," she corrected at her aunt's glare. "At high tea?" *Who would've guessed?*

"Enough about the tea," Aunt Marigold said. "We want to hear about you, Bailey. What's happening in your life? Tell us about your new book."

"Tell us about your new book later," her other aunt interjected. "I'd rather hear if you've got any new beaus."

"New *beaus*?" Granny Bee asked, coming back in from the kitchen, cradling the teapot in her hands. She set it on the table, then offered her sister a withering glance. "We're not *that* old, sister. Most people these days just call them *boyfriends*." She planted a hand on her hip. "Or their *boos*. Right, Daisy?"

The teenager blinked at her great-grandmother as if she didn't know exactly how to respond.

"Oh, hush up," Marigold said, leaning forward to pour Daisy a cup of tea. She passed it to the girl, who was still staring at her great-grandmother. "She can call them beaus if she wants to. What do you care? You're more concerned with bees than beaus . . . or boos . . . anyway."

Granny Bee still had her hand on her hip, and she gave it a little sashay as she leveled her sister with a cool stare. "That's not true. I could have a boo anytime I want."

"Yeah, right," Marigold said. "When would you have the time? Would you just squeeze your 'boo' in between candle making and the cattle auction?"

"I could *squeeze* my boo anytime I want to," Granny Bee declared, giving another saucy swing to her hips. "And besides, having a boo doesn't take up that much time. Right, Dottie?"

Dot gave a little start. "Me? Why would you ask me?"

"You're the one who said you've been seeing a new man."

"No, not me."

"You most certainly did," Granny Bee said, sitting down next to Bailey and reaching for her mug. "Last time you mentioned him, I swear you giggled like a schoolgirl."

Bailey picked up a cup. Apparently, she was expected to pour her own tea. She looked over at Dot, whose hands fluttered to the neckline of her modest blouse. "I think it's exciting that you're seeing someone."

Dot worked at the library and, as far as Bailey knew, she'd been single her entire life. She was active in her church and volunteered at the hospital and had always claimed that Leopold, her orange and white tabby cat, was the only man she needed in her life.

"I'm sure it's nothing," Dot said, her gaze bouncing around the room, looking everywhere except at Bailey.

"*Nothing?*" Granny Bee said, barreling on, apparently unable to read the room or notice Dot's discomfort. "You've been talking about this mystery man for weeks. You said you've been out on a bunch of dates with him."

Mystery man? And beer? High tea had gotten a lot more exciting than Bailey remembered.

"He's not really that much of a mystery," Dot said quietly, staring down into whatever was in her cup. "He's just new, and I'm not quite ready to share him yet. And maybe I don't want to jinx it by talking too much about it."

"That makes sense to me," Bailey said, hoping that the mystery man turned out to be something wonderful for Dottie. Just because she didn't believe in finding a happily ever after for herself didn't mean that she didn't hope it still happened for others. And she couldn't think of a sweeter woman to have a late-in-life romance. She turned her attention to her aunt. "What about you, Aunt Aster? I thought you told me you'd been out on a few dates recently too."

"Oh well, yes, a couple, but I don't think it's going to work out," Aster said, looking down into her cup.

What was so interesting in the bottom of these cups? Were these women trying to read their tea leaves?

"Why not?" Granny asked. "I thought you liked him. You were acting all moony after that last date, flitting around the kitchen like you were walking on air and calling him a poet." She lifted her voice into a romantic breathy pitch. "You told me he said your silvery gray hair reminded him of moonbeams and made him want to dance under the stars with you."

Bailey heard Dot's quick intake of breath before Aster shushed and swatted at her sister's leg. "Who are you all of a sudden? The dating detective? Digging into everyone's love life like you don't have enough to do." She lifted her chin and gave an indignant huff. "I swear, half the time you don't even listen to a word I tell you, but now you're quoting something I *may* have said weeks ago."

Granny shrugged. "That's because most of the stuff you say isn't that interesting, but gray-haired moonbeams caught my attention."

"Who wants more tea?" Used to refereeing her sisters, Aunt Marigold deftly changed the subject as she lifted the teapot Bailey was pretty sure had the beer in it. "And we'd better decide which book we're *pretending* to read next."

Laughter rippled through the group, even as Dottie muttered, "I *always* read the books."

But the conversation shifted, and after a brief argument over which novel to read next, they decided on a title, and the book club finally wound down. After another round of hugs, the members of The Hive piled into Marigold's sedan and headed out. As they turned out of the driveway, they waved to the man in the tow truck hauling Bailey's car into the drive.

For the second time that day, Bailey felt a fist squeeze her heart as a tall, dark-haired man stepped from the tow truck and flashed a grin in her direction that had her insides melting into goo and sent her lady parts atingle. He wore a black T-shirt snug across his muscular chest, and the top half of his coveralls were pulled down and tied low around his waist.

Holy hot mechanic.

"Dang, Evie, I didn't think your brother could get any hotter, but I was wrong."

"Eww," Evie said, wrinkling her nose. "And I thought you were all atwitter over seeing Sawyer."

"I'm not *atwitter* over anyone. But I'm also not blind," she said quietly before waving a hand and breaking into a smile as the man sauntered up the stairs. "Hey, Mateo," she said, a little more breathlessly than she'd planned.

"Hey Bailes." His voice was even deeper than she remembered as he drawled the nickname only he and his sister used for her. He leaned down and wrapped her in a bear hug, then lifted her off the ground as he swung around. "You look amazing." His whiskered chin scraped her neck as he did a quick inhale before setting her down. "You smell good too. Like honey and flowers and raspberry cookies."

She playfully swatted his arm, trying not to fall into the smoldering gaze of his dark chocolate-colored eyes. "More like road trip, cold fries, and golden retriever."

"Still," he said, keeping his gaze on her as he reached down to ruffle the neck of the golden retriever in question while Cooper wiggled around his legs, his tail thumping the wooden slats of the porch. "I like it."

He smelled like a heady mixture of aftershave, Irish Spring soap, engine oil, and manliness. Like a sexy race car.

Okay, maybe she was *slightly* atwitter.

She nodded to her daughter standing to the side of Evie. "Mateo, you remember Daisy?"

He stepped forward and pulled the girl into a hug. "I thought I did, but I remembered a little girl, not this gorgeous teenager."

"Gah, don't say that. She's not a teenager. Not yet. She's only twelve."

"Mo-*om*!" Her daughter's cheeks flushed pink.

Bailey knew the feeling.

Chapter Three

The next morning, Bailey drove through Humble Hills and marveled at how much it hadn't changed from when she was growing up there. It was a town out of simpler times, where neighbors still sat on front porches and kids spent their summers at the city pool or hanging around the Tasty Freez. Some of the storefronts had faded, and a few had been replaced with newer businesses, but it still felt unchanged to her as the tires of her car rumbled over the same brick-lined streets.

After Evie and Mateo had left the night before, she and Daisy had gotten unpacked, then stuffed themselves on Granny Bee's fried chicken, homemade mashed potatoes and gravy, and fluffy biscuits slathered in Honey Bee Good, Gran's latest sweet honey recipe. After supper, they'd sat on the porch and played cards as they'd watched the sun go down.

As they'd been cleaning up before bed, they'd found Werner Humble's suit jacket where it must have fallen behind a chair in the living room. Bailey had offered to return it this morning so her grandmother wouldn't have to see, *or threaten*, him again.

Although after hearing all the details of Werner putting the moves on her grandmother, Bailey had a few murderous intentions of her own. It would take all her strength to just drop the jacket off and not lay into him herself. She liked to think she had more composure than Granny Bee, but most of it flew out the window where her family was concerned.

She'd left Daisy in the kitchen with Granny Bee, learning how to make her famous honey-do pancakes, with Cooper stretched out on the floor by their feet waiting for errant crumbs to drop. Her stomach growled, and she wished she had grabbed more than one small pancake on her way out of the house.

Turning the corner, she drove into an upscale section on the edge of town. Its wide streets with enormous elm trees arching overhead held stately older homes owned by the wealthier set of Humble Hills, including several sizable Victorian houses. Most, like the one her great-aunts Marigold and Aster owned, had been restored to their original look on the outside but had been renovated and modernized on the inside.

Lavender Manor, her aunts' monstrous Victorian, held a place of honor at the end of the street. True to its name, its grand façade was painted in variegated shades of purple, periwinkle, and blue, and the lush lavender bushes surrounding the house were a bee's paradise.

The splendid home had been passed down in the Briggs family; it had been their place in town when they weren't at the ranch, but her aunts had lived there for as long as she could remember. Memories of herself and Evie racing down the long hardwood hallways, polished to a bright sheen, and spending hours exploring the attic and the grounds flooded Bailey's mind. She was eager to take Daisy there again, now that she was old enough to appreciate some of the more unique qualities of the house, like the reading nook in the gazebo and the boxes of family photos in the attic.

She pulled up in front of Werner's house, another renovated Victorian. It was smaller in scale, but still as grand, with a wide front porch and soaring turret. Although, as Bailey pushed through the gate, she noticed a few areas of disrepair—overgrown flower beds choked with weeds, peeling paint, and cracked sidewalks. She noted one of the porch steps was loose as she made her way up the walk and knocked on the door.

Shifting from one foot to the other, she tried to think of something to say that didn't involve chewing the man out for getting handsy with her granny. But there was no answer to her first knock or her second.

A wicker love seat flanked by two rocking chairs sat in front of the wide front windows, and she crossed the porch and laid the jacket in one of them. Glancing through the window, she could see the grand foyer, the main living area, and into the dining room. She gasped at the sight of the town founder lying on his back on the dining room floor, one arm outstretched next to the overturned chair.

She rapped loudly on the window. "Werner?! Can you hear me?" She ran back to the front door, calling his name again as she tried the knob. *Locked.*

Maybe the back door was open. Her heart raced as she turned and ran smack into the hard muscled chest of Sawyer Dunn.

"Bailey? What are you doing here?" He reached for her arms to steady her, then his brow furrowed as he must have caught the alarm in her face. "What's wrong?"

"It's Werner. He's on the floor in the house. I could see him through the window. He's not moving."

Sawyer pushed past her, taking two seconds to peer through the front glass, then returned to the door. "Werner," he called, rattling the knob.

"I tried that," she said. "It's locked . . ." Her words were lost in the crashing crack of wood as Sawyer put his shoulder to the door and broke it open, the shards and splinters raining down on the porch.

"Okay, I didn't try *that*," she muttered, following him in.

He raced to the dining room and dropped down next to Werner's body. His expression was grim as he placed two fingers against his neck, searching for a pulse. "He's gone," he said, shaking his head.

"Gone? As in *dead*?"

He nodded.

She couldn't seem to catch her breath. "Like dead-dead?" she whispered, trying to keep her anxiety in check and not hyperventilate.

Sawyer arched an eyebrow. "Yes, Bailey. Like that."

Her hands fluttered to her mouth as she slumped to the floor next to Werner. Praying he was wrong, she picked up Werner's hand, just as Sawyer had done to her the day before and tried desperately to find the flutter of a beat.

"Just breathe, Bailey," Sawyer said, firmly cupping the side of her shoulder, the same way he used to when she'd had panic attacks back in high school.

The pressure of his hand calmed her, just as it always had, and she matched her breathing with his, taking in a deep breath, then slowly letting it out. "I'm okay, but we've got to call someone," she said, pulling her phone from her pocket and stabbing at the screen as she tapped 9-1-1.

"It's okay, Bailey. I've got this."

She shook her head. How was he so calm? "No, we need an ambulance. Or a fireman. Or the police." Her heart rate climbed even higher. "Oh my gosh, do we need the police?"

"Yes, but—" he started to say, but Bailey cut him off as the line was picked up.

"Nine-one-one. What is your emergency?" The operator's voice sounded familiar.

"Yes, hello. We just found Werner Humble on his dining room floor, and we think he might be dead."

"He is," Sawyer confirmed. *Again.*

Bailey shot him a quick glare as she heard the operator say, "I'm sending an ambulance now."

"Tell her there are suspicious circumstances," he instructed.

Suspicious circumstances?

"Well, shoot fire," the dispatcher whispered, then recognition set in as she said more clearly, "I heard him. I'll contact the sheriff now."

"Linda? Is that you?" Bailey asked.

"Yes, this is Linda Johnson."

"This is Bailey Briggs." She and Linda had gone to high school together and been lab partners for chemistry. Linda had been notorious for diving in without reading the lab notes, and Bailey had heard that whispered "Well, shoot fire" many times as their experiments literally went up in smoke.

"Oh hey, Bailey, I heard you were back in town. Hold on, I'm ringing the sheriff."

Bailey turned toward Sawyer as she heard the theme song of *Mission Impossible* coming from his pocket.

He pulled out his phone and tapped the screen. "Dunn here."

Bailey heard Linda say, "Hey, Sheriff, you need to head over to Werner Humble's house. I already sent an ambulance, but apparently he's dead and they think there might be suspicious circumstances."

"Thanks, Linda, I'm already at the scene."

"How'd you get there so fast?"

"I'm the one who discovered the body."

"I thought Bailey Briggs did."

"She's here with me."

"Oh, then why did I need to call you?"

Bailey spoke into the phone. "Because he didn't tell me he was the *sheriff*."

Sawyer shrugged as the corner of his lip tugged up in a grin. "I tried."

"Not hard enough," she muttered.

"Why don't you call off the ambulance, Linda," Sawyer told the dispatcher. "And send the coroner instead."

"I'm on it, Sheriff. But he was doing a lecture at the hospital in the next town over today, so it may take him a half an hour or so to get to you."

"That's fine. I'll wait here."

"Okay, well, I've got another call coming in," Linda said. "Welcome home, Bailey."

What a homecoming.

"*You're* the sheriff?" Bailey asked as she pushed her phone back into her pocket.

He nodded.

"Why didn't you tell me that yesterday?"

"Didn't come up."

And why hadn't her grandmother or her so-called best friend informed her of this fact? Oh yeah, Evie thought it was just *so much more fun* this way.

I'll be sure to let her know how much fun I'm having.

"Why does he look like that?" She pressed her fingers together and tried to rub the tackiness of them on her jeans. "And why is he sticky?"

"I'm assuming he's sticky from the honey-slathered biscuit it appears he was eating." He nodded to the evidence lying on the floor a few feet from his outstretched hand.

It was partially under the table, so she hadn't noticed it before, but now she could see the biscuit had a large bite out of the side. "There's no way Werner was eating that. Granny Bee just told us he's deathly allergic to honey. And that's not something you eat by mistake."

"I'm not the medical examiner, of course, but the way his lips are swollen, the hives, the . . ." He waved his hand in a circle around his head. "The way he *looks* leads me to believe he died from anaphylactic shock, presumably from eating that honey we *know* he was allergic to. It's hard to see around the hives, but it looks to me like there are also traces of the honey on his chin and around his mouth." He furrowed his brow as he leaned closer and sniffed at Werner's face.

Bailey drew back, wrinkling her nose. "What are you doing?"

"I know this scent." Realization lit his eyes, then his expression changed to dread as he leaned back and gazed around the room.

"What is it?"

His shoulders slumped as he shook his head. "I sure wish I hadn't heard Granny Bee threaten to kill this man yesterday."

"Why? What does Granny Bee have to do with this?"

He pointed to the jar of Granny Bee's signature Honey I'm Home hot spiced honey sitting open on the table, a spoon covered in the amber substance next to it. "Because it looks like it was *her* honey that killed him."

Chapter Four

"What are you suggesting?" Bailey sputtered, her anxiety ramping back up. "That just because it was a jar of Granny Bee's honey, that she might had have something to do with his death?"

"His *death* is lookin' a whole lot more like a *murder.*"

"A *murder*? In Humble Hills?"

"Yeah, I'm not too thrilled about it myself," Sawyer said absently as his gaze tracked around the room. He pulled a note-pad from his front pocket and began to jot down notes.

She huffed out an affronted laugh. "You don't seriously think my grandmother killed this man."

Sawyer shrugged as he scribbled something on his pad. "I don't get paid to *think*. I get paid to look at the evidence."

"What evidence? A little jar of honey? Granny Bee sells thousands of them."

"Yes, I'm sure she does. Just not to a man who she herself told us has a deathly allergy to bees and honey."

"Lots of people are allergic to bees."

He sat back on his haunches and fixed her with a cool stare. "How many of them just knowingly ingested Honeybuzz

Mountain honey? And how many of them did Granny Bee threaten to kill?"

She swallowed. Dang. *Why couldn't Granny be sweet and demure like the old ladies on television?* "I can assure you it wasn't her."

"Oh yeah? You know as well as I do that your grandmother has a bit of a wild streak and a short fuse. Why, just last week, she about tore the head off one of my deputies for daring to have sixteen things in the fifteen-item self-checkout lane."

She tilted her head. "Well, that *is* against the rules. And as a deputy, he should have known better."

Sawyer sighed. "Yes, that's what your grandmother said too. But in his defense, he had a twin pack of Twinkies and most people would count that as one."

"Let's forget about my grandmother's temperament and her propensity for keeping folks in line at the checkout lane. What makes you think this is . . ." She lowered her voice to a whisper. ". . . a *murder*?"

"You don't have to whisper." He glanced down at Werner. "He's not going to hear you."

"Good point," she replied in her normal voice.

"I'm more interested in what *you* think." He gestured to the body. "Do you see anything suspicious? Or anything that suggests foul play?"

She studied him for a moment, narrowing her eyes to try to judge if he was being serious, but his expression held no amusement. She swallowed as she turned her gaze to the body, her breathing evening out as she put on her professional author hat and tried to see it from a different perspective. A perspective of "foul play."

"Okay, so this is happening. I may be staring at a murder victim. No problem. I can do this. I toss my characters into murder scenes all the time. And they don't usually hyperventilate or vomit on the victim," she muttered more to herself than to Sawyer.

He pulled back the slightest. "Are you going to vomit on the victim?"

She shook her head. "What? No." She offered him a quick glance. "Was I talking out loud?"

He nodded.

"Sorry, I tend to do that a lot, but I'm usually alone at my desk, and my dog is the only one who hears me."

"No problem. I like to hear how your mind works."

Warmth heated her neck. *Ignore the handsome cowboy*, her brain commanded. This was her chance to be part of what could possibly be a real crime scene. *Focus on the scene.*

"Okay, here's what I see. The table is set for one, and it's set with what looks like the good dishes." She pointed to the large china hutch set against the wall. "It matches the plates in that far cabinet, and from here it looks like the door of that cabinet isn't completely latched, which suggests someone recently took the plates from there. Although maybe the town founder uses his good china at every meal. But this doesn't look like a meal."

"Why not?"

"There's no dinner plate—only the dessert plate and a cup and saucer with what looks like the remains of tea inside. So this looks more like dessert or breakfast. It's too early for midday tea."

"I agree. The teapot and plate of chocolate-covered strawberries and those little cake things suggest you're right so far."

"Petit fours."

"What?"

"The little cake things. They're called petit fours. And they're not usually for breakfast. They're more of a dessert thing. Although he's dressed oddly for dessert." She raked her gaze over the body, ignoring the red swollen hives on his skin and trying to concentrate on the other details.

He was wearing an expensive blue dress shirt, the front unbuttoned and opened to reveal a white undershirt, and navy blue boxer shorts. His legs were stark white against the dark blue shorts and the navy dress socks that rose to his mid-calf. His silvery white hair, normally combed back in the style of Michael Douglas and still pretty thick for a guy who had to be in his late seventies, was mussed across his head, and Bailey couldn't tell if it was disheveled from the fall or due to fingers running through it. *Eww!* to the thought of old guy romance. And what even had her brain going there? Maybe it was the chocolate-covered strawberries or that he was in his unmentionables, but something about the scene made her wonder if romance—*eww* again—was a factor here.

She leaned a bit closer, wrinkling her nose at the smell of the corpse, and tilted her head to get a different view. Her writer brain was cataloging every image, every scent, and already creating prose in her mind on how to capture it all for her latest manuscript. "There's something odd there," she said, pointing to the man's hands. "I mean odd*er*. This whole thing is weird. But I'm starting to agree with you about the foul play. Besides the fact that there is no way a man who is deathly allergic to bees and honey would intentionally ingest it, the way he fell from his chair and landed on his arm is strange. Like, why wouldn't he put his hands out to stop his fall? And it looks to me like there are ligature marks on his wrists, like maybe his hands were tied to the chair."

"*Ligature* marks?" Sawyer asked. "How do you know about ligature marks?"

"I've spent the last decade researching murders and attending forensic classes, and I've studied a lot of crime scenes. You know I *have* written a mystery novel or two."

"Or eight," he muttered.

But she caught it, and another flush of heat traveled up her neck. *He knows how many books I've written.* It seemed unfair that he knew something about her as an adult when she knew nothing about him. Other than the fact he'd somehow become sheriff, moved back to their hometown, and still had the most gorgeous blue eyes she'd ever seen and a smile that made her knees weak.

Down, girl. Remember the dead guy?

"I've spent so much time researching this stuff, I would hope that I've picked up *some* terminology," she told him, trying to focus her attention back to the scene in front of her. "It is kind of exciting, though."

"Exciting?"

"Well, not exciting, like *woo-hoo—Werner's dead*. I feel awful about that. Okay, well, *mildly* awful. I *was* pretty mad at him." She held up her palms as she back-pedaled. "I mean not mad enough that I wished him dead." She lowered her voice to a whisper. "Or that I had anything to do with this."

Sawyer offered her a bemused half grin as he made a circling motion with his hand. "I don't think you wished him dead, or that you killed him, but I do think we need to focus our attention back to the body. I've kind of got a crime scene to process here."

"Yes. Right. Of course. That's the exciting part. I've written a dozen crime scenes and interviewed tons of cops and coroners and firemen, but this is the first time I've gotten to experience a live one." She frowned. "Well, not a *live* one. You know what I mean."

"I do. And I think you may be right about the ligature marks." He used his pen to point toward the red areas on his wrists.

Bailey reached out to lift Werner's hand, but Sawyer blocked her with his arm. "Careful, you can't touch anything. Contaminating the crime scene and all that."

"Right. Sorry, I forgot for a second," she said, pulling her arm back against her side. "But look at his wrists. I didn't see it at first because of the redness, but doesn't it look like there's some kind of little red or orangish threads there?" Her gaze traveled over Werner's body, and her voice rose as she caught more glimpses of the odd-colored fibers. "Look, you can see more of them on his boxers and his socks too. They stick out against the dark-colored fabric."

"Yeah, I noticed them before, and they are a weird color. Weird enough that they make me think they're from something unusual or something we wouldn't normally see around."

The color *was* odd, but something in the back of Bailey's mind made her feel like she'd seen it somewhere before. "Do you think they came from whatever was used to tie him up?"

Sawyer shrugged. "I don't know for sure. But that's a good guess. Or they could have shed from the killer's clothing."

A shiver ran through Bailey's shoulders as she snuck a peek behind her and lowered her voice again. "You don't think the killer is still here, do you?"

He shook his head. "I doubt it. We'll have to wait for the medical examiner, but from the state of the body, I'd guess that Werner died sometime last night. That's a lot of time for a perp to just hang around."

This was too crazy. Bailey couldn't believe she was staring at a dead body while discussing ligature marks and perps with her old boyfriend who was now in law enforcement—which made the whole thing even crazier since the reason she'd assumed he'd been sent away was for grand theft auto, or grand theft tractor in their case. The whole thing was surreal.

She would have thought seeing an actual corpse would be the scary part of this equation, but the part that really scared her was the fact that Sawyer thought Granny Bee had something to do with this guy's death. She had to do something. And soon. Before Sawyer got it in his head to pull out his handcuffs and arrest her grandmother.

"Sometime last night, you say? That's when you think he died?"

Sawyer shrugged. "That'd be my best guess."

"Well, then that settles it," she said, slapping her knee just a little too hard. And why was she slapping her knee anyway? Like she was an old geezer who'd just fired off a lame punch line. The sound was too loud in the room and seemed wrong. Kind of like the lie she was about to spin. But she was going to tell it anyway.

"Settles what?"

"The question about Granny Bee." She crossed her arms over her chest. "Now we know it wasn't her."

He leaned back on his haunches. "And what makes you so sure?"

"Besides the fact that she's incapable of killing anyone or anything—she takes spiders outside for goodness sakes—I know she didn't have anything to do with this because I was with her when it happened."

"We don't even know for certain what time Werner was killed."

"Doesn't matter. You just said it was probably last night sometime, and I've been with her the whole time since I've been home."

He arched his eyebrow again. "All night too?"

"Yes."

"You slept in her bed?"

She faltered. But only for a second, then caught herself. "Yes," she said with what she hoped was a casual shrug. "I crawled in with her because I had a nightmare when I tried to fall asleep."

His bemused grin told her he wasn't buying what she was selling. No matter how hard she was trying. "What was your nightmare about?"

"It was about my old boyfriend moving back to our hometown and becoming the sheriff."

"You only found out I was the sheriff half an hour ago."

"I guess dreams really do come true."

He huffed out a laugh. "Even if I believed that you slept with your grandma last night because you had a bad dream, how do you know she didn't get up and leave sometime in the middle of the night?"

"Because I would have known. I'm a very light sleeper."

He let out another laugh, this one loud enough to fill the room. And something inside of Bailey's chest. She used to love to make him laugh. But not about this. Not when Granny's innocence was on the line.

"Now I *know* you're lying. You sleep like the dead." He leaned toward the body. "No offense, Werner."

"None taken," she mumbled, unable to help herself from continuing their riff. She hadn't seen him in thirteen years, yet he still felt so familiar, and they had so easily fallen back into their old rhythm of banter.

"I can remember one time when you fell asleep on the bus on the way home from a field trip," he said. "It was that time our class went to Denver to visit the Museum of Natural History. You remember?"

She nodded. Of course she remembered. Sawyer had held her hand the whole day, and they had snuck off from the group at one point and he'd kissed her in front of the triceratops display in the Prehistoric Journey exhibition. She hadn't been able to see a dinosaur without thinking of him since.

"What you don't remember is Kevin Young standing up in the back of the bus to announce he wasn't feeling well right before he tossed his cookies all over Amy Robinson's backpack, which caused her to lose her mind, screaming and hollering before she picked up her ralphed-on bag and whacked Kevin in the gut with it." Sawyer grinned as he recounted the tale. "And the reason you don't remember any of that is because you *slept* through the entire upchuck incident."

"I heard Amy Robinson got her teaching degree and ended up back at Humble Hills High. I think she teaches English."

He cocked an eyebrow her direction. "Don't try to change the subject. You know the point I'm trying to make is that you are *not* a light sleeper, and I don't believe you've suddenly become one. And that's just the start of what I don't believe about your story."

"People change, you know," she muttered. "You sure did." She looked around the room, anywhere but at him. She didn't like the way he thought he still knew her so well. Not after all this time.

Her gaze caught on something just under the china hutch. She leaned closer to try to decipher what the yellow and orange cylinder could be. "Look, Sawyer," she said, pointing to the object just as she figured out what it was. "Isn't that an EpiPen?"

Sawyer crossed the room and bent down to peer under the hutch. "That's exactly what it is. And it hasn't been used."

"How can you tell?"

"The blue cap is still on, and I can see liquid through the clear part on the side."

"Why is it under the china hutch? Do you think he tried to use it but dropped it, and it rolled over there?" she asked, mentally measuring the distance between his hand and the cabinet.

Sawyer's expression was grim. "Either that or he tried to use it and someone knocked it out of his hand and kicked it over here so he couldn't."

Chapter Five

"Then that couldn't have been Granny Bee," Bailey said. "She's terrible at kicking. *And* she has a broken foot."

Sawyer sighed. "Come on, Bailey. You know I'm going to have to take your grandmother in for questioning. If I didn't, I wouldn't be doing my job. Or wouldn't be doing it very well. For now, can we just focus on the facts and the crime scene? I need to get some pictures of this. And the ME should be here any time now." He pulled out his phone and aimed it at Werner, taking several photos of the scene and of the body from all different angles.

"Yeah, of course. I don't want to be in the way." Bailey stood and took a single step back, careful not to touch anything or step any place but where they'd come from.

She waited until Sawyer's back was turned, then used her phone to quickly snap as many shots as she could as well. She wasn't exactly hiding the fact that she was taking them, but she wasn't announcing it either. And they would make great photos for research and for helping her to remember all the details of an actual crime scene. Even though she was already trying to memorize every moment of this day to be able to use in her next book.

A knock on the front door sounded, then it swung open and a tall man with a bushy head of salt and pepper hair stepped in. He had on a white jumpsuit and what looked like safety goggles strapped around his head, barely visible in the jumble of hair, reminding Bailey of Doc Brown from *Back to the Future.* "Hey, Sheriff," he called out as he entered the house.

"Hey, Doc," Sawyer answered, shaking the other man's hand. "Good to see you. Wish it were under different circumstances."

He looked down at Werner Humble with a somber expression. "We always do."

Sawyer pointed at her. "Doc, do you know Bailey Briggs? She grew up around here and is home visiting her grandmother. Bailey, this is Dr. Leon Foster, our local ME."

The medical examiner smiled and nodded as he shook Bailey's hand. "Good to meet you. I've read all your books."

"Oh gosh, really?"

"Absolutely. I enjoy them. I'd be happy to help if you ever need advice or have questions about a procedure or medical detail."

"Really? That would be great. I never turn down an offer to help. And it seems like I always have questions that are totally weird or might put me on a watchlist if I tried to google them."

Doc nodded. "Totally weird questions are my favorite. I'll give you one of my cards. Call or email me anytime. I love talking shop. And I know tons of stories."

"Thanks. That's really nice of you."

"No problem. Just because we work with them doesn't mean we're all *stiffs*," he said with a wink.

"Wow. You're funny too."

He offered her a modest shrug. "I'm just a coroner, not a comedian, but I still get excited when it's *open Mike* night."

Bailey's eyes widened, and a laugh escaped her lips. "That's awful."

"I know. But I've got a ton of them. If you have time while you're here, stop by the morgue. We can talk shop while we crack open a cold one."

"All right, Doctor Stand-Up Comedian, I wouldn't quit your day job," Sawyer said, then motioned to Werner. "And speaking of your day job, how about we focus on the actual cold one we've got in front of us."

Doc hung his head, acting properly scolded, but snuck another wink at Bailey before he knelt beside the body. "Yes, Sheriff, back to business. I might be going out on a limb here, but I'm going to say this man is dead."

Bailey laughed again, a small chuckle, but Sawyer stayed straight-faced as he stared at the medical examiner.

Doc held up his hands in surrender. "All right, I'll stop. It's just hard to turn it off once I get on a roll. And I'm not used to having a *live* audience." He peered up at Sawyer. "No? Nothing? Not even a hint of a smile? Tough crowd." He opened the medical bag he had brought in with him and set to work.

Sawyer looked up at Bailey and shook his head, but she caught the ghost of a smile playing around his lips. She liked the medical examiner. And she was thrilled by his offer to answer questions for her books. Although Sawyer was right, this probably wasn't the best time to be networking and thinking about her career.

Another knock on the front door, and Bailey turned at the familiar voices of her aunts calling out greetings.

"Yoo hoo, anyone home?" called Aster, while her older sister headed toward Bailey.

"We saw your car, and the sheriff's, then the medical examiner's," Marigold said. "Are you all right?"

Sawyer took a step toward them. "I'm sorry, you ladies can't be in here." He glanced at Bailey. "Get them out of here before they contaminate the crime scene."

"*Crime scene?*" Marigold asked, glancing behind Bailey then letting out a gasp. "Oh no, what happened?"

Aster didn't say anything. She must have already seen Werner's body because she was staring down at him, her hands covering her mouth as her eyes filled with tears.

Bailey opened her arms to corral her aunts back to the front porch, giving a nod to Sawyer as he gestured to the body, then to her aunts as he mouthed "Don't tell them anything."

"Come on, Aunties," she said, a little too loudly, putting an arm around each of them.

"What's going on? Did Werner have a heart attack?" Marigold asked as she pulled open the door.

"I'll tell you all about it later," Bailey said, her voice still loud enough to carry. "You take Aunt Aster home now and get her a cup of tea. It looks like she's had a bit of a shock." She hugged Aster. "I'm sorry," she said, pressing a kiss to her aunt's cheek.

Bailey understood how a crime scene worked and knew she shouldn't say a word, but it was her grandmother's innocence at stake here, she thought as she pulled Marigold in for a hug and whispered quickly into her ear. "It looks like he was killed with Granny Bee's hot spiced honey, so they're sending a car out to bring her in to the station. You need to call and warn her."

Her Aunt Marigold could have been an actress in a former life for the calm way she took the news, hugging Bailey back, then giving her a quick nod as she took her sister's arm. Either that, or she'd been involved in another murder investigation that Bailey had never heard about. Either way, she was cool as a cucumber as she led her sister down the steps. "Yes, a cup of tea sounds just right, dear."

"I'll call you both in a bit," Bailey called out, raising her hand in a wave.

"You told them, didn't you?"

Bailey jumped at Sawyer's voice in her ear and then inhaled a quick breath as he put a hand on her shoulder to settle her. "Holy cow, you scared me," she said, trying to focus on anything other than the heat of his large hand resting on her arm.

"You're avoiding the question," he said.

But she'd already ducked from under his hand and was heading back inside as she said over her shoulder, "I'm sure I have no idea what you're talking about."

He followed right on her heels as she hurried back through the living room, but before he could ask anything more, they were interrupted by another slam of the front screen door, and both turned to a see a man of about thirty wearing khaki pants, a navy polo shirt, and scuffed brown boat shoes. His face held enough of the same features, but it was the shock of too-long dark hair worn in the same style that told Bailey this man was related to Werner.

"What's going on here?" the man asked, not bothering with a greeting as he barreled through the living room. "Has something happened to my uncle?" He called into the house, "Uncle?" before his gaze fell on the body lying on the dining room floor. "Uncle?" he asked again, although this time his voice had lost its bluster.

Sawyer stepped forward, holding out his hand. "Hi, Edward. I'm not sure if you remember me. We met at that Humble Hills Museum fundraiser a week or so back. I'm Sheriff Dunn, this is

Bailey Briggs. We're the ones who found your uncle. I'm sorry for your loss."

"What happened to him?" Edward asked, ignoring Sawyer's hand as he tried to peer around his shoulder.

"Looks like he died from anaphylactic shock," the medical examiner said, pushing to his feet and approaching the nephew. "My best guess is that it had to do with an allergic reaction to something he ate. Do you know if he has any food allergies?"

"He's always going on about his allergies to bees and honey."

Doc nodded to the overturned jar of honey. "That'd do it."

Edward followed Doc Foster's gaze, then shook his head. "No way. That can't be how he died. He was terrified of the stuff. Wouldn't even have it in the house for other people. There's no way he'd eat honey on purpose. And even if he did it by accident, he *always* carried one of those EpiPen things with him, wherever he went. And I know he's got several here at the house."

"He must not have been able to get to one in time," Doc said. "I'm sorry for your loss."

"Do you know anyone who might have something against your uncle or who would want to harm him?" Bailey asked. She ignored Sawyer's wide-eyed look of disbelief. There was a possibility she probably shouldn't be the one asking the nephew questions. But oh well, she could always act innocent later.

"Apparently half this town has something against him," he said, then paused. "Wait. What do you mean, *harm* him? Do you think someone *did* something to him?" Edward took another step closer.

"We don't know anything yet," Sawyer told him, blocking his way. "But it might help to know when you saw your uncle last. Or if you knew if he was expecting company last night."

Edward shook his head. "I saw him yesterday. We met for lunch at the club. He didn't say anything about meeting anyone else. But he was always doing something or seeing someone. He has . . . *had* . . . a more active social life than I do."

"Well, if you think of anything else, I'd appreciate you letting me know," Sawyer said, handing him a business card.

Edward's gaze traveled around the room and up the stairs. "I should probably move in here. You know, to take care of things now that my uncle is . . . gone."

Wow. That was fast.

Sawyer shot a quick glance at Bailey. Apparently, he was thinking the same thing. "I don't think the house will be available for a few days, at least. Could possibly be a week or two," Sawyer told him.

"A week or two?" Edward asked, sounding annoyed. "Why would I have to wait that long?"

"Your uncle just died, son," Sawyer explained.

"So? It's not like I'm afraid of his spirit or his ghost or whatever sticking around to haunt me. I don't believe in that garbage."

"It has nothing to do with his spirit, although I think a little respect *is* in order here," Sawyer said, taking on a bit of a sterner tone. "It's more that it's going to take us a bit to process the scene."

Edward shrugged, either ignoring or oblivious to Sawyer's admonition. "Can't you do that while I'm staying here? Like you could rope off the dining room or something? I don't need to use that room anyway."

Sawyer shook his head. "No. I'm afraid that's not possible."

"Well, let me know as soon as I'm clear to move in."

"Will do." Sawyer turned his back on Edward, dismissing the man as he and Doc returned to the dining room area.

Bailey followed them but snuck a glance back at Edward, just to see what he'd do. She half expected him to take off with some of Werner's belongings. That whole business of him wanting to move in so quickly didn't sit well in her stomach.

But Edward didn't appear to be shoving anything into his pockets. Instead, he was peering around the foyer and up the stairs, a thoughtful expression on his face, and Bailey couldn't tell if he was trying to appraise the value or imagining how he'd redecorate.

On the floor by the front door, two pair of Werner's shoes were neatly lined up against the wall, one a basic pair of sneakers, the other a pair of Gucci Italian leather loafers that Bailey knew cost a serious chunk of change. They were the kind of shoes a man wore to show he had wealth.

Edward stared down at the shoes, then to Bailey's surprise, toed his scuffed boat shoes off and slipped his feet into the Gucci loafers.

Leaving his shoes next to the empty space, Edward turned and walked out the door. His steps were light, and Bailey couldn't help thinking that Werner's nephew had quite literally just stepped into his dead uncle's shoes.

Chapter Six

B ailey stared at a poster proclaiming "5 Tips to Improve your Pet's Dental Health" and wondered how many people sitting at the sheriff's department were worried about their dog's tooth decay. She certainly wasn't. Although Cooper had great teeth. But right now, all she was worried about was Granny Bee. And Daisy. What would happen to her daughter if they took Gran away?

She chewed on her bottom lip. Had the aunts gotten a message to Granny in time to warn her? And warn her of what? It's not like Gran could have anything to do with Werner's death. *Could she?*

No, of course not.

Bailey was dying to talk to her. To reassure Gran, *and herself,* that everything was going to be okay. But Sawyer had instructed her not to talk to anyone until she'd given her official statement.

They had stayed at Werner's house another half an hour, long enough for several of Sawyer's deputies to show up and for the medical examiner to take the body away. Then she rode with Sawyer to the station.

They hadn't talked much during the car ride, except for him to assure her that someone would drive her back to her car when they were finished. And she did tell him about the weird thing she'd witnessed with Edward essentially stealing Werner's shoes. He'd agreed it was weird but didn't comment further. Although she still recognized his *thinking* face, and it was most definitely the expression he wore for most of the ride.

Her phone buzzed in her pocket. A short buzz indicating a text. Sawyer said she couldn't talk to anyone, but that didn't mean someone couldn't talk to her. She looked across the station to where she could see him through the top section of the glass of his office. He was sitting at his desk, his phone pressed to his ear, a frown creasing his forehead as he listened more than he talked.

She nonchalantly twisted her wrist to peer at her smart watch, acting as if she were just checking the time, but really checking the text message that was displayed there.

It was a group text, and the screen didn't show all the participants, but she could read both her aunts' names and Rosa's, so she assumed it was from The Hive. The message was only two words, but they were two words that made her pulse race and sweat pop out in the center of her back: OPERATION ALIBI.

Oh. Shit.

There were no responses, no follow-up texts, just the two words. But she knew what they meant. They all did.

She took a deep breath, forcing herself to relax. This was all going to be fine.

The front door of the sheriff's department burst open, and a deputy walked in, his hand on the elbow of a spitting mad Granny Bee.

"Gran, are you all right?" Bailey asked, pushing to her feet.

"No, I'm not all right," her grandmother hollered, her wrists held together in front of her. "Does it look like I'm all right? This young whippersnapper showed up and dragged me out of my house in handcuffs and then hauled me down here to the station to be thrown in the slammer. Like I'm a common criminal."

Granny had on jeans and a yellow T-shirt with a large bee on it that read "I'm a Keeper." Her long silvery-blond hair was disheveled, pieces of it falling free from the ponytail at the back of her neck. She wore the blue boot fastened around her broken foot and a slipper on the other, making Bailey think this callous deputy hadn't even given her a chance to put on proper footwear.

"Miss Briggs . . . ," the deputy, who wasn't that young—the guy looked like he was in his forties—tried to say. He had short dark hair, but a few gray strands were visible in his thick mustache.

But Granny Bee interrupted him, raising her voice even louder. "I've got rights, you know." From behind the deputy's back, she snuck a quick glance at Bailey and gave her a wink, a sly grin curving her lips for just a moment before her angry scowl returned. "I protested for women's rights in the sixties and burned my bra with the rest of them. So I know a travesty of justice when I see one."

Bailey grimaced, not wanting to imagine her grandmother swinging her brassiere around before tossing it into a bonfire. She also had no idea what bra-burning had to do with Gran's current situation, but it was getting the results she was trying for. Everyone in the station was staring in their direction.

Sawyer must have finished his call because he yanked open his office door and strode across the room, already pulling a ring of keys from his pocket. "Geez, Riggs, I told you to bring her in for questioning, not handcuff her and drag her out of her house."

"I didn't handcuff her," the deputy sputtered. "She's just holding her wrists together."

Sawyer looked down at Granny's hands where she had her wrists pressed together, then cocked an eyebrow as his gaze returned to her face.

She gave an innocent shrug, then crossed her *un*handcuffed hands in front of her. "Wellll," she huffed indignantly. "He might as well have handcuffed me. It was still humiliating."

The deputy, who apparently *wasn't* that callous, shook his head. "I tried to tell her that if I put the cuffs on her then I'd have to arrest her, but she kept insisting. It's a wonder I got her here at all."

"Where's Daisy?" Bailey asked, ignoring her grandmother's theatrics as she craned her neck to look around the deputy.

"Don't worry," Granny said. "She's with Rosa."

Bailey let out a sigh of relief.

"You're not under arrest, I just need to ask you some questions," Sawyer told Granny. "How about we get you some coffee? Or a glass of water?"

Granny Bee's shoulders slumped, and her chest caved inward as if her whole body was an ice cream cone that was melting in the sun, as she let out a long, tortured sigh. "You know, I'm just a poor defenseless little old lady who was only minding her own business."

Sawyer arched an eyebrow again and lowered his voice as he leaned closer to her. "You can cut the act, Granny. I'm not buying it. You're not *that* old. And just a minute ago, you were making a fuss and hollering about your rights."

She huffed again, straightening her shoulders. "Well, I have the *right* to call myself a defenseless little old lady if I want. That's what we protested and burned our—"

Sawyer held up his hands. "I don't need to know what you burned. Can you just come back to my office and give me a statement?"

"Wait!" a voice yelled as Aster and Marigold pushed into the sheriff's office.

"Don't say anything, Bee," Marigold commanded, hustling past the deputy. "Sheriff, I'm here to tell you that my sister had nothing to do with this unpleasant business with Werner."

Now it was Sawyer's turn to sigh. And his was almost as long-suffering sounding as Granny's had been. "I appreciate your concern, Miss Marigold, but I still need to ask her some questions."

"You can't arrest her," Marigold barreled on as if Sawyer hadn't said anything. "Because I was with her the whole night, so she couldn't have been with Werner."

"Yeah," Aster said, stepping up to stand with her sister. "I was too."

Sawyer looked from the aunts to Bailey, then back to the aunts. "You mean you're here to tell me that you were with your sister *the whole night*? In the *same room* with her?"

"Yep," Marigold said, without missing a beat. "It was like a slumber party."

"A slumber party?" Sawyer asked, but before he could say anything more, Rosa, Evie, and Daisy burst through the door.

"We're here to make a statement," Rosa declared.

Evie put a hand on her hip. "Yeah, we're here to declare that we were with Granny Bee all night last night. We slept over."

Bailey's heart swelled as Daisy followed Evie's lead, planting her fist at her waist and calling out, "Me too."

Sawyer scrubbed a hand over his face and rubbed the whiskers on his jawline. "So, all three of you were at this so-called slumber party?"

"*Sí*," Rosa confirmed with a hard nod.

"We stayed up all night," Evie told him, embellishing the story ever more. "We played truth or dare and tried to put Granny's bra in the freezer."

Sawyer winced. "Can we please stop talking about Granny Bee's br-r . . . undergarments?"

A blast of warm summer air came through as the station door pushed open one more time and a disheveled Dottie came striding in holding a pink bakery box. "Sorry I'm late, I stopped to pick up some cupcakes." She blew her damp bangs up and off her forehead.

"Oh, I'll take one," Deputy Riggs said, reaching toward the box.

"Sure thing, honey. There's chocolate, vanilla, and strawberry. And they've all got that yummy whippy frosting. And a few have sprinkles." Dottie opened the lid. "Take your pick. I brought them for you all. But they're not like a bribe or anything. I would never do that. I watch crime shows and know that bribing a police officer is against the law."

"But lying to one is apparently okay," Sawyer muttered.

Deputy Riggs picked up a strawberry frosted one covered in rainbow-colored sprinkles and grinned like he'd won a prize.

Marigold cleared her throat in an exaggerated, "Ahem."

Dottie looked up, then closed the lid and rearranged her expression into a more serious one. "Oh yes, of course. I'm so sorry. I'm here to make a statement that I was with Granny Bee all night last night."

Sawyer groaned and slapped a hand to his forehead. "She's *not* under arrest. We just brought her in for questioning."

"Then you won't mind if we wait," Rosa said, planting her fanny in one of the plastic chairs and pulling a ball of yarn and knitting needles from her bag.

"Suit yourself," Sawyer said, holding his arm out to Granny Bee. "Despite the sizable slumber party that supposably happened at your house last night, I do still need to ask you some questions. Would you please come into my office to do that now?"

Granny Bee lifted her chin. "Well, since you asked so nicely."

Sawyer let out a low growl as the door to the station opened one more time, then his eyes widened at the teenager holding three boxes of pizza.

"I got a delivery here for Briggs," he said, snapping his gum as he peered around the station.

"That's me," Marigold said, raising her finger. She offered Sawyer a shrug. "I wasn't sure how long we'd be here. But we're prepared to wait it out if you end up throwing my sister in the slammer."

"No one is throwing anyone in the slammer," Sawyer said, then held up his hand. "Enough already. You're not turning the lobby of my station into a party." His voice took on a sterner tone. "In case you've forgotten, a man is dead."

The women lowered their heads, accepting the chastisement as if they had just now remembered the reason they were all gathered there.

Sawyer narrowed his eyes, keeping his tone firm. "Now, I'm taking Granny Bee back to get her statement, and I'm not sure how long we'll be. Could be twenty minutes, could be several hours. Either way, I would suggest that you all *not* be here when

I come out. If you are, I will be forced to take all your statements and will arrest anyone who I find out has perjured themselves."

"Can he really do that?" Dot whispered to Deputy Riggs as Sawyer took Granny's arm and led her toward his office.

"Oh yeah, you bet he can. It's against the law to purposely impede an investigation, and you can go to jail for perjury."

Bailey swallowed. The charge was severe, but it was hard to take it seriously when the deputy had a dab of pink frosting and three rainbow sprinkles stuck in his mustache.

Marigold put her knitting back into her bag, then stood up and peered around at the group. "It sounds like Granny may be a bit. I suggest we all go back to the ranch and wait for her there."

"Good idea," Deputy Riggs said, eyeing the pizza boxes. "Any chance I could get a slice before you go?"

Chapter Seven

It took several hours before both women had finished giving their statements and were free to leave the police station, and Bailey was glad there was still some pizza left when they finally made it back to the farm.

It was well past noon, and her stomach had made an embarrassing growl toward the end of her interview. It must have been loud enough for Sawyer to hear since he finished typing the last sentence he was on and told her he had enough for now. She'd hoped so; they'd gone over her statement four times already. Which was a little annoying since he'd been there with her the whole time.

A deputy had taken her and Granny Bee back to Bailey's car where she'd left it in front of Werner's, and she was glad to see the women of The Hive were all still waiting when they arrived at the ranch. She let her aunts make a fuss over Granny while she got them each a glass of iced tea and heated up a couple of slices of pizza.

"Well, this is a fine kettle of fish," Marigold said, settling back into her favorite wingback chair and picking up her knitting. "You just *had* to tell Werner Humble that you were going to *kill* him the day before someone actually did."

Granny shrugged nonchalantly, but Bailey could see the mischief in her eyes. "Seems like someone just beat me to it."

Rosa shook her head and muttered, "You are one *señora loca*."

"I'm not crazy," Granny Bee insisted. "Just frustrated at that man who thinks he can do whatever he wants and get away with it."

"He's not getting away with anything anymore," Evie said.

"Point taken," Granny said before stuffing another bite of pizza into her mouth.

Aster's teacup rattled against her saucer, and she quickly set it on the table next to her and stared down into her lap.

Bailey reached a hand out to touch her shoulder. "Are you okay, Auntie?"

Aster shook her head. "I don't know. I'm all mixed up inside. I mean, yesterday I was so mad at the man. He made me feel foolish that I'd gone out to dinner with him several times, then he had the nerve to make a pass at my sister. But as mad as I was, I sure didn't wish him dead." She waved her hand in front of her face as she blinked back tears. "Oh, don't listen to me. I'm just out of sorts. I'm mad and sad and scared for Bee and embarrassed that I thought love was even still in the cards for an old gal like me."

"You're not that old," Evie said. "And you don't have to give up on finding someone. Look at Miss Dot, she found a great guy."

They all turned to Dottie, who was wringing her hands together in her lap. A lone tear slipped down her cheek as she bit her bottom lip to keep it from trembling.

"Oh no," Bailey said. "Your wonderful mystery man wasn't . . . ?" She couldn't bring herself to say Werner's name.

Dottie gave the slightest nod as she dipped her chin closer to her chest.

"Oh no," Granny Bee whispered.

"Oh yes," Dottie whispered back.

Oh shoot.

Bailey pressed her fingers to her lips. What could she say now?

Apparently, she didn't have to say anything. Instead, the lovely well-mannered child that she birthed said it for them all.

"You mean to say that guy was dating *both* of you *and* made a pass at Granny Bee?" Daisy asked. "He sounds like a real douche nugget to me."

Dottie looked up at Daisy, her eyes round in surprise, then a small giggle bubbled out of her. She covered her hand with her mouth, but another laugh escaped. Then the room erupted as they all burst out laughing.

"Yes, great-granddaughter," Granny Bee said, as the laughter settled down. "I think you hit the nail right on the smarmy bastard's head."

"The smarmy *dead* bastard," Bailey reminded her. "Which brings us back to the kettle of fish we started this conversation with. The one where you're a 'person of interest' in his death."

Aster sighed as she peered around the room. "Anyone have any great ideas how we're going to get my sister out of this mess? Or even semi-mediocre ideas?"

"I still don't know all the details of what happened," Evie said. "Other than he's dead, and it was Granny's honey that possibly killed him. Why don't you start by telling us everything you know?"

"Obviously this information is confidential and can't leave this room," Bailey said before filling them in on everything that had happened that morning.

"Hmm. That does sound bad for Bee," Marigold said, patting her sister's good leg. "But only because she threatened him.

Otherwise, anyone could have gotten ahold of a jar of her honey. They sell it in half the stores in town for goodness sakes."

"*Getting* the honey would be easy," Granny Bee agreed, "But the hard part would be getting him to eat it. The man was ridiculously careful about avoiding any kind of exposure to bees or honey. Frankly, I'm surprised he even came out to the ranch yesterday since he knows there are numerous hives here."

"That is a mystery," Rosa said.

"A mystery that I plan to solve," Bailey said.

Granny jerked her head toward her granddaughter. "*You?* No way. The police think Werner was *murdered*. Which means there is a *murderer* out there. Someone who *murders* people. Which means I don't want you anywhere near this business."

"Gran, murder *is* my business. That's how I make my living."

"You make your living off *fictional* murders. This is for real, Bailey. A man is dead."

Bailey nodded. "Yes, I know. I saw him this morning. And the police think you had something to do with it. So, if I can figure out who the real killer is, then you'll be off the hook."

"Makes sense to me," Evie said, having her back, like always. "What can I do to help?"

"I want to help as well," Marigold said, putting her knitting to the side and leaning forward.

"Me too," Dottie said.

Aster raised her hand. "Me three."

Granny smacked her forehead. "Now look what you've done. You've got half The Hive thinking they're private detectives. What do any of you know about solving a crime or finding a murderer?"

"Excuse me," Bailey said. "Solving crimes *is* what I do."

"And we watch a lot of murder mysteries," Aster said, pointing to herself and Marigold. "And we almost always guess the killer correctly."

"You solve mysteries that *you* create," Granny told Bailey, then turned to her sisters. "And this isn't like on television. This is dangerous. And I've watched mysteries with you all, and saying you *almost always* guess correctly is a gross overstatement. The only reason you ever get the identity of the killer right is because you've guessed half the suspects before the show is over."

"Doesn't mean we couldn't get it right this time," Aster said, lifting her chin.

Granny Bee sighed as she peered around the room. "Are you serious about this? You *all* want to try to solve Werner's murder?"

Every woman nodded, even Daisy.

Granny threw up her hands. "Okay, fine. If you're all in, I'm in too. So I guess we're doing this." She looked toward Bailey. "The Hive is temporarily transitioning to The Hive *Mind*. Where do we start?"

Oh shoot. Now she'd done it.

"Why are you all looking at me?" Bailey asked.

"You were just bragging that you knew everything about solving mysteries," Granny said. "Start solving."

"What would you have the characters in your books do first, Mom?" Daisy asked.

"Good question. Thanks, hon," Bailey said. "First, they would either compile a list of suspects, or if they didn't know of any suspects, then they would have to interview people to figure out who might have had a reason to want Werner Humble dead."

"Good," Marigold said, pulling a pad of paper and a pen from her knitting bag. "List of suspects," she said, writing it across the top of a blank page. "Number one is Blossom Briggs."

Aster swiped at the notebook. "Don't put Bee on there."

Marigold held the notebook out of reach. "Why not? She *is* a suspect. The police questioned her. And I want to have at least one person on our list that we'll have the satisfaction of crossing off when we prove she didn't do it."

"Thanks," Granny Bee said, a note of sarcasm in her voice. "Please tell me we've got at least one other person to add to the list."

"I think we can add Werner's nephew to the list," Bailey said. "That thing with the shoes really bothered me."

"Me too," Evie said. "And the fact that he was so anxious to move into the house. Plus, I just don't like him. He comes into the café for breakfast quite often, and he treats our waitresses like trash. *And* he's a terrible tipper. I just don't get a good vibe from him."

Evie and Rosa ran a small coffeeshop and café in town that served breakfast and lunch. Many of their recipes had been handed down in their family and had a sweet and spicy flair reminiscent of their Puerto Rican heritage. Bailey's mouth watered just thinking about their crispy cinnamon-crusted quesitos and breakfast sausage empanadas.

"A bad vibe doesn't mean he killed his uncle," Marigold told Evie. "But I'll add him to the list."

"Anyone have any other suspects to add?"

"I'm sorry to say it," Bailey said. "But there *are* a couple of other names we need to add. And I'm sure I'm not the only one who's thinking of them. The sheriff is going to want to talk to anyone who might have been close to Werner, and that would include any romantic interests. Which puts Aster and Dottie's names on that list just as surely as Granny Bee's."

Marigold gave a solemn nod. "You're right, of course. Sorry, gals," she said as she wrote down their names.

Aster shrugged and Dottie went back to wringing her hands.

"Did he have a butler?" Daisy asked, grinning at her mom. "It seems like the butler always makes the list."

"No butler," Aster said. "But he has a housekeeper who cooks and cleans for him. Olive something."

"Not anymore," Dottie said. "He fired her a few weeks ago. Under suspicion of theft. And her name is Olive Green."

Bailey winced. "Olive *Green*? That's an unfortunate name."

"And an unfortunate circumstance," Granny Bee said. "Her getting fired gives her motive. We can definitely add her to the list."

"Really?" Marigold asked. "Lots of people get fired from their jobs. That doesn't mean they kill their ex-employer."

"Well, she's at least a person of interest," Bailey said. "And our list is pretty slim, so I think we should add her. It seems like she'd be a good person to talk to."

Evie nodded. "I agree. Most people ignore the waitresses and the housekeepers, but they're the ones who usually hear all the juicy stuff. I think we should talk to all of the douche nugget's staff." She winked at Daisy.

"What staff?" Granny Bee asked. "Dot just told us he fired his housekeeper."

"She could still know things," Evie insisted. "And she worked at his house. What about his staff at the courthouse? He's the freaking mayor—he has to have people who work for him. A secretary or some kind of administrative assistant, at least."

"He does," Granny Bee said. "Her name is Susan Dodd. She's worked at the courthouse for years."

"Then that's where we need to start," Bailey said. "We need to go to his office and talk to Susan Dodd first, then we need to talk to anyone else who is . . . er, *was* . . . close to Werner. That's the only way we're going to find out who had a motive, who had an opportunity, and who wanted him dead." She checked her watch. "We might still have time to catch her if we head to the courthouse now."

The women all started to collect their things and stand up from their chairs.

"Wait," Bailey said. "We can't *all* go."

"Right. I see what you mean," Aster said, dropping back into her chair. "Poor woman wouldn't know what to think if we all went traipsing in there and started grilling her for information about her recently departed boss."

"I should go, though," Granny said. "Since I'm the one who knows her. Maybe she'll open up and spill all the dirt on Werner to me."

"Oh sure. A few minutes ago, you thought our plan to find the killer was ridiculous and dangerous, now suddenly you're the lead investigator digging up dirt on the case."

Granny shrugged. "What can I say? I'm a joiner."

Bailey laughed. "You are sooo *not* a joiner. And you can't go. You're the lead suspect in the case."

"Well, she might not know that."

"This is Humble Hills *and* she's the mayor's secretary. I guarantee she knows," Bailey said. "And if she doesn't know yet, then maybe she's not the person we need to be chatting up to find out all the dirt in this town."

"Fine," Granny said, with a huff as she sat back down on the sofa.

"Besides, you need to rest your broken foot. You've been walking around all day," Bailey told her, gently propping Granny's foot up on a pillow. "I can go talk to her. I'll say I'm doing research for a new book, and I've got a scene set in a mayor's office. People love to help writers."

"I'll come with you," Evie said. "I know Susan. She comes in every Friday for a coffee and a honey-glazed quesito. Maybe she'll open up more to a familiar face."

"Good idea," Bailey said.

"What should we do while we wait?" Marigold asked. "We can't just sit around here and twiddle our thumbs."

"Keep working on the list."

"I can look him up on my laptop," Daisy said. "Since he's the mayor, I'm sure he has public profiles out there. I'll check his socials to see if I can find out anything useful about his personal life or people he might know."

"Good idea," Bailey said.

Marigold leaned toward Aster. "What are socials?"

"Social media," Aster said. "You know, if he twitters."

"*Twitters?*" Marigold said, making a face.

Aster waved a hand her direction. "I'll explain later."

"I want to help too," Dottie said. "But I'm afraid I have to go in to work. I've got the evening shift at the library, and I'm supposed to be there in an hour."

"That's okay," Bailey assured her. "You can still help from there. If you get some down time, why don't you help Daisy with researching Werner's life? Although, if she's looking into his personal life, then why don't you see if you can do some digging into his business life? See if he's ever started any companies or had any business deals that fell through or any jilted business parties. We all know money makes people do crazy things."

"Okay," Dot said, slinging her purse over her shoulder. "I'll try to see what I can find."

* * *

Fifteen minutes later, Bailey and Evie pushed through the tall glass door of the ancient courthouse located in the town square. The foyer was cool compared to the heat outside, and Bailey inhaled the scents of old wood, floor wax, and a faint smell of lemon furniture polish.

If they'd been in Denver, there would have been several armed guards and a line to search your bag before going through a metal detector, but this was Humble Hills, population sixteen hundred (and that may only be if they counted the dogs). So instead, there was just a simple desk with a low counter and a lone uniformed man sitting behind it.

He looked to be in his mid-twenties, his shoulders still a little too thin to completely fill out his uniform shirt. He looked up from the paperback he was reading, and his ears turned red as he spotted them. "Hey there, Miss Evie."

"Hi Charlie," her friend all but purred.

"What are you doing here . . . er . . . . I mean, what can I help you with?" He ducked his head, and Bailey couldn't help but feel a little sorry for him. Evie had always had that effect on most men—they either got tongue-tied or fell all over themselves trying to help her with something. "You're not in any kind of trouble, are you?" Charlie asked, his expression one of general concern.

"No, of course not," Evie said. "My friend Bailey here is back in town and we were just playing tourist, and I thought I'd show her around the courthouse. If that's okay."

For the first time, his gaze shifted to her, and his eyes widened. "You're Bailey Briggs?"

She laughed. "Yes, I am."

"Cool. I've read all your books."

"Thank you."

He looked down the hall behind him. Most of the doors were closed and there weren't many people around. He lowered his voice. "It's probably not the best day for a tour. Because of . . . you know, the mayor passing away and all. But I guess you could go in for a few minutes. You want me to show you around?"

Evie shook her head. "You're sweet for offering, but we're okay. We'll just do a quick look, then pop right back out. You'll never even know we were here."

He looked around again. "Yeah, I guess that would be okay. Best to stay away from the third floor, though. Since that's where the mayor's office is . . . er . . . was."

"Oh sure, of course," Evie said. "Thanks, Charlie." She took Bailey's arm, and they walked past him and into the grand foyer.

He waved, then picked up his book as he sank back into his chair. The elevator dinged, and the doors opened. A man in a navy suit holding a cell phone to his ear strode out, ignoring them as they stepped into the empty elevator and pushed the button displaying the number three.

Chapter Eight

The mayor's office was at the end of the hall, Werner Humble's name emblazoned on the door in large gold letters. Unlike the loud tapping their heels had made on the linoleum when they'd come in, thick beige carpeting camouflaged the sound of their steps as Bailey and Evie approached the office.

The door was barely ajar, and they looked questioningly at each other at the sound of a woman's voice swearing from inside. Carefully pushing through the door, they saw the receptionist's desk was empty.

The room itself was tastefully decorated in muted golds and wood tones. Two burgundy leather chairs sat against the wall opposite the desk with a small magazine-covered table between them, forming what looked like a waiting room. Behind the receptionist's desk, another door, presumably to the mayor's inner sanctum, stood partly open.

A file folder came flying through the air and hit the side of the door. Papers fluttered to the floor as a voice proclaimed, "Mother freaking heck of a biscuit!"

So maybe not *exactly* swearing, but a darn good substitute for it.

Bailey pointed toward the door, and she and Evie crept closer. Peering inside, they saw a huge oak desk with four file cabinets against the wall behind it. The drawers of three of them were open, and stacks of file folders were piled up on the desk and the floor. Two doors on the left wall were open, revealing a large closet and a spacious en suite bathroom. An open bottle of expensive scotch was sitting on the desk next to a cut-glass crystal rocks glass with only a thin line of the dark alcohol still in it.

A dark-haired woman wearing a navy skirt and matching jacket sat on the floor amid the stacks, frantically flipping through one folder after another. She looked to be in her sixties, and the silk blouse and string of pearls around her neck led Bailey to think she was normally well-dressed and put together. But today, her sensible black heels sat discarded by the desk, several locks of her hair had come free of her French twist and hung in her face, and a large snag had traveled up the shin of her suntan-colored panty hose.

"Hello," Bailey called out tentatively.

The woman let out a startled shriek and threw the folder she was holding in the air as she jumped.

"I'm sorry. We didn't mean to scare you," Bailey said, as she and Evie entered the room and bent to retrieve the flying papers.

The woman pressed a hand to her chest. "I'm fine. I just didn't see you there." She took the papers they held out, pushed them back into the folder, and slapped it on to a teetering pile. "I just didn't think they were letting anyone up to this floor today."

"Are you Susan?" Bailey asked, ignoring the fact that no one actually *let* them up here.

"Yes," the woman said, pushing her hair back from her face and straightening her blouse.

"I'm Bailey Briggs, and I think you know my friend, Evie."

"Yes, of course," Susan said, arranging her mouth into a smile as she nodded at Evie. "Any chance you've brought pastries?"

Evie shook her head. "No, but I may have to bring some back to you. It looks like you've got quite a project going on here. What are you looking for?"

It was obvious she was on the hunt for something, and Bailey's spidey senses were on full alert since Susan just happened to be tearing her boss's office apart within hours of hearing of his death.

Susan shook her head, her eyes wide, reminding Bailey of a deer caught in the headlights, or in this case, a secretary caught in the mayor's private files. "Oh no, I'm not looking for anything in particular . . . I'm just . . ." She paused as if trying to come up with a plausible explanation for the state of the office. "I'm just organizing some paperwork. Is there something I can help you with?"

"I think the bigger question," Evie said, peering around at the file folders, "is if we can't help you. This looks like a huge job."

She waved away the offer as she pushed up from the floor and plopped down in Werner's leather desk chair. "No, I can get it." A wave of sadness seemed to wash over her, and she appeared to shrink into Werner's chair as her shoulders sank inward. "On second thought, yes, I will take some help." She poured more scotch into her glass and took a healthy swig, then pointed to the stacks of folders. Her voice had just a hint of a slur, enough to make Bailey think this might be more than her second glass. "I've already gone through all of these . . . um, I mean, organized all of them, so they just need to go back into the file cabinet drawers."

"We can do that," Bailey said, straightening a pile before lifting it up and placing it back in the open drawer. "Do we need to keep them in any particular order?"

She started to nod, then shook her head. "No, just put them in however you can make them fit. What do I care? I don't even know if I have a job anymore." She let out another sigh as she looked out the window. "I've been Werner's secretary for the past twenty-three years, but I can't be the mayor's admin if there's no mayor."

"Oh gosh, I hadn't thought about that," Evie said, pushing a stack of folders into the drawer behind the ones Bailey had put in. "Who's supposed to step in when a mayor dies?"

"I'm not sure who the city will appoint, but I think the city council member who has served the longest is supposed to take his place." Susan tilted her head as she looked up to the ceiling. "I think Lon Bracken has been on the council the longest, so my best guess is that he'll step in."

"I'm sure if they're appointing an interim mayor, they'll keep you on too," Bailey said.

"I hope so," Susan said. "I've only got two years left until I can retire with full benefits. It would be just my luck that I've hung on to this darn job this long, then I end up getting sacked right before retirement."

Bailey noted the bitterness in her voice and was dying to ask a million questions, but felt she needed to tread carefully. "You and Werner worked together a long time. You must have got along pretty well."

Susan gave her a knowing side-eye as she took another swig. "If that's your subtle way of asking if I had any reason to want the guy dead, then the answer is no. I told you, I needed him alive, at least for the next two years, then I could care less if he kicked the bucket."

"Oh."

"Sorry, that came out harsher than I meant. But Werner was a hard man to work for. He wasn't as bad when his wife was still alive, but she died close to ten years ago, and he's changed a lot since then. The last decade he's gotten more demanding, twice as chauvinistic, and I think he invented mansplaining. And don't get me started on the women, and how he came to believe he was God's gift to them."

"Eww," Evie said with a shudder.

Susan shrugged and took another sip. "He might be *eww* to you, because you're young, but for a guy in his seventies who was fit, charming, and still had a great head of hair, he was catnip to anyone over the age of sixty."

"Apparently to *several* someones over sixty," Evie muttered.

"But he wasn't catnip to you?" Bailey asked. Normally, she wouldn't be so bold, but she noted Susan wasn't wearing a ring *and* her grandmother's innocence was on the line.

"Not even close," Susan said. "He tried a couple of times, once in the early days of my working with him and then again after my husband died. But I shut him down both times. He wasn't really interested in me anyway. I wasn't his type."

"No?"

"No. You could say Werner liked his women to be plus-sized— not their bodies, but their bank accounts." She narrowed her eyes as she peered at Bailey over her glass. "I'm assuming you're going to talk to them. If you haven't already."

"Talk to who?" Bailey asked.

"Oh, come on now. Do you gals really think I don't know why you're here? I know you didn't sneak up to the third floor to help me clean up this office." She offered them a sly smile. "I've lived in this town my whole life. I heard about Werner hours ago. I know he died under 'suspicious' circumstances, that the police are investigating this like a murder, *and* that they've already brought your grandmother in for questioning. I know you're here to try to find out something about our dearly departed mayor that might clear Bee."

Busted.

"Okay, yes, that *is* why we're here," Bailey said. "We figured if anyone knew any reasons why someone would want to take Werner out, it would be you, the person who works with him every day. So, *do* you know anything that might clear my grandmother?"

She was really going for broke here. But Susan seemed to be in a chatty mood; whether that was due to the stress of her boss's death or the amount of alcohol she'd consumed, Bailey didn't know. But as long as the woman was talking, Bailey was going to try to get as much out of her as she could.

Susan let out a loud hiccup, then covered her mouth as she shook her head. "No. I'm sorry. I don't."

"Do you have any suggestions of who we *should* be talking to?" Evie asked.

"You mean besides Alice and Helen?"

Evie looked as confused as Bailey. "Alice and Helen?"

"Yes. Alice Crawford and Helen Dobbs. The ones we were just talking about. The women Werner was currently dating."

Chapter Nine

E vie shot her a quick look, and Bailey knew they were think-ing the same thing.

These were not the droids, or in this case old ladies, we were looking for.

Poor Aunt Aster. And poor Dottie.

Susan caught the look, and her lips curved into a knowing smile. "Oh. You heard he was dating some *other* women?" She shrugged. "He probably was. I couldn't keep up with his dating life." Her smile transformed into a sneer. "The snake."

"Were the women you mentioned more Werner's type?"

"Oh yeah. And I'm sure they were both contributing to the mayor's *private fund*."

"Private fund?" Bailey asked at the same time Evie said, "It sounds like the motive for his death had to be about money."

Susan's face went pale as she shook her head. "I didn't say that. I'm sure it wasn't just about money. The mayor had plenty of enemies. He loved the ladies, but he was also a shrewd business-man and didn't like to lose, especially when it came to business. Maybe you should think about who else he was in bed with . . . so to speak." She took another sip, then slid lower into the chair.

"Besides, it's not like you could get into his accounts or anything. There's no way for you two to check into his finances, even if you wanted to. And crooked politicians always seem to know how to hide their funds."

"Was Werner a crooked politician?" Bailey asked.

"I didn't say that either," Susan said, backpedaling a little. "But Werner had a way of taking advantage of people when they were at their most vulnerable." Another loud hiccup escaped her lips, and she pressed a hand to her mouth. Her face went from pale white to a shade of green. "I don't feel very well." She pushed up from the chair and stumbled toward the bathroom, yanking the door shut behind her.

"Poor woman," Bailey whispered.

"Bad for her, good for us," Evie said, reaching into her designer purse and pulling out two pairs of disposable plastic gloves. She passed a pair to Bailey.

"You brought gloves?"

"No, I just had them in my purse. They're from the restaurant, but they should work to keep our fingerprints off anything Susan didn't see us touch." She pulled the gloves on and hurried toward the mayor's desk. "Don't just stand there, help me look around." She jerked at the desk drawers, but they didn't budge. "Sh . . ." She stopped herself with a growl followed by a frustrated, "Sugar nuggets. They're locked."

Bailey had to chuckle at Evie's attempts to cut back on her swearing. The woman was creative. She had to give her that.

"Look at this," Evie said, pointing to a letter opener on the desk, then at several scratches on the top desk drawer's lock. "It looks like we aren't the first ones trying to get a look at what's in the mayor's drawers." She looked up at Bailey then made a gagging motion. "Gross. Pretend I didn't say that. You know what I mean."

Bailey laughed again as she pulled on her gloves, then crossed to the open closet door and quickly scanned its contents. Three white dress shirts and two ties hung inside, all still secured in the dry cleaner's plastic. A blue sport coat hung next to them, and Bailey quickly checked the pockets, coming up with a tube of lip balm, a tin of mints, a crumpled receipt from a local restaurant, and a white handkerchief that she prayed was clean.

The top shelf held a spray bottle of wrinkle releaser and a can of air freshener, and the floor showed fresh vacuum tracks and held only a pair of sneakers and an umbrella. No critical clue, no smoking gun pointing to the mayor's killer.

Bailey winced as she heard the distinct sound of retching coming from behind the bathroom door and figured they only had a few more minutes to search. She turned back to Evie, who had squatted down in front of the desk and was stabbing two straightened paper clips into the lock of the drawer.

"What are you doing?" Bailey whispered. "Since when do you know how to pick a lock?"

"Since never, but this is how they do it on television," Evie said, then her eyes grew wide. "I got it! I can't believe that worked."

"No way," Bailey whispered as she practically ran back to the desk, both excited to see what was in the drawer and a bit awestruck at her friend's lock-picking abilities. Although there wasn't much Evie Delgado couldn't do once she set her mind to it.

"Ohhh shit," Evie said, then shrugged at Bailey's scolding look. "Sorry, but sugar nuggets wasn't gonna cover it this time."

Bailey peered into the drawer to where Evie was pointing. The drawer held an assortment of items, and all of them made Bailey cringe. A silver monogrammed flask, a prescription bottle of Viagra, a half-smoked cigar, a United States passport, a motel key card wrapped inside a pair of lacy thong panties, and tucked behind a small leather address book sat a box of ammunition and a steely gray handgun.

Evie reached in to grab the address book but yanked her hand back at the sound of the bathroom door lock releasing. She pushed the drawer shut, and she and Bailey yanked off their gloves and were shoving them into Evie's purse just as the door opened and Susan came staggering out.

"I'm sure you have a peppermint in here somewhere," Bailey said, trying for a reasonable excuse for why they both had their hands crammed into Evie's bag.

"Here they are," Evie proclaimed, pulling out a plastic case of mints. She shook one into her hand and passed it to Susan. "You don't look so great, hon."

"I don't feel so great," Susan said, taking the mint and putting it in her mouth. "I'm not much of a drinker. Apparently, an occasional glass of wine at a party does not have the same effect as half a bottle of aged scotch."

"Why don't you let us take you home?" Bailey said.

Susan let out a heavy sigh, as if the weight of the world rested on her narrow shoulders. "Yes. Okay. There's not much else I can do here today anyway. And I'm suddenly very tired." Her bangs were damp and plastered to her sweaty forehead. "I don't want to be a bother."

"You're no bother. We're happy to do it. Let's just grab your purse and shoes, then we'll lock up and get you out of here."

"Let's use the back door," Susan said, weaving a little as she tried to put her foot into her shoe and not fall over. "I don't want anyone to see me like this."

Bailey put a supporting hand under her elbow. "Good idea. We'll all just slip out, and no one will even have to know we were here."

* * *

Twenty minutes later, Bailey and Evie had locked up the mayor's office, and Evie had followed in Susan's car while Bailey drove Susan home. She lived in an adorable yellow two-story house only a few blocks from downtown, the yard lush with several colorful flower beds.

Susan had changed into a pair of blue floral pajamas while Evie rummaged through her kitchen and came up with a can of ginger ale and some bread to toast. Bailey got her settled on the sofa with a pillow and a comfy knitted throw. A black and white tabby cat had jumped up and curled in next to her legs, and she reached out to absently stroke the cat's side.

"Try to drink some of this," Evie said, handing Susan a glass of ginger ale and then setting a plate of lightly buttered toast on the end table next to the sofa. "Small sips at first to rehydrate you, then try a little of the toast to help settle your stomach."

"Thank you." Susan took a sip, then set the glass next to the toast. She pulled the throw up around her shoulders as she laid her head on the pillow and closed her eyes. "I'm so embarrassed."

"Don't be," Evie said, lightly patting her shoulder. "We've all been there."

"You're home now," Bailey said, peering around the beauti-fully decorated living room and kitchen area. "I love your house."

"Thanks. We loved it so much. And worked so damn hard to get it. It was our first home, and we moved in right after we got married. We always thought it was a sign that our anniversary was November sixteenth and that's how much our mortgage was—eleven hundred and sixteen dollars." She choked back a sob. "My Charlie died five years ago, and I still miss that man every single day."

"I'm sure you do," Bailey said. "And all your hard work was worth it. Your house is gorgeous."

Susan's voice transitioned from sad to sleepy and still held a hint of a slur as she was drifting off. "It'd better be . . . since I sold my soul to the devil to keep it."

* * *

"What now?" Evie asked as she and Bailey got into the car and drove away from Susan's house. "Do we still want to head to the nephew's house, or should we try to talk to the two women Susan told us about first?"

"I say we still try for Edward. We know that he's aware of the suspicious stuff surrounding his uncle's death. The other women may not have even heard about it yet, and I don't want to be the one to tell them Werner died."

"Good point."

"I'm not sure how we're going to get him to talk to us."

"I've got an idea," Evie said. "We just need to make a quick stop first."

"I just keep thinking about my Aunt Aster," Bailey said after they'd made the stop and were on their way to Edward's. "I feel so bad for her. And for poor Dottie. It was awful enough when they both found out they were being *two*-timed, but now we're

86

going to have to tell them they were being . . . what? *Four*-timed? Quadruple-timed? I don't even know the word for it."

Evie made a gagging motion. "Slimeball is the word that comes to mind for me. It's like he was a geriatric gigolo."

Bailey couldn't help but laugh at the description as she pulled into the parking lot of the Lutheran church and cut the engine. Granny Bee had told them Edward had been renting the small blue cottage behind the church. She took a deep breath, then turned her head to look at Evie. "Do you want to be the good cop or the bad cop?"

"Oh please," Evie said, arching a perfectly shaped eyebrow. "You know I'm *always* gonna be the bad cop."

Bailey grinned. "I was counting on it."

Apparently, Edward didn't take any better care of his yard than his uncle did, Bailey noted as she and Evie walked up the cracked sidewalk to the cottage. The lawn was patchy, too long in some spots and practically bare in others, and the green grass was dotted with yellow dandelions.

"I don't take kindly to solicitors," Edward said, frowning as he opened the door. Then his frown curved up into a sleazy smile as his gaze raked up Evie's curves. "But in your case, I'm interested in whatever you're selling."

It seemed the "slimeball" trait ran in the family.

"We're not selling anything," Evie said in a tone Bailey recognized as her "fakey nice but you're really getting on my last nerve" voice. "We just brought you some fresh pastries from my café and wanted to stop in and say how sorry we were to hear about your dear uncle's passing."

"Well, come on in then. I love fresh pastries," Edward said, opening the door wider and practically salivating as he watched Evie walk by him.

It was a small consolation that Evie had told her she'd filled the box with some of the week-old stuff they were getting ready to toss.

As happened frequently in their long friendship, most people barely noticed Bailey when Evie was around—her friend was just too tall, too gorgeous, too charismatic, too . . . everything. But in this case, Bailey didn't mind. It gave her a chance to study Edward, and to look around the house as she followed him in.

He had on the same outfit as that morning and was still wearing Werner's loafers. It was a testament to the power of Evie's beauty that he hadn't even realized Bailey was the same person who had discovered his uncle's body.

"So tell us, how are you coping?" Evie said, setting the box down on the kitchen counter.

"Oh, well, you know, of course I'm sad," Edward said after a moment, as if he couldn't quite remember what he was supposed to be coping with.

"You poor thing. Were you and your uncle close?"

"Oh yeah. Real close. He planned to leave me everything." He shook his head. "Of course, I'm just broken up by his unexpected passing, but I'm about to become a very rich man. This time next week, I'll be out of here and moved into my uncle's house on the avenue. You'll have to bring me some pastries there, and I'll show you around."

"Mmm-hmmm," Evie hummed noncommittally, then leaned a little closer to whisper. "I heard there might be some suspicious circumstances surrounding your uncle's death. Nothing like that ever happens in this boring town. You seem really brave to me, but aren't you a little worried about a killer being on the loose?"

Evie was laying it on a little thick, but Edward seemed to be eating it up with a spoon. He pushed his shoulders back and puffed out his chest. "Me? Nah. Why would anyone want to hurt me? I'm a great guy."

Wow. Conceited much?

Evie leaned closer still, keeping her voice low as if they were in on a secret together. "Do you have any ideas of who might have had something against your uncle?"

Edward barked out a derisive laugh. "Who *didn't* have something against my uncle? I swear that guy had his thumb in every pie in this town. And I don't know many who were excited about his dirty hand being in their pie, if you know what I mean."

Bailey knew what he meant. Even though he wasn't talking to her—he may have even forgotten she was there. But it was a gross image just the same.

While Evie was talking, Bailey was scoping out the house, nonchalantly looking for clues. Not that she was seeing much. It's not like he had a folder lying on the counter labeled "Uncle's Killer." Although that would have made this whole thing much easier.

"Speaking of pie," Edward said, inching closer to Evie. "Maybe we could go get a slice sometime. I heard there's a great coffee shop and bakery downtown."

Um, yeah. There is. It's *Evie's* bakery, Bailey wanted to yell. This guy really was clueless. And so, it seemed, was his house.

A knock on the front door saved Evie from having to answer.

Edward frowned. "Be right back," he said, but they followed him toward the door, thinking this might be their best chance to sneak out of there without Evie having to give this creep her number.

Edward pushed open the screen door, and Bailey caught her breath as Sawyer stepped inside. Even though she'd spent most of the morning with him, she still wasn't used to the sight of him, especially this new version of him, all grown up and broad-shouldered.

Although *his* presence was sending her pulse pounding, she didn't seem to be having the same effect on him. In fact, he appeared a bit annoyed. His eyes were narrowed as he tipped his hat to her and Evie.

"Sorry to bother you, Edward," Sawyer said. "Especially when it looks like you're entertaining. But I've got some questions I need to ask you."

"This isn't a real great time," Edward said. "Maybe you could come back later."

Really? For a guy who said he was so close to his uncle, it would seem like he'd want to know more about what happened to him.

"We should probably get going anyway," Bailey said. Edward's back was to her, but she had Sawyer's attention, and she pointed down at the loafers. She'd told him earlier that she'd witnessed Edward taking them.

He gave just the slightest nod, but she caught it.

"You sure you don't want to wait around?" Edward asked Evie. "I'm sure this won't take long."

"No, sorry," Evie said, not sounding sorry at all. "We need to scoot. Enjoy the pastries."

They escaped out the front door but could still hear Edward's exasperated voice as he told Sawyer, "Can you make this quick? I've got things to do."

Bailey couldn't help but smile as she heard Sawyer's terse reply. "Considering you're wearing a pair of shoes that you *stole* this morning from an active crime scene, I'd suggest you make us much time as we need. But I'm happy to take you down to the station if you'd rather talk there."

Chapter Ten

Bailey and Evie made it inside the car before they started cracking up. But just barely.

"I think I need a shower," Evie said with a shiver. "That guy gave me the creeps."

"Thank you," Bailey said, cranking the engine and pulling out of the parking lot. "That's what I thought this morning too. He sure didn't seem too choked up about his uncle's death. I'm surprised he hadn't already started packing to move into his house."

"I thought the same thing."

"Sawyer didn't seem too thrilled to see us."

Evie laughed again. "Maybe not, but I was sure glad to see him. I was ready to get the heck out of there."

"Me too." Bailey turned onto the highway to head back toward the ranch. "Sorry you never got to play the bad cop."

"I was working up to it," Evie said with a shrug.

"I was working on my best detective skills, but I didn't deduce much. Other than the weird vibes we got from him and the fact that he didn't seem too broken up, the only other thing I noticed is that it looked like he was dating someone. Not that you could tell from the way he was treating you."

Evie nodded. "I noticed that too. I looked down the hall and could see a second toothbrush in the bathroom, and a pair of pink slippers with green frogs on them were next to the sofa."

"I noticed the slippers too. Didn't seem to be Edward's style. Good catch on the toothbrush, though. I noticed the coffee cup in the sink had a hot pink lipstick stain on the rim."

"Good job. I didn't see the cup. But I made sure to set the pastries down next to a pile of mail and it seems like Eddie-boy hasn't been keeping up on his bills. I saw at least three envelopes with overdue notices on them."

"I noticed a couple of blue mac and cheese boxes and several ramen wrappers in the trash can too, so he's not spending much on groceries."

Evie held up her hand for a high five. "Give it here, lady. I'd say we found out a lot of shh—stuff for only being in that dude's house for like five minutes. I think we make a pretty good investigative team."

"Yeah, we do. But what does any of that tell us? Besides that the guy is broke and he's dating a woman with questionable taste in lipstick."

"I think it tells us a couple of things. Number one, once we figure out who the pink frog slippers belong to, we'll have another person to talk to who might give us more insight into Werner's life, or at the very least Edward's relationship with his uncle. And number two, it tells us that Edward desperately needs the money an inheritance would bring him. Which, to me, sounds like another way to say *motive*."

* * *

Rosa and the aunts had all left by the time Bailey and Evie got back to the ranch. They filled Granny Bee and Daisy in on what they'd found, then Evie took off too.

"Any luck with digging into Werner's social life?" Bailey asked Daisy as they sat down to supper that night.

Granny Bee had thrown together a simple pot of chili, but the addition of warm cornbread covered in melted butter and drizzled in her fresh honey made the meal a feast for the taste sensations.

Daisy pushed the last bite of her cornbread into her mouth, then dropped her hand down to let the dog lick the remains of the dripping honey from her fingers. "Not much. He has a Twitter account and a pretty set routine of daily tweets, but they're mostly political or just feel-goody enough that it makes me think he's got a PR person creating and scheduling them for him. He has a Facebook profile, but it's more of the same. Not as many posts, but also nothing really personal. Sorry."

"Don't be sorry," Granny Bee. "It can be just as important to figure what *doesn't* matter and what to rule out."

"Granny's right." Bailey put her hand on top of her grandmother's. "How are you doing, by the way? I don't think I've really checked in with you all day. Is your foot hurting? Are you freaking out about the investigation? What can we do to help you?"

Granny p-shawed her with a wave. "I'm fit as a fiddle, honey. Don't you worry about me. And you're already helping. Just having you two here is help enough. Being with my great-grandchild is the best medicine I could ask for."

Bailey smiled at her grandmother and squeezed her hand, but she noticed a quick look on Daisy's face—not quite sadness and not quite confusion, but maybe somewhere in between.

* * *

Later that night, Bailey knocked on Daisy's door. "You got a second, hon?"

"Sure." Daisy was already tucked in bed, a large golden retriever cuddled against her side. Cooper had his head resting in her lap, and she had her book leaning against his neck so she could scratch his head in between turning pages. "What's up?"

"I just wanted to check in with you," Bailey said, settling on the edge of her bed. Cooper stretched his neck out to be able to give her hand a quick lick, then settled back in Daisy's lap with a sigh. His soulful brown eyes swept back and forth between mother and daughter. "You doing okay? Having fun?"

"Yeah, I'm good. I like being here. It feels like home."

It should. They'd lived at the ranch for the first four years of Daisy's life, before Bailey had moved them to Denver to finish school and pursue her dream of becoming an author. Granny Bee had designed the room especially for her great-granddaughter, updating and changing it as she grew so that it now held matching white bedroom furniture, bookshelves, a corner desk, and cozy bedding, all in a soft pink color with big white and yellow daisies printed on it.

Bailey was glad she felt at home here, especially now, with their future so up in the air. But she'd think about that later. Right now, she was more concerned with what *didn't* feel right with her daughter. "I just noticed a funny look you had at supper."

Daisy's gaze dropped to her lap, and she picked at a loose thread on the seam of her pajama top. "I didn't have a funny look. I'm fine. Everything's fine."

"That was one too many fines than I'm comfortable with." Something *was* bothering her daughter. Bailey nudged her arm. "Come on, kid. Talk to me. What's got you upset?"

"I'm not exactly upset. I guess I'm just a little worried."

"About what?"

Daisy's face pinched as if saying the words caused her physical pain. "I don't know if I should say anything."

Alarm bells went crazy in Bailey's chest. "Did someone hurt you? Or make you uncomfortable?"

Daisy rolled her eyes. "No, Mom. It's nothing like that. It's something I saw. It was weird. Well, I guess two somethings I saw."

"And both of them were weird?"

Daisy nodded.

"Like you saw a shadowy presence and think the house is haunted weird? Or like extraterrestrial, beam me up Scotty weird? Because the truth *is* out there."

Her daughter gave her an annoyed huff. "Neither of those kinds of weird." She took a deep breath then let it out slowly. "It was last night, like around midnight. I woke up. I'm not sure why. I don't know if I heard something or it was being in a different place, or maybe I just had to pee. Anyway, I got up to go to the bathroom and get a drink of water, and Cooper got up to come with me, like he always does. But when I came out of the bathroom, he must have seen Granny's door open because he ran in there, and I heard him jump up on the bed."

"Oh no." Bailey winced, all too familiar with the golden retriever launching himself onto her bed, *and her*, in the middle of the night. "Did he land on Granny?"

Daisy shook her head. "No, that's what was weird. I was so worried that he'd hurt her, so I ran in there after him, but she wasn't in there. Her bed was empty."

"That's not too weird," Bailey told her, although something niggled at the sides of her belly. "Maybe she was just downstairs. Maybe she couldn't sleep and went down to make a cup of tea or get a snack."

"That's what I thought too. But when I went back to my room, Cooper went running over and jumped up on the window and when I looked out to see what he was making a fuss about, I saw Granny Bee outside."

"Outside?"

"Yeah, she was kind of hurrying across the yard like she was coming in from the barn."

"Maybe she was just checking on some of the animals. Was she in her pajamas?"

Daisy stared down at the comforter as she shook her head again. "No, she was dressed. She had on pants and a sweatshirt. I could see her when she went under the yard light. And that was the other weird thing. She didn't have that funny boot on her foot. And she was walking pretty fast. Like she wasn't even limping at all."

Chapter Eleven

Bailey had been waiting all morning for a chance to talk to her grandmother, but Granny Bee had been outside most of the time, either caring for the bees or deep in discussion with Lyle.

She hadn't had much of a chance to get a good read on the new farm manager yet. He was probably somewhere around Granny's age, although he might already be in his seventies. Like Granny, he was fit and healthy, striding around the ranch in jeans and boots, feeding cattle and taking care of the horses. His western shirts were neat and ironed, and he had thick salt and pepper hair under the straw Stetson he wore. The ranch seemed to be running smoothly, and he seemed nice enough, with an easy smile and gentle manner. He'd let Daisy feed the chickens that morning and showed her how to collect their eggs.

He'd taken on quite a lot of the responsibilities of the farm, more than the last ranch manager had, so Granny Bee obviously trusted him. She'd have to make a point to spend some time with him today, to get a chance to know him better herself.

She was starting to think her grandmother might be avoiding her when she texted to say she'd left sandwich fixings, a plate of relishes, and a jar of honey lemonade in the fridge. It wasn't like

Granny Bee to not put on a spread for lunch, especially so soon after they'd arrived. But Bailey's brain had been going a million miles an hour, so she didn't mind the mental break as she and Daisy sat on the front porch, and each read a book while they ate.

Bailey was glad, but a little surprised, when Evie showed up shortly after lunch. She was in the kitchen just finishing up their dishes when her friend strolled in, looking gorgeous and chic in black ankle pants, a teal wrap shirt, and black wedge sandals. A silver-wrapped aquamarine stone hung from a silver chain around her neck and matching earrings sparkled from somewhere in the depths of her thick dark hair.

She looked down at her boyfriend jeans, low-top white tennies, and her plain black V-neck T-shirt, sans any sparkling jewelry, and wondered if she'd even brought anything remotely dressy with her. Oh well. There were more pressing things to worry about than her boring wardrobe, she reminded herself. "How'd you get away from the café so early? I figured I wouldn't see you until after the lunch crowd died down."

"Abuela told me she'd cover for me so we can get back to our *investigating*." Evie grinned and winked as she reached for one of the crispy honey butter cookies Granny had left on a covered plate on the island counter. She groaned as she took a bite. "These are so good."

"Everything Granny Bee makes is so good. I swear I've already gained ten pounds." So many of her grandmother's recipes were infused with or incorporated variations of her honey products, from the hot spiced honey-drizzled ricotta cheese dip to the honey vanilla banana bread she'd made them for breakfast.

Bailey just prayed one of those honey recipes hadn't been used to murder the town's mayor.

"Who should we talk to first?" Evie asked, nibbling on the crispy corner of her second cookie.

"I was thinking we try to talk to the housekeeper and the women Susan told us about yesterday." Bailey wrinkled her brow. "Gosh, speaking of Susan, I hope she's feeling okay. Maybe we should check in on her."

"I already did. I ran a plate of cream cheese quesitos and some coffee over to her house this morning."

"Aww. You're so sweet. How'd she look?"

Evie shrugged. "About how you'd think—like she'd tied one on the day before. She appreciated the food and said she planned to stay home today and binge some new reality series on Netflix. And I *was* doing something nice—I felt sorry for her after yesterday—but I also spent a little time chatting with her and she ended up giving me the addresses of the three people you just mentioned and a little more dirt on the housekeeper."

"Really?"

She shrugged again. "You know how it is, people just tell me things."

"You *are* easy to talk to." She poured Evie a glass of lemonade and set it on the counter in front of her. "So spill it. What'd you find out."

Evie took a sip of the lemonade, then settled on the stool next to the island. "She said this Olive pretty much hated Werner, but she was in dire financial straits, so she put up with him because she needed the job."

"Sounds familiar. Just like Edward. Did she say why her finances were so dire?"

"Apparently, she's been living with and helping to support her grandmother, and they had to move her grandma into a nursing home earlier this year. It's a crime how much they charge for those senior living centers anyway, but I guess they just had to move her to the Alzheimer's wing, which costs even more since it's round-the-clock care."

"You have to respect her for taking care of her grandmother, but all that only lends credence to the allegations that she may have stolen something from Werner's. Not that I'd blame her. It had to have been hard, surrounded by all those expensive things while she was trying to scrape together enough to cover her grandma's care."

"Agreed. But Susan says she'd met her several times and had a hard time believing she'd steal from Werner."

Bailey took a sip of her lemonade. "Yeah, but people can act out of character when they're desperate."

"But what would killing Werner accomplish for her? She might get rid of a bad reference, but she'd blow any chance of getting her job back."

"Unless she really did take something from the house. Something worth enough that it would be missed. Something worth enough to warrant killing someone for."

Evie looked down at her hands and twisted one of her silver rings around her finger. "Speaking of taking something . . . I have a *tiny* confession to make . . ."

Bailey arched an eyebrow at her friend but didn't say anything.

"Wellll . . . I may have sort of taken something from the mayor's office yesterday."

"What?" Bailey asked, but she already had a sinking suspicion what it was. Evie reached for her purse, and Bailey prayed she didn't pull Werner's handgun from it. But it wasn't a firearm she pulled out. It was the small leather book that had been in the drawer. "You took his address book?"

Evie set it gingerly on the counter. "That's what I thought I was taking. I figured there must be something important in it for him to keep it locked up with a gun. But it's not an address book. It's way better." She paused as if for dramatic effect. "It's a *password* book."

"A password book?" Bailey reached out her hand to touch it, then thought better of it and pulled her hand back.

"Yeah, it's got all his usernames and passwords in it. I looked through it last night, and some of them are obviously in some kind of secret code, but some are perfectly labeled and clear as day. Granted, those are mostly the ones we don't really care about, or are so old they don't matter—does Blockbuster even still *have* a website? But there are a bunch pertaining to his finances." She planted a hand on her hip. "And I know Miss Susan told us yesterday she was sure Werner's death had nothing to do with money, but her saying that just made me want to dig into his finances even more."

A shiver ran up Bailey's back. "I thought the same thing. But this . . ." She pointed to the book. "This is freaking me out a little. I mean, talking to people is one thing. There's no harm in that. But hacking into someone's bank accounts—I'm pretty sure that's illegal."

"We're not *hacking* into anything. Unless you've acquired some new skills in the past few years, I don't think either one of us could do *any* kind of hacking, even if we were offered a million dollars to do it. But it's not hacking if we use his username and password. Is it?"

"Yes," she said, rolling her eyes at her friend. "It still is. Of course it is."

"But it's for a good reason. We're trying to help Granny Bee."

"I'm sure the judge would accept that excuse."

Evie let out a groan of frustration. "Okay, what if we found someone to do the hacking for us?"

"Do you know any computer hackers?"

Evie tapped her lips as she thought then shook her head. "No. But with all your writing connections, surely you do."

Bailey let out a sigh. "Yeah. I do."

Evie clapped her hands and grinned. "Yes. I knew it. Who is it? A contact from the seedy underbelly of the crime syndicate?"

"Yes, because I have a ton of contacts in the seedy underbelly of the crime syndicates."

Evie shrugged. "Well, how should I know? You did go to the prison a few years ago to interview that mobster guy for one of your books."

"He wasn't a mobster. He was a white-collar criminal who was in jail for check fraud." She pulled her phone from her pocket and scrolled through her contacts. "This guy isn't a mobster, although I'm sure he'd appreciate the notion of it. He's a friend. A retired cop. His name is Griffin Yates."

"Wow. Cool name." She narrowed her eyes. "I'm picturing an old guy keeping guard over his neighborhood from a rocking chair on his front porch, white beard, baseball cap, a limp from an old injury on the job. He smokes cigars, plays poker on Thursday nights with the guys, and can't stop thinking about that one cold case he never solved."

Bailey barked out a laugh. "I think you just described Clint Eastwood in his last three movies."

"But did I get it right?"

She shook her head. "Not even close. Except for the limp. Griff is closer to our age, maybe a few years older, but still in his early thirties, and the only reason he's retired is because he got shot when he was trying to take down an active shooter. Took a bullet to the leg that ended his career. It took him a while to recover, then he opened his own private investigation and security firm."

"How'd you meet him?"

"It was years ago. A cop I knew introduced me to him. Thought he could help me with researching one of my earlier books. We went to dinner, talked the whole night, and have been great friends ever since."

"Talked all night? That sounds like more than friends."

They'd tried that. Had one awkward date and realized they were much better suited as good friends. "Oh, come on now. You know I would have told you if I had a 'more than a friend.'" She found his number in her contacts. "Let me call him and see if he can help."

Twenty seconds later, she smiled at the gruff tone of Griffin's voice. "Yeah, what do you need?"

"Who says I need anything?"

He waited, saying nothing. Dang. He knew her too well.

"Okay. I need a little something."

"How little?"

"Let me ask you this—how experienced are you in hacking into people's finances? And if it helps, I have their username and password."

"Then that doesn't sound much like hacking."

"It is if the person whose accounts you're trying to look at is the mayor of the town who was just possibly murdered and your grandmother is just possibly the main suspect."

She heard him chuckle softly. "I'm listening."

She filled him in on the details, leaving out the part about how exactly they had gotten hold of the mayor's password book. "So what do you think? Can you use the dark web or whatever it's called so you won't be traced and take a look into the mayor's financials? Something just tells me there's going to be some interesting things to find."

"Yeah. What the hell. You've got me just intrigued enough by this crazy story to want to shake some trees and see what falls out."

"He'll do it," she whispered to Evie, who gave her an enthusiastic thumbs up. "Thanks, Griff. Now the only problem is that we're in kind of a time crunch, since we're pretty sure the guy was murdered and all, and I'm not sure how to get this book to you."

"You don't have to," he said. "I'll come to you. The city's too hot this week anyway. I could use a little mountain time. That town you grew up in big enough to have a motel?"

"Of course, but you don't have to come all the way up here."

"I could use the drive. Give me an hour or so to take care of some things and throw my laptop and some stuff in a bag. I'll be there by supper. Which *you're* buying."

"Better yet. I'll serve you a home-cooked meal."

"Since when do you cook?"

"Hey. I can cook. Mostly. When I have to. But my grandma can *really* cook. Bring your appetite because you're in for a treat. I'll send you the address of the ranch. Text me when you're on your way. And hey, Griff?"

He gave a grunt of response.

"Thanks. You're the best."

Another grunt, then he disconnected.

"He'll be here for supper," she told Evie.

"Then we'd better get going if we're going to try to talk to one disgruntled housekeeper and two grieving girlfriends."

* * *

It turned out they only got to talk to one grieving girlfriend, Helen Dobbs, since the other one, Alice Crawford, was currently on a Viking cruise in the Mediterranean and had been for the past two weeks. So they weren't able to glean much information about Werner from her, but at least they could rule her out as a suspect.

They'd left Daisy at the ranch with Cooper and a stack of library books, which was exactly the way her daughter loved spending an afternoon. Bailey had said they'd be back in a few hours, but Daisy had waved her on, telling them to take their time.

They stopped at Helen's house first, although calling it a house was a bit of an understatement. It was more of an estate. It was hidden among the pine trees right outside of town, and they drove up a long, curved driveway to a sprawling two-story with a four-bay garage and a rock water feature outside the front door. All stone and cedar, it had the look of a mountain lodge with a black tile roof and a wraparound veranda with a large seating area at one end, complete with an outdoor fireplace and a big-screen television.

The inside was just as lavish, with a stacked-stone fireplace that rose two stories and ten-foot-tall glass doors that opened onto the veranda and showcased a magnificent view of the mountains.

They were shown into the grand living room by a woman wearing traditional maid attire, complete with the short black dress, white pinafore apron, and the tiny white cap pinned into her hair. Bailey and Evie sat on the edges of a white leather sofa, both afraid to mess anything up and wondering if they should have taken off their shoes.

A petite woman wearing black slacks, a soft blue cardigan twin set, and a warm smile greeted them as she came in from another room. "Oh, how wonderful. I love having guests."

Bailey and Evie stood up and started to introduce themselves, but she waved them back down. "Oh sit, I know who you are. I've played bridge with both of your grandmothers for years. Evie, I think your pastelón recipe is to die for, and Bailey, I've read several of your books and thoroughly enjoyed them."

"Thank you," Bailey said, feeling at a disadvantage for not knowing more about Helen Dobbs.

"Now what I can I get you to drink? I've already told Marietta to put together a cheese and fruit plate."

A light gray cat with a white belly ambled into the room and paused to regard the visitors before jumping up on the far end of the sofa and settling in on one of the posh throw pillows.

"Oh, you don't have to go to any trouble," Evie told her.

"It's no trouble. Like I said, I'm glad to have the company."

Bailey could imagine how the big house could get lonely. "I'll have some water. Or iced tea, please, if you've got it." She settled back into the lush sofa.

The same woman who met them at the door came in carrying a tray with a pitcher of iced tea and a platter of assorted cheeses, crackers, and sliced melon.

"Help yourselves," Helen told them, passing them each a plate. "That white cheese is imported. It spreads like soft butter. You've got to try it with those round crackers. They're rosemary and sea salt."

Bailey marveled at the thin bone china plate as she and Evie each took a sampling of cheese and crackers that probably cost as much as a meal at the local steakhouse. Marietta poured them each a glass of iced tea and set it on the table in front of them.

Helen spread a thin cracker with cheese, inhaled the scent of it, then closed her eyes as she bit into the crispy cracker. "Oh, I just love these. I've been known to eat a dozen of them and call it lunch."

"I can see why. They *are* good," Bailey said, trying to hold back a groan and wondering if it would be bad form to take seconds already.

"When you're a widow and live alone . . . well, almost alone . . ." She nodded to the cat. "You can do pretty much whatever you want." She heaved a slight sigh, as though getting to do whatever she wanted didn't hold as much appeal as one would think. She picked up her glass of tea, then leaned back against her chair. "Now, I'm assuming you're here to discuss the recent incident with the mayor." She held up her hand before either of them could protest. "It's a small town, dears. And I've heard that they think Bee is involved. Which I'll tell you right now, sounds like absolute nonsense to me. Your grandmother is a bit on the wild side, but she treasures her bees, and I can't imagine her using them to harm someone."

"Thank you," Bailey said. "I appreciate you saying that. And yes, we are here to learn more about Mayor Humble. And to see if you had any ideas of who might have wanted to hurt him."

"Oh, I'm full of ideas. And unfortunately for me, I'm probably at the top of someone's list. I half expected it to be that handsome sheriff when I heard the doorbell chime."

"Why would the sheriff want to talk to you?"

"Because I hated Werner's slimy guts. He stole thirty thousand dollars from me, and we got into an argument a few weeks ago at a museum fundraiser, and I threatened to expose him for the conniving con man that he was."

Chapter Twelve

"Oh" was all Bailey could manage to say. Her brain was screaming *"Motive! Motive!"* but she wasn't sure what the best response was to say to the widow.

Helen Dobbs sighed. "I know what you're thinking. *Sounds like motive.* And it is. I almost wish I had killed the man. And I'm not the least bit sorry he's dead."

"I have so many questions," Evie said, reaching for another cracker and slathering it with cheese. Evie never seemed to be at a loss for words. And thank goodness. Because her bestie had barely finished chewing when she started rattling off questions. "How did he steal your money? Did you get it back? Did anyone *hear* you threaten him? And I'm totally confused because I thought you were *dating* him. Oh, and tell us more about this con man business because we're jonesing for more suspects in this case."

Helen stared at her for a moment, then burst out laughing. "I like you. You remind me of Rosa. In a good way. She doesn't mince words either. Even though some of hers are often in Spanish." She toasted them in the air with her glass. "Buckle up, ladies. I'm in a good mood, so I will answer *all* your questions."

"Thank you," Bailey said softly, not wanting to break the camaraderie of the mood.

"First of all," Helen said. "I was not *dating* Werner. We went out on some dates, in the beginning, when he was wooing me. Or should I say, wooing my bank account. That one's a charmer, for sure. He knew all the right things to say to a lonely widow and all the right buttons to push to get me to invest in what I thought was the good of our town. Apparently, I was only investing in the good of the town *founder*."

"What do you mean?" Evie asked, reaching for another piece of melon.

"Werner knows that when you *have* a lot of money, you're expected to *donate* a lot of money, and in most cases, donating money is a wise tax move. I didn't know all this back then. My husband had always taken care of our finances, and he left me well taken care of. Although a house like this"—Helen waved her hand toward the spacious ceiling—"takes quite a lot of money just for its upkeep. I've learned a lot in the years since he's been gone. I've had to. If there's one piece of advice I could give you gals, make sure you know how to manage your own money. I didn't even know how to sign on to our online banking." She pointed a finger in the air. "Oh, but Werner, he was so *kind* and *sweet*, he knew how to set it up and offered to 'help' me. Which really meant he 'helped' himself to my username and password and then several transfers to his own accounts."

"Oh no. That snake," Bailey said. "But couldn't you go to the bank and have them help you get the transfers reversed?"

Helen shrugged. "I don't know. Maybe. Maybe not. It took me a long time to figure out what he'd done. That was my mistake for trusting him. Once I did, I changed all my passwords.

And some of them were legitimate transfers to what I thought were reputable charities. I've since learned that some of them were dummy charities that he had in his own name. So I was essentially donating to *him*."

"But that's illegal," Evie said. "You could have had him arrested."

Helen's lips curved into a small sad smile. "You would have thought so. But Werner was a man of many talents, and one of them was finding out your secrets and using them against you. My secrets weren't that terrible, especially by today's standards, but they were enough that I, as an upstanding woman in this community and a deacon in my church, would not want them to get out. And would pay to keep them under wraps."

Bailey shook her head. "So he stole from your accounts *and* was blackmailing you?"

Helen nodded. Just one slight dip of her head.

Evie huffed. "So why in blue blazes do people think you were *dating* this man?"

Helen sighed. "Because I do go out on dates with him. Well, not dates like to an intimate restaurant or out to the movies, but we have come to an understanding, and we have . . . or I guess, *had*, a mutually beneficial relationship. You see, I'd gotten my real estate license before I was married and had always kept it current. After my husband died, I went back into real estate and, over the years, have built quite a successful business for myself. But being a realtor depends a lot on contacts and word-of-mouth referrals. So, when the town had fundraisers or fancy events where it was important to be seen or to network, Werner often took me as his 'date.' But all that meant was that he picked me up, brought me home, and we sat at the same table if there was a dinner involved. We didn't have to speak the whole evening, but it looked good for both of us to be seen on the other's arm. It helped my business to be seen with the mayor, and it helped him to be seen with one of the wealthiest women in town. It's shallow, I'll admit. But it worked."

Helen clasped her hands together in her lap. "I'm not proud of these things. I'm embarrassed that I let myself be taken in by a man of such low standards. And after the last *request* for a new donation he made, I'd had enough. He must have really gotten himself into some kind of jam because I'd never seen him quite like that. He's always been charming and sweet when he asks, like he's trying to fool me into believing he's not really blackmailing me. He's just asking *for the town*. But this time was different. There was no sweet talking, no charm, and there was a desperation in his eyes that told me he was in trouble."

"Did you ever find out what kind of trouble?" Bailey asked.

"No. And I didn't really care. I'd had enough. I was tired of worrying about him and what would happen if he exposed my secrets. I'm too old to lose sleep over what *might* happen. And who knows, a little scandal might have livened up my life and maybe been good for business. So I told him I was done paying him, and I was going to expose him as a con man. I'd had a little too much chardonnay that evening, and it was probably giving me too much liquid courage, so I may have been talking a little too loud and saying too much, and maybe someone overheard me. I don't know. I do know that I've spent the last few weeks fretting about when and where and how he was going to expose me. But nothing happened. So I guess we'll never know if my secrets would have caused a scandal or not."

"Wow," Bailey said. "That's quite a story."

"And you're right," Evie said. "It totally gives you motive."

"Yes, it does." Helen calmly took another sip of her tea. "Which I might be concerned about if I hadn't been out of town at a charity gala in Atlanta that night. I just flew home late yesterday afternoon. My phone's been going crazy since it happened, so I know all about it, but luckily, I wasn't even in the state when it happened."

Luck? Or cunning? Bailey couldn't help but think Helen Dobbs knew more than she was telling them. And she could say she was old all she wanted, but the woman was still sharp as a tack.

They chatted for another twenty minutes, but despite Evie's attempts at more invasive questions, they didn't find out anything new.

"Dang," Evie said as they were heading toward her car. "I was dying to find out what Helen's scandalous secret was."

"Me too," Bailey said, then her heart skipped a beat at the sight of the county sheriff's SUV pulling into the drive. Not so much at the vehicle, but at the handsome sheriff at the wheel. He parked next to Evie's car and pushed his hat onto his head as he got out.

If his frown was any indication, it would seem Sawyer wasn't exactly happy to see them again.

"Hey, Sawyer," she said, keeping her tone light as a battalion of butterflies took off in her belly.

Oh for heaven's sake. She was a grown woman. And he was just a man. No need for her stomach to get topsy-turvy just at the sight of him.

Yeah. Tell that to the dozen butterflies dive-bombing my guts.

"What are you two doing here?" Sawyer asked, the frown firmly in place.

"Oh, we were just visiting our friend Helen." Evie leaned her hip casually against the side of her car. "What are *you* doing here? Is Helen some kind of suspect in your investigation? Did she know Werner?"

"You know darn well that she did." He pointed a finger back and forth between her and Evie. "You two need to stop 'visiting' all of my suspects . . . er . . . persons of interest."

"Ah ha," Evie said, like she was an inspector at Scotland Yard. "So she *is* a suspect." She lowered her voice at Sawyer's glare. "I mean person of interest."

"It doesn't matter which one she is. You two are impeding a criminal investigation."

"You say *impeding*," Bailey said. "I say *helping my grandmother*. We'll stop right now if you tell us you're no longer interested in *her* as a suspect."

Sawyer sighed. "I'm sorry, Bailey. I can't do that."

She folded her arms across her chest and lifted her chin. "Then I can't stop talking to people to try to find out what really happened."

"One thing about you hasn't changed. You're just as stubborn as you've always been."

"I could say the same for you." Although so many things about Sawyer seemed to have changed. And it was taking up too many of her thoughts imagining what they all were. Thoughts that should have been focused on helping her grandma. "Okay, I'll admit I am stubborn, but I'm not stupid, and I know that the best way to solve this case is for us to share information."

Sawyer raised an eyebrow. "You've got that half right."

"Oh, so you just want us to tell you what we know, but you don't want to share what you know?"

"Yes. That is correct. Because I am the police officer and held to a certain standard of procedure. Especially in a homicide investigation. Which I'm not saying that this is. But no matter what kind of investigation it is, I will *not* be sharing all the details of it with two civilians. Especially when one of them is related to one of my suspects."

"Persons of interests," Evie interjected, then shrank back at another of Sawyer's glares. "Sorry, just helping."

"I think you two have helped enough."

"I hear where you're coming from, Sawyer," Bailey said. "But know that we want you to find the real culprit just as much as you do. So we'll tell you that Helen has a *lot* to say. And also, I know Granny's making her famous honey cake with marshmallow frosting if you want to stop by later and compare notes."

Sawyer studied her for a moment, then gave a slight nod. "Good try. I may stop by after supper, but only because I love Granny's desserts. And to make sure Ms. Dobbs shared all the same information with me. But remember, anything you tell me is just hearsay. It doesn't count unless Ms. Dobbs tells it to me herself."

"Well, I'd head in there," Evie said. "Because she's feeling chatty. And the cheese plate is delicious. Make sure to try the soft one. It spreads like butter."

He held Bailey's gaze for a little too long—long enough for heat to rise to her cheeks and enough pressure to build in her chest to make it hard to breathe. Then he tipped his hat and headed toward Helen's door. "We'll talk later. And stop talking to my witnesses," he called over his shoulder.

"Holy hot staredown," Evie said, as she and Bailey slid into the car. She cranked up the air conditioner and fanned her face.

"Oh, stop it," Bailey said, nudging her friend's arm but still thankful for the cool air on her heated cheeks.

"So are we still going to Olive Green's house or are we going to do as Sawyer said and stop talking to his witnesses?"

"What do you think?"

Evie's lips curved into an impish grin as she put the car in gear. "Off to Olive's it is then."

Chapter Thirteen

Olive Green lived in a small white ranch-style home a few blocks from downtown. The yard was neatly maintained, and colorful blossoms exploded in long flower beds on either side of the front porch steps. Two rocking chairs sat on the porch, and a whimsical dancing frog holding a sign that read "Welcome to our Pad" stood next to the door. There were no cars parked on the street in front, but the garage opened to the alley running behind the house, so they just hoped that Olive was home.

A woman in her mid-twenties with long red hair pulled into a messy bun on top of her head answered the door. Her expression was guarded as she pushed open the screen door. "Hi, can I help you with something? I already believe in Jesus, so you can save your pamphlets for someone else."

Bailey shook her head. "No, that's not why we're here. We just wondered if we could talk to you for a few minutes."

Her expression stayed guarded. "About what?"

They'd discussed their plan in the car and had wavered between the ruse of talking to Olive about a job opportunity or just telling her the truth about why they were there. They'd decided to go with the honest approach.

"We want to talk to you about your recent employment with Werner Humble," Evie said.

"No way," Olive said as she started to close the door. "I didn't steal anything from that old curmudgeon."

"Wait," Bailey said. "We don't think you stole anything. But this is important. My grandmother is Granny Bee—you know, the lady with all the honey? The police think she may have had something to do with Werner's death. And I'm just trying to help prove that she didn't. I love my grandma, and I'm just trying to protect her. Surely you can understand that."

Okay, it was a little bit of dirty pool, using their knowledge of Olive's relationship with her grandmother, but hey, if it worked . . .

Olive stared at them a moment, the door still half closed, then finally let out a sigh and opened it again. A yellow and white cat weaved its way through her legs, paused to scrutinize Bailey and Evie, then sauntered back into the house. "Okay, but just for a few minutes. And we can talk out here."

"That's fine," Bailey told her, even though she was trying not to crane her neck to see into Olive's house behind her. Not that a giant clue would be sitting inside the front door, but she could still hope. "Can you just tell us what you know about Werner? And about why you were fired?"

"I don't know that much. Except that he tries to act like he has it all together, but he's actually kind of a slob. Always leaving his dirty towels on the floor and dishes all around like he was used to having someone pick up after him. I feel sorry for anyone who had to be married to that guy."

"How'd you get the job?"

She lifted one shoulder in a half-shrug. "He goes to the Lutheran church downtown, same as us. He must have told somebody there he was looking for a housekeeper and it got back to my grandma. I'd done some cleaning and helping out at the church, so she told me I should go talk to him. So I just walked over to his house and knocked on the door. I told him who I was and that my grandmother had taught me how to cook and clean. He hired me on the spot—asked if I could start right then. Didn't even have to fill out an application."

"Wow. That was lucky," Evie said.

Olive shrugged again. "I don't know. It was a bit weird. His house was a total mess. It took me all afternoon just to clean it up. And he was all stressed out that day, pacing around the house and talking to himself and pulling at his hair."

"What was he stressed out about?"

"I don't know. And I didn't ask. I was just so happy I got the job. I can remember being so proud of myself for negotiating the salary. I may have taken advantage of the fact he was stressed and just went for it—asked for a dollar more an hour than he was offering, but he said okay. We did argue a little bit, though. Mainly because he made me wear this little maid outfit deal when I was there. Nobody wears those—not unless you work in like an English mansion, or you're trying for some kind of sexy Halloween costume. It was weird. And a total pain to work in. I'm very serious when it comes to cleaning. But he insisted, and the pay was good, so I'd just put it on and get to work."

Bailey shivered. Even though she'd just seen Helen's housekeeper wearing something similar, it did sound creepy that Werner had expected Olive to wear what sounded like a skimpy version of it. "That does seem weird. But I'm glad the job worked out for you. It seems like you were in the right place at the right time."

"Maybe. I guess it was okay for a while. But then it didn't work out so great for me in the end. I got fired, and now I can't get housekeeping work because everyone thinks I'm some kind of thief."

"What does he think you took?"

Olive shook her head. "I don't know, really. Money and some jewelry, I guess. You know he dates all these rich old ladies, and they're always stopping by the house. Personally, I don't know how he keeps them all straight and keeps them from running into each other. It makes my head hurt to think about it. But anyway, he said one of his *lady friends* ratted on me and told him I stole something. That she saw me. But I didn't. And that's what sucks so much, because he *knows* I didn't."

All the rich old ladies part of Olive's story didn't surprise Bailey, but the conviction with which she proclaimed her innocence did. "What do you mean? How does he *know* you didn't?"

"Because he's got cameras all over the house. All he'd have to do is watch the recordings. I wasn't even upstairs that day."

"Cameras?" Evie made a face like she'd just tasted something sour. "*Eww.* What was he recording?"

"I don't know. Everything, I guess." Olive turned to look back into the house. "Look, I gotta go. I hope you can help your grandma."

"Me too," Bailey said.

"Hang in there," Evie told her. "And hey, my abuela and I run the coffeeshop and bakery on the corner of Fourth and Main downtown. Come in and fill out an application if you want."

Olive narrowed her eyes in suspicion. "Really?"

"Yeah, really."

"Why? I already told you everything I know."

"It doesn't have anything to do with this. We're just always looking for great help. No promises, but we'd be happy for you to apply."

"Okay," she said, with almost a smile. "Maybe I will."

"Cute frog," Bailey said.

Olive's lips curved into a genuine grin. "Thanks. I know it's silly. But I just love frogs. They're so cute. And they're green—like me." She waved before going back inside and shutting the door.

Bailey and Evie hurried toward the car but waited until they were inside and pulling away before they spoke.

"The frog slippers," they said at the same time, then cracked up laughing.

"You know they had to be hers," Evie said.

"Absolutely. And if I weren't a hundred percent sure, what I saw in her living room sitting on the floor in front of the sofa totally convinced me."

Evie offered her a knowing grin. "You mean the pair of Italian leather loafers?"

"You saw them too?"

"You bet I did. And all I could think about was whether that weasel, Edward, was in the living room with his ear to the wall listening to everything we said."

"I thought the same thing," Bailey said. "But that *was* nice of you to offer for her to come in and fill out an application at the bakery."

"Nice has nothing to do with it. We're always looking for good help, and I'd heard that she was great at keeping Werner's place clean. But I also don't believe for a second that she told us everything she knows. And if she comes down to the bakery to fill out an application, I'll sic my abuelita on her. She's like a mafia security man with a pastry—she can get anyone to open up and tell her everything they know."

* * *

"I should go," Evie told Bailey a few hours later as she drained her second glass of honey lemonade.

"You sure you don't want to stay for supper?" Bailey asked. "You know Granny Bee will make plenty."

Evie nodded. "I know she will. I'm just beat. Although that was odd the way she kicked us out of the kitchen when we got back. She normally loves having us hang out with her while she cooks."

"Oh, I'm sure that's because she's avoiding me. She knows I want to talk to her about what she was up to the night of Werner's death, so I think she's purposely avoiding me." Bailey had told Evie earlier, under a solid oath pinkie promise not to tell the rest of The Hive, about Daisy seeing Granny coming in from the barn in the middle of the night.

"I don't get why, though. But the fact that she's avoiding the subject makes me want to know even more."

"Me too."

"Speaking of avoiding the subject, are we ever going to talk about the fact that Sawyer is coming over here tonight?"

"Oh? Was that tonight?" Bailey said, trying for casual nonchalance. And coming nowhere close to pulling it off.

"Oh, girl. Don't even try to fool me. I know you."

"So does he. Or he used to. And it feels like he sometimes still does. And I feel like I know him. But I also feel like I've changed so much. And so has he. I never could have imagined him going into law enforcement. And now I'm just rambling."

Evie smiled. "It's okay to be nervous. He looks good, though, doesn't he?"

"Yeah, he does," Bailey answered with a bit too wistful of a sigh.

"So are you going to tell him what Olive told us? About the cameras?"

Her starry-eyed wistfulness came crashing to the ground. "I don't know. Yes. Maybe. I know I should . . ."

"But?"

"But I was thinking that it does sound a little preposterous, so maybe we should sneak into the house and see for ourselves."

Evie's eyes widened. "You mean see if we can watch them first to make sure Granny Bee isn't really on them."

Bailey lowered her gaze as she raised her shoulders in a tiny shrug. "Maybe," she said in a soft voice.

"So let me get this straight . . . you're suggesting that you and I, two people who have zero experience with burglary tactics or video equipment, sneak into an active crime scene to see if we can find some hidden cameras and then watch the footage before we alert the sheriff?"

Bailey nodded. "Yeah, that sounds about right."

Evie grinned. "Okay. I'm in."

Before they could say anything more, they were interrupted by a black Toyota 4Runner with dark gray tinted windows pulling into the driveway. A dark-haired man wearing a black T-shirt, jeans, and scuffed square-toed cowboy boots got out and stretched. He was well over six feet tall, with broad shoulders and thick hair that was just long enough to have a slight curl at his collar.

"Oh yay," Bailey said, pushing up out of her chair. "Griff's here."

Evie grabbed her arm and pulled her back, her voice a little croaky as if she were finding it hard to breathe. "*That's* Griffin Yates? The grizzled old retired cop guy?"

Bailey chuckled. "I told you you missed it by a mile."

"More like by a *thousand* miles. That guy's not Clint Eastwood, he looks like Hugh Jackman when he first played Wolverine, except without the wings in his hair and the steel claws."

Bailey laughed again. "Yeah, I can see that. I'll tell him you think so."

"Don't you dare." She reached to fluff up her curly hair. "Why didn't you warn me? I would have at least put on some freaking lip gloss."

"What was it you said about not telling me about Sawyer?" She grinned at her friend. "It's much more fun this way."

Evie blew her a quick raspberry before turning back toward the driveway and smoothing out her shirt.

"Hey, Slick," Griffin said, his gaze raking over the house, then the two women as he sauntered toward the porch.

"Hey, Griff. Good to see you." Bailey met him with a hug at the top of the stairs. "Have any trouble finding the place?"

"Nah. It was a nice drive. Good to be in the mountains again. And this farm is really cool. It's kind of hard to imagine you growing up here, though." He grinned down at her. "Not a coffeeshop or takeout joint in sight."

"I'm really just a country girl at heart. And I've got my best friend here to prove it." She took a step back. "Griffin Yates, this is Evie Delgado Espinoza. We grew up together. She's the closest thing I have to a sister."

Griffin took Evie's hand and held it, and her gaze, just a fraction of a second too long. "Nice to meet you, Evie."

"You too," was all Evie said in return, but she couldn't take her eyes off the tall man.

Hmm. Bailey had never seen Evie with nothing to say.

"I hope you brought your appetite," Bailey told him. "Granny Bee's been cooking for the last two hours. She's making chicken fried steak and mashed potatoes. And homemade biscuits with honey butter. Of course."

"Sounds great. I'm starving." He glanced sideways at Evie. "Will you be joining us for supper?"

"No," Bailey said. "She was just getting ready to leave."

"Don't be silly, Bailey," Evie said, her voice a little breathless, as she stared up at Griffin. "Of course I'm planning to stay for supper. You know how I love Granny's biscuits and honey butter."

"Nice," Griffin said.

Bailey followed them inside, wondering if Evie was imagining Griffin as the main course or just the dessert.

*   *   *

Bailey held her stomach as she pushed away from the table. "Granny Bee, you outdid yourself with those biscuits. Everything was so good. But I ate way too much."

"I second that," Griffin said, setting his napkin next to his empty plate. "I can't remember when I've had a better meal. Now, if you'll tell me where to find the dishwasher, I'd like to show my appreciation by cleaning up the kitchen."

"I'll help you," Evie and Daisy said together. Bailey wasn't sure which one of them was more smitten with the private investigator.

"Don't you dare," Granny told him. She held up her hands. "These are the only dishwashers in this house. And I don't mind cleaning up. I do some of my best thinking when I'm elbows deep in soapy water."

"If you're sure," he said, then continued after Granny nodded. "Well then, I think I'll head back to the motel."

"Are you sure you don't want to stay here?" Bailey asked. "We've got plenty of room."

"I'm sure," he said. "But I appreciate the offer. Besides, I've got some work to catch up on tonight, so I'll probably be up late. And now that you've filled me in on this Werner Humble stuff, I'm anxious to get started and see what I can dig up."

"I'm anxious for that too," Bailey said.

"Any suggestions on where I can get a decent cup of coffee and some breakfast in the morning?"

"I can help with that," Evie told him. "Our family coffeehouse and bakery is on the next block from your motel." There was only one motel in town, so they all knew where he was staying. "Come by in the morning, and I'll set you up with coffee and breakfast."

He offered Evie a smile that seemed to carry something more. "I look forward to it."

"Me too," Evie said, her voice just a little breathy.

His grin widened, then he turned and tipped his chin toward Granny. "Miss Bee, thank you again for supper." He pushed back his chair and stood. "Bailey, you want to walk me out?"

"Sure," she said, following him toward the door.

They stopped on the porch, and Bailey gave him another hug. "Thanks again for doing this, Griff. I owe you." She heard the rumble of an engine and looked past Griffin to see Sawyer's truck pulling into the driveway.

"You don't owe me a thing," he told her. "I just hope I can help." She'd already given him Werner's password book. He looked down at his feet then back up at her. "I don't know if I should mention it, because she was so sweet at dinner, and I really like your grandmother, but . . ." His voice trailed off.

"But what? You secretly think she might have murdered the mayor?"

He chuckled. "No, I don't think that, not that she's not capable of it. I wouldn't put much past your Granny. But there *is* something going on with her." He scrubbed at the scruff of dark beard on his jaw. "I'm not sure why she's pretending, but I can assure you, her foot is not broken."

Bailey frowned. Although she'd begun to suspect as much herself. "How can you tell?"

"Besides the fact that half the time she forgets to limp and the other half she limps on the wrong foot?"

Chapter Fourteen

"I knew it," Bailey said.

"Knew what?" Sawyer asked, stepping up on the porch. His eyes were narrowed as his gaze took in Griffin as if sizing the other man up.

"That Granny Bee's foot isn't actually broken."

"Oh yeah. I thought you knew that all along and were just going along with it," he said.

Bailey's mouth dropped open as she stared at him. "You knew she was faking it?"

"Sure. The first time I came out here, she had that boot on her left leg, then yesterday when she came in to the station she had it on her right. Plus, half the time she forgets to limp."

Griffin nodded his agreement. "That's what I just said."

Sawyer turned toward him and held out his hand. "I don't think we've met. Sawyer Dunn." He didn't have to add the sheriff part. The shiny gold badge on his uniform shirt spoke for him.

"Griffin Yates," he said, shaking Sawyer's hand.

Sawyer's shoulders were back as he stood his full height, but Griffin was just as tall. "I don't think I've seen you before. You from around here?"

Bailey's emotions were jumping all over the place, from the jittery feeling she got in her chest from having Sawyer standing so close to her, to the heart-thudding notion that he might be jealous of Griffin.

Griff shook his head. "Nope, just drove up from Denver." He turned back to Bailey and gave her arm a quick squeeze. "I'll see you in the morning."

"I'll call you later," she told him as he strode off the porch and back to his 4Runner.

"Who's that guy?" Sawyer asked, and Bailey caught the slight edge to his voice. "Your boyfriend?"

"Ha. If you'd seen the way he's been looking at Evie all night, you wouldn't have to ask. But no, he's just a friend. A good one, but just a friend."

His stiff shoulders relaxed . . . a little. "*Will* your boyfriend be joining you while you're here?"

She raised an eyebrow. "Why, Sawyer Dunn, are you jealous?"

"Are you avoiding the question?"

"Will *your* girlfriend be joining *you* while I'm here?"

The side of his lip quirked up in the tiniest of grins. "I don't have a girlfriend."

"Well, I don't have a boyfriend either."

His shoulders relaxed all the way as his grin widened. "Now that we got that settled."

She grinned back. She'd been afraid to ask Evie or her grandmother if he was seeing someone. Now she knew. *Not that it mattered*. Her stomach betrayed her feigned nonchalance as it did a tiny little flip.

Sawyer took a seat on the porch swing and patted the cushion next to him.

She sat next to him, her heart reminding her of all the nights they'd spent like this—sitting on her grandmother's porch, his arm thrown casually around her shoulders as she leaned into his chest. They used to talk about everything. And nothing. Happy to be together whether they were sharing stories of their day or just listening to the creak of the swing's springs as Sawyer pushed them slowly back and forth with his foot.

"It's good to see you, Bailey," he said, his voice softer than before.

"It's good to see you too."

"I'm glad you're doing well. I've read your books, you know."

"You have?" she asked, both thrilled and nervous. Would he have recognized himself in the description of just about every hunky hero figure she wrote? "Which ones?"

"All of them."

"*All* of them? All eight?"

He nodded. "They're great. You were always a good writer."

Heat traveled up her neck at the compliment. "Thanks."

"But writing about murder doesn't mean you know how to solve one."

Her shoulders stiffened. "It doesn't mean I don't."

"Come on, Bailey. You know enough to understand that what you and Evie are doing could actually be screwing up my investigation."

Which might not be a bad thing, if it steered it away from Granny.

"I'm just trying to help."

"I get that. But you have to trust me that I know what I'm doing. I take this job seriously. And I'm damn good at it."

"I believe you. Which is why I know that you won't back down if your investigation points toward Granny Bee."

"There might be a *reason* the investigation is pointing that way."

"All the more reason for me to help."

He sighed. "Fine. Do you want to tell me what you found out so far?"

She filled him in on the conversations they'd had, only omitting the information Olive had shared about the hidden cameras in Werner's house. It wouldn't hurt to share what they'd learned with him, especially since so much of it could be viewed as motives that could steer him toward other suspects.

He leaned back against the porch swing's cushion when she'd finally wound down. "Is that all?"

"What do you mean? That was a lot. I easily just gave you at least two other suspects."

"Maybe. But there's still a lot missing between point A and point B."

"There's got to be a lot missing in those same points when it comes to Gran too."

He nodded. "I'll give you that."

"Do you want to give me anything else? I told you all this stuff. Don't you want to share what you've found out with me?"

He sighed. "You know I can't do that."

She slumped back against the cushion, all too aware of how her shoulder now rested against his. "I had to try."

"I'd expect nothing less."

Her heart pounded hard against her chest as she looked at him, the half smile on his lips, the warmth in those gorgeous blue eyes she knew so well.

His gaze dropped to her lips, and all the moisture dried up in her mouth as she inhaled a quick breath.

"Bailey . . ." was all he said before the screen door slammed open and Evie stepped out.

"Oh, sorry," she said, seeing Sawyer. "I didn't know you were here."

He stood up. "It's okay. I should probably get going anyway." He looked down at Bailey. "We'll talk tomorrow."

"Sure." She watched him cross the porch. "Hey, Sawyer?"

"Yeah?"

"How come you didn't tell me sooner? About Granny's *un*broken foot?"

He shrugged. "I figured she had her reasons, and you'd either figure it out or she'd fess up soon enough."

"Sorry," Evie told her as they walked back inside. "Didn't mean to interrupt."

"It's okay. I wasn't gonna get anything out of him anyway." She pointed toward the kitchen where Granny Bee was drying the dishes. "But I'm going to get something out of *her*. She's going to tell me what's going on right now."

"I'll leave you to it," Evie said, grabbing her purse from the side table by the door. "Daisy said she was in the middle of a great book, so she already headed up to her room to read. Call me tomorrow. Or tonight if you find out anything good."

"I will," she promised before heading into the kitchen to face her grandmother.

"Whew. Just finished," Granny said, flipping the tea towel over her shoulder as she sagged into a kitchen chair.

She looked wiped out, and for the first time Bailey noticed the dark smudges under her grandmother's eyes as if she hadn't been sleeping well. She almost backed down. They could talk in the morning, after Granny had a good night's sleep.

"You want a cup of tea or something, sugar?" Granny asked, starting to stand up.

Bailey waved her back down. "No, I'm good. I can get you one if you want, though."

Granny shook her head. "No, honey. I'm fine."

"That's kind of what I wanted to talk to you about," Bailey said, unable to ignore the opening her grandmother had just given her. "It seems like not only are *you* fine, but your *leg* is too."

"What do you mean?" Granny asked, trying to arrange her expression into one of innocence.

"You and I, and apparently everyone else, know that your foot is not actually broken. So come on now, fess up. What's really going on?"

Granny held her stare for a few seconds, then slumped down in her seat. "Fine. You caught me."

"So you admit your foot isn't broken?"

Granny lowered her chin to her chest and gave the slightest nod.

Even though she knew the truth, she was still shocked that her grandmother would flat out lie to her and concoct this crazy fake injury. "Why on earth did you act like it was?"

Granny sat up and slapped the table, making both Bailey and the sugar bowl sitting on it jump. "Because it was the only way I could think of to get you to come home. You haven't been up here to see me in two years, and it was time for you to get your fanny back home for a visit. I'm sorry I lied to you, and I'm even more sorry that I picked an ailment that involved wearing this stupid thing . . ." She paused to wrench the straps of the boot free, the sound of the Velcro ripping through the air. "But I'd do it again if it meant getting you to come home."

"Oh, Granny, I'm sorry," she said, lowering her head in shame. "You're right, I should have come home sooner. I've just gotten so caught up in my career and keeping up with Daisy the last few years, I haven't had time for anything else. Between writing deadlines and managing social media and marketing and trying to handle Daisy's schedule and middle school and . . . well, I guess I just didn't make the time to visit that I should have. I really am sorry."

Her grandmother let the blue cloth boot fall to the floor with a thud. She patted Bailey's hand. "It's all right, honey. You're home now. That's all that matters."

Bailey raised her head, and they smiled at each other—those tender smiles that expressed their love for each other while also saying all was forgiven.

"How'd you figure it out?" Granny asked. "I've always considered myself a pretty good actress."

Bailey laughed. "Apparently you're not that good of one, because you kept either forgetting to limp or you were limping or wearing the boot on the wrong foot."

"Dang. I caught myself doing that once, but I'd hoped nobody else noticed."

"Oh, they noticed." Bailey's laughter died as she took on a more serious tone. "Daisy is actually the one who told me first. She saw you walking fine without the boot."

Granny's brow furrowed. "How? When? I've worn it every time we've been together."

"We *weren't* together. It was in the middle of the night. The night Werner was murdered. She got up to go to the bathroom, and she saw you out the window, walking in from the barn."

"Oh." She had the wide-eyed stare of a deer who'd just heard a twig snap under a hunter's boot. "I wish she hadn't seen that."

"Me too. But she did. And now all three of us know that you weren't in bed the night Werner was killed, like you said you were. Like we *all* said you were."

Granny let out a huff as she lifted her chin. "Well now, I didn't tell you all to say that. You came up with that on your own."

"Seriously?" Bailey couldn't believe her ears. "You're going to bash all of our attempts at providing you an alibi?"

She lowered her chin *and* her righteous indignation. "You're right. I did appreciate the effort."

"I don't want your appreciation. I want to know what the heck you were doing out of bed, fully dressed, and coming in from the barn in the middle of the night."

Her chin went up again. "Well, I'm sorry. But that, young lady, is none of your beeswax."

Chapter Fifteen

Bailey stared at her grandmother. "It *is* my beeswax. Besides the fact that a man was *murdered*, and the police are looking at you as their prime suspect, I also put *my* behind on the line providing you with an alibi. As did your great-granddaughter and every other member of The Hive."

"Like I said before, I never asked any of you to do that."

"But we did. And I think that means we deserve an explanation. What were you doing roaming around in the middle of the night on the same night that a man was killed?" She stared at her grandmother, waiting for an answer.

Granny Bee stared back, her lips pressed tightly together. But Bailey was determined to outlast her on this one. She had to get to the bottom of this, so she could wait all night if she had to.

Granny lasted all of thirty seconds before she let out an exasperated huff. "I swear, Bailey Jeanne, you always were the most stubborn child." She took a deep breath then blew it out slowly. "Fine. I'll tell you. If you must know. I was *not* out in the middle of the night *killing* a man, I was canoodling with one."

Bailey's mouth fell open. She blinked. Then blinked again as she continued to stare at her grandmother. "*Canoodling?* With who?" she finally managed to croak.

"Don't you mean with *whom?*"

"Stop correcting my grammar," Bailey sputtered. "And just answer the question." Bailey pressed the ends of her fingers against her forehead. "And please Lord, do *not* say Werner Humble."

Granny Bee made a gagging sound in her mouth. "Oh no. That man makes my skin crawl. I can't believe your Aunt Aster *and* Dottie both got sucked in by his snake-oil salesman charm." She smoothed out the front of her blouse and dabbed at a damp spot from where she must have leaned against the sink when she was washing dishes. "I have been involved for some time now with a perfectly lovely man. Who also happens to manage my ranch."

"Lyle Ambrose?"

Granny nodded, still staring at the wet mark on her shirt. Then she raised her chin and looked directly at Bailey. "I am a grown woman, and still in the prime of my life. I can canoodle *who*ever I want, *when*ever I want."

Bailey covered her ears. "La, la, la. Please stop saying canoodle, Gran. And I agree, you can do whatever . . ." *Or whoever . . . Eww.* ". . . you want. I just wish you wouldn't have done it the night Werner was murdered. Or that you would have stayed there the whole night."

Granny shrugged. "Lyle is willing to talk to Sawyer, tell him he was with me that night."

"But depending on when they place Werner's time of death, you still might not have an actual alibi." Although what a testament to her grandmother that so many people were willing to lie for her.

She looked back down at her shirt. "Yes, I know. But there's nothing I can do about that now."

Bailey sighed then shook her head. "Well, there's one thing you're going to need to do now. Tell your great-granddaughter what you were doing. Or let me tell her. She's been making herself sick trying to keep the secret of your whereabouts that night."

Granny winced. "Oh dear. Sweet girl. I hadn't thought about that. Of course you can tell her. Just use your discretion. It's not that I'm embarrassed, I just don't want to hear all the ribbing I'll get from The Hive. They already gave me enough razzing when I was with Ellis. I don't want them to think I get together with every farm hand I hire."

"Ellis? I knew it." Bailey tilted her head. "I loved Ellis. Why aren't you two still together?"

"Oh, I loved him too. But we wanted different things. All his kids are in Austin, and he's got six grandkids. They've been wanting him to move down there with them, and he asked me to come along. But we both knew there's no way I was leaving this ranch. Or my bees. It's okay, though. We're still friends. Always have been. Always will be." She pressed a hand to her chest. "I'll tell you, though, as much as I cared for Ellis, he never made my heart race the way being with Lyle does. I don't care how old I am, that man just does something to me."

Bailey covered her ears again. She did not want to hear what anyone *did* to her grandmother. "On that note," she said, "I'm going upstairs to talk to Daisy, then I'm going to brush my teeth and go to bed and pretend we never had this conversation."

Granny chuckled. "I think I'll do the same." Her smile turned wistful as she placed her hand over Bailey's. "Sometimes you remind me so much of your mother, it tears my heart in two."

Bailey caught her breath and fought the sudden sting of tears as she turned her hand over and squeezed her grandmother's palm. "I know. I miss her too," she whispered.

They didn't often speak of Holly, her mother and Bee's daughter. Bailey's dad had never been in the picture, and she and her mom had always lived at the ranch with Granny.

Holly had struggled with depression and anxiety, a fact that made Bailey's own anxiety even worse with the fear that she would turn out like her mother. She'd already become a single mom to a daughter who had no relationship with her father. But Bailey would never abandon *her* daughter.

She'd been ten years old when Holly had left to "run errands" one afternoon and never come home. At first, they'd thought something nefarious had happened to her.

Then they'd gotten the letter.

Holly hadn't been kidnapped or in an accident that left her comatose in the hospital. She'd just chosen another life. One that didn't involve her ten-year-old daughter.

* * *

The next morning, Bailey found herself standing outside the barn door working up the gumption to go inside and talk to Lyle. It would have been no big deal to talk to him yesterday. Or the day before. But that was before she knew about the *canoodling*.

Now she wasn't sure if she could look at the man and keep from blushing.

"Somethin' I can help you with?" Lyle asked, poking his head out of the barn.

Bailey jumped. "What? No. I mean, yes. I mean . . . wait, what do you mean?"

He chuckled, and his laugh had an easy deep timbre to it. "I just noticed you've been standing there a few minutes now. Seems like you've got something on your mind."

"Yes. I guess I do."

He waved her toward him. "Come on in then. I'm just tinkerin' with this tractor engine. It's been making a funny sound when I drop it into low gear. You can keep me company while I work."

"Sure. Okay. That would be fine." Geez. What was wrong with her? For someone who wrote mystery novels, complete with clues, multiple motives, and red herrings, she suddenly couldn't seem to string together a complete sentence. She sat on a small stack of hay bales across from where Lyle was working.

The tractor, with its faded green paint and metal seat that got so hot in the summer it would burn the back of your legs if you didn't stay exactly in the center of the cushion, sat in the middle of the barn's alley. Further down were six horse stalls, three on each side, but only two were occupied—one holding her grand-mother's palomino mare, Ginger, and the other holding a brown quarter horse she didn't recognize.

"That your horse?" she asked Lyle, nodding her head toward the stall.

"Yep," Lyle answered without looking up from his task. He was twisting some kind of tool around in the engine of the trac-tor. "That's Ranger. We've been together about fifteen years now. Your grandma likes to go for a ride most every morning, so I keep these two in the barn so I can have them tacked and ready to go when she's ready."

"Have you seen her this morning?" Bailey asked, wonder-ing if Granny Bee had already given Lyle a heads-up about their conversation.

"Not yet, but I'm sure she'll be along shortly. She likes to spend some time with the bees early, then sometimes she spends a few hours in the shop working on this or that with the honey or making candles or some of her lip balm. She usually shows up before lunchtime, though. Why? Do you need her? She doesn't always carry her phone with her, especially when she's with the bees." He continued to work on the engine, but Bailey caught the amused grin that creased his face. "She says she only likes to hear *their* buzzing and doesn't want the sound of the phone to confuse them." He looked up and toward Bailey. "But I'm sure I can track her down if you need her."

Bailey shook her head. "No, that's okay. It was more you that I wanted to talk to this morning anyway."

"Okay. What's on your mind?"

"You, actually. You're on my mind."

He kept his focus on the engine, switching out one tool for another. "All right."

All right? What kind of response was that?

"I guess I'm just wondering what your intentions are with my grandmother."

His lips curved into a grin. "So I take it she told you about us?"

"I kind of forced it out of her. The night Werner was killed, Daisy found her bed empty, then saw her coming in from the barn in the middle of the night. She was pretty stressed about it."

"Ah no. Poor kid. Well, I'm glad Bee told you then." He lifted one shoulder in a shrug. "Doesn't bother me who she tells. I'm not ashamed to admit that I'm real fond of your grandmother, and I don't care who knows it. But she's a little more private, and I respect that."

She studied him for a moment, feeling like she had a better read on him. He seemed genuine. And she had always trusted her grandmother's opinion when it came to assessing people. She gave him a small nod. "All right."

He gave her another wry grin, this one full of mischief, and she liked him even more. "All right?"

She let out a laugh. "Yes. All right."

"All right then." He took off his hat and drew a rag from his back pocket to wipe the sweat from his brow. "Now that we've got that settled, you want to split a cup of coffee with me? I've got just enough for two left in the thermos I brought with me this morning." His face still held that easy smile as he looked over at her.

But Bailey couldn't answer. She couldn't speak at all. Her mouth had gone dry, and her heart was pounding so hard and so fast, it made her chest hurt. She tried to swallow as she raised her hand and pointed to the rag Lyle was now using to wipe the engine grease from his hands.

Except it wasn't a rag.

It was a silk scarf, an odd reddish orange–colored scarf that looked just like one her Granny owned . . . and it exactly matched the color of the fibers of what they thought was used to tie up Werner's wrists and legs.

Chapter Sixteen

"Where did you get that?" Bailey finally managed to croak out.

Lyle's brow furrowed as he held up the reddish orange material. "What? This old rag? I found it in the barn this morning when I was feeding the horses. It was stuffed between two bales of hay. It was ripped and one side was sticky, so I figured it was a rag and just folded the sticky part in and tucked it in my pocket." He held it out toward her. "Is it yours?"

She shook her head as she held her hands out. "No. It's not mine. And I don't want it." Her voice caught as she whispered, "But it might be Granny's."

"Oh shoot. I'm sorry if I got grease on it. I really thought it was just a scrap someone was getting rid of."

"Oh, I do think someone was trying to get rid of it," she said, then pointed to the workbench. "You need to put it down. Now."

His expression was a mixture of confusion and worry as he dropped the cloth on the bench. "Bailey, what's going on?" His voice was stern and had that grandfatherly tone to it.

It was enough to ground her, though, and she let out a shaky breath. She pointed to the fabric again. She knew she'd seen that odd color somewhere before. "Fibers were found on Werner's wrists and ankles that suggested some type of fabric was used to tie him up. And the fibers were a really unusual blend of reddish orange—exactly the color of that scarf. So, I'm not saying it was for sure, but there's a chance that rag you just wiped your brow with . . ." *And got your DNA on.* ". . . was used in the murder."

"Well, hell."

"Yeah." She pulled her phone from her pocket and scrolled to find the group text of The Hive. Her hands were still shaking as she typed in a message. "9-1-1. Emergency meeting of The Hive. Get to the ranch ASAP."

* * *

Thirty minutes later, all the members of The Hive, including Bailey, Daisy, and Evie, had arrived at the ranch and were gathered in the living room.

"I don't know what's going on," Granny Bee said as she carried a tray holding glasses, a pitcher of lemonade, and a plate of cookies in from the kitchen. "But I have a feeling we're going to need some sugar."

Dot took the tray from Granny and set it on the coffee table, then helped to pour and dispense glasses of lemonade. Marigold raised a cool eyebrow as she glanced down at Granny's leg, sans the blue medical boot, but didn't comment. And neither did anyone else.

Which meant that either no one had noticed yet, or they had all been in on the broken foot ruse of trying to get Bailey and Daisy to come home.

None of that matters now.

Bailey wiped her sweaty palms on her jeans-clad thighs. She'd realized she needed the whole Hive together, because it wasn't just Granny who had a reddish orange scarf like the one now sealed in a Ziploc bag, but every member of the book club had a matching one too.

And they needed to know where they all were.

Bailey let out a long breath before calling for the room's attention. "I'm sorry to call you all out here on such short notice, but something happened this morning and we all need to talk."

"Good heavens," Aster said, pressing a hand to her chest. "Your message made it sound urgent—like someone had died."

Someone had died.

"Just tell us what's happened," Marigold said.

"I will," Bailey told them. "I promise. But first I need to ask you all a question, and you need to think really hard before you answer." She looked each of the women of The Hive in the eye. "You all remember several years ago when Marigold and Aster went on that trip to Mexico, and they brought us all back those reddish orange silky scarves? The ones they said reminded them of Humble High's school colors, and they thought we could all wear them to football and basketball games and cheer them on?"

Marigold made an annoyed huff. "You're telling me I left bridge to race out here to talk about some silky scarves we bought in Mexico five years ago?"

"Yes, I am," Bailey said, keeping her tone stern. "And I need you all to tell me where those scarves are now." She looked around the room and her gaze landed on Dot, who was looking everywhere but at her. "Dottie, you want to go first?"

The ice clinked in Dot's glass as she almost lost her grip on it. "Oh, I'd rather not. I'm sure mine is at home somewhere."

"Could you put your hands on it? Bring it out here?"

She looked stricken as her gaze bounced from Marigold to Aster, then back down to her glass. "No, I'm sorry. But I don't think I can."

Bailey was confused. Why was Dottie acting so weird about it? "Why not?"

Dot lifted her shoulders but kept her gaze trained on her glass. "I'd rather not say."

"I'm sorry, but this is important. I need you to tell us."

She raised her eyes and looked at Bailey, her expression practically pleading with Bailey not to make her say. Then she lifted her chin. "Oh, all right, fine. I'll tell you. I'm sorry to say it, because it was such a lovely gesture and so thoughtful of you all to buy them for us, but that color was just ghastly. And every time I brought mine out to try to wear it to work or to a football game, it scared poor Leopold to death. He'd hiss and scratch at it, and it was so upsetting to him that I finally gave it away to Goodwill." She looked back down at her hands. "I'm sorry. I know it was a gift. And it was so sweet. But it was upsetting my cat."

"Don't feel bad, *amiga*," Rosa said, resting a hand on Dot's arm. "Those scarves were *repugnante*. I gave mine away to an aunt I was annoyed with years ago. I wrapped it up in a box and giggled a little inside as I watched her face when she opened it at Christmas."

"Abuelita," Evie said with a mock gasp. "You are wicked."

Rosa shrugged. "Eh. Maybe. But it still makes me smile when I think about it." She turned to Aster and Marigold. "Sorry, my loves."

Aster's lips quirked up in a sheepish smile. "Don't feel bad. Either of you. I thought they were a little ugly too, and I may have accidentally on purpose left mine on the bleachers at a basketball game last year."

Marigold gasped. "You never told me that."

"Well, I'm sorry, sister. You had picked them out and you seemed so excited about them being the school colors, so I didn't want to hurt your feelings. And I just thought maybe someone with a little more school spirit might find it and appreciate it more than I did."

Bailey couldn't blame any of them. She hadn't given hers away, but she had no idea where it was. Probably stuffed in the back of her closet somewhere.

Marigold sniffed. "Well, I've got mine at home in my scarf drawer. I know exactly where it is."

"Me too," Evie said. "I don't know what you all are talking about. I love the color. I've worn mine several times."

Granny Bee smiled at Evie. "That's because with your gorgeous coloring and fashion flair, you were the only one of us who could get away with wearing it and looking good in it. I tried it a few times, but that color washed me out and made me look like I was ill."

"So did you give yours away to charity too, Gran?" Bailey asked, praying that her grandmother would say she'd given hers away years ago too.

"Oh no. It's probably upstairs somewhere. Although I did think about using it a few months ago for something with the bees, and I couldn't find it. So I'm really not sure where it is."

Bailey groaned. That was not the answer she'd been hoping for.

"What is this about, Bailey?" Marigold snipped, her feelings obviously hurt from everyone disparaging her thoughtful gift.

"Why did you make us all rush out here just to ask us about some apparently ugly silk scarves that no one wanted and half of you gave away?"

"Because . . . ," a stern male voice said, and they all turned to see Sawyer standing in the archway of the living room, an unhappy frown on his face. "We think a silk scarf similar to the one you all are talking about was used in the murder of Werner Humble."

Shocked gasps and murmurs sounded in the group of women.

"What are you doing here?" Bailey asked, confused as to how he knew about the scarf and also terrified that he was here to take Granny away. She prayed he hadn't heard her say that she had no idea where her scarf was.

"My job," he said, his voice carrying an official tone with no hint of the friendly camaraderie they'd shared the night before. "Can I speak to you in the kitchen a moment? *Now.*"

That felt more like an order than a request, and Bailey stood up from her chair and followed him into the kitchen. "Seriously," she said, when they were out of earshot of the others. "Why are you here?"

"To collect what might be evidence," Sawyer said, his tone still serious. "Lyle called me and told me what you'd found. I came out to pick it up." He scrubbed a hand through his hair, then looked down at her, and she swore she caught hurt in his eyes before he blinked and looked away. "Why didn't *you* call me?"

"I was going to."

He cocked an eyebrow. "I'm not sure I believe you."

Ouch. That hurt. But probably just as much as her not calling had hurt him. "I was. I swear."

He let out a pained sigh. "But you knew what you'd found, and first you wanted to account for the whereabouts of all the matching scarves that your grandmother and apparently all the women in her family and her book club own." He said it as a statement, not a question.

She stared down at her hands clasped in front of her, feeling embarrassed and a little ashamed of herself. "You're right," she said, her voice soft. "And I'm sorry. I should have called you right away."

"Yeah," he said. "You should have."

"But I was just trying to help."

"That's what you said last night. And the day before. But it seems to me like you're not trying to help *me*, you're only trying to help Bee."

She put a hand on his arm. "She's my grandmother."

"I know." He looked down at her hand, and for a second she thought he was going to brush it off, but he let it sit there. "What I don't know is if you recognized what those fibers were when we saw them the first time. On the body."

She shook her head vehemently. "No. I didn't. I swear. I mean, for a second when I first saw that weird color, I felt a little niggling, like maybe I had seen it somewhere, but I didn't realize where until Lyle pulled one of those scarves out of his pocket this morning and used it to wipe his sweaty head and greasy hands on."

He stared at her, hard, as if trying to decipher whether she was telling the truth. He must have believed her because he nodded, and his features softened. "Okay. So tell me about when you saw it. Did you touch it?"

She shook her head again. "No. No way. Like I said, I didn't know until Lyle pulled it from his pocket. Then I just felt ill. I swear I almost threw up. He said he found it in the barn, stuffed between two hay bales, and it was ripped and had something sticky on it. That's got to be the honey, right?" She rubbed her arms as if to ward off a sudden chill. "I mean, I don't want to believe it, especially since it was found out here on our ranch, but it's got to be the thing used to tie Werner to the chair." Her voice dropped to a frightened whisper. "Doesn't it?"

This time, Sawyer put his hand on Bailey's arm and the solid strength and warmth of it settled her. "I don't know, Bailes. It looks to be, but we won't know anything until we turn it in and they run some tests on the fabric to see if they find Werner's DNA on it."

"They'll find Lyle's too, since he wiped his sweaty head on it." *And they might find Granny Bee's on it too*, she couldn't bring herself to say. "But you heard what The Hive said, half of those scarves went to charity or were given away or left on the bleachers. There's no way to tie that scarf to one of these women."

"There *is*, Bailey. You know there is."

She *did* know. And her stomach flipped over as she fought the bile trying to rise in her throat.

A knock on the front screen door sounded, then it opened, and Griffin poked his head inside. "Hello, anyone home?"

Sawyer dropped his hand from Bailey's arm as she called out, "Come on in, Griff."

"I'd better get back to the station," Sawyer said. "Lyle already gave me the evidence, and I've got it in my car. Thanks for sticking it in the sealed bag. That was good thinking."

"Yeah, of course," she said, but he was already walking away.

He paused to tip his head to Griffin as he passed him standing inside the door.

"Sheriff," Griffin said, his voice carrying a tone of respect. He had also spent years wearing a badge. Although Bailey hadn't told Sawyer that yet. Or that Griffin was here helping her investigate *his* murder case.

For some reason, she didn't think he was going to be real happy about her not telling him that information either.

"Hey, Griff," she said, wincing as the wooden screen door slammed behind Sawyer. "Come on in. We found something, and I want to tell you about it."

He offered her one of his trademark cocky grins. "I found something too."

Chapter Seventeen

"Oh gosh," Bailey said, pressing her hand to her chest, as if to stop the sudden spike of her heart rate. Her smart watch would be sounding the heart rate alarm if she'd only remembered to charge the thing and stick it back on. "Am I going to be happy with what you found? Or am I going to be searching for her passport, dyeing her hair, and trying to get Granny out of the country?"

He chuckled. "No, it's nothing like that. Well, I hope it's not. I don't want to be responsible for you and your grandma going on the lam."

She motioned toward the living room. "The Hive, otherwise known as Granny's book club, are here. Can you share what you found with all of us?"

"Sure," he said, following her in.

Bailey introduced him around but noticed the way his gaze caught on Evie. She'd come straight from the bakery, so she had her thick dark hair pulled up in a high ponytail and wore jeans and a snug V-neck T-shirt, and even with the light dusting of flour visible on her shoulder, she still looked drop dead gorgeous.

Granny motioned for him to sit as she passed him a glass of lemonade and a couple of cookies. "Tell us what you've been working on, Griffin."

"I've spent hours digging into the mayor's and the county's finances, and I've uncovered quite a few inconsistencies. And some very glaring evidence of blackmail."

"What kind of evidence?" Dottie asked. "Like pictures?"

He shook his head. "No, nothing like that. I'm just tracking the money. His statements show lots of deposits—some cash, some checks, and a lot of the checks have the word *donation*, or something similar, written in the memo line, which is troubling in itself. But the deposits are spread out over several accounts, and all of them are just under the limit to keep from having currency transaction reporting done on him. He might have been a creep or a snake, or whatever, but he was a smart snake."

Daisy was sitting next to Griffin, and she raised her hand, as if she were in school.

Griffin grinned. "Yes, Daisy." He leaned closer. "You don't have to raise your hand, ya know."

She laughed, but Bailey knew it was a nervous laugh and noted the pink coloring her cheeks. Still, she was proud of her daughter for wanting to contribute to the conversation. "Um, so I was doing some digging this morning too," Daisy said. "I thought I'd poke around on the secretary of state website and see if Werner . . . um . . . Mayor Humble . . . was involved in any businesses. And I found a bunch of businesses that had his name or versions of it, like Humble Homes, an LLC for a construction company. But I couldn't find any other evidence of the businesses, like no websites or reviews or any kind of online presence."

"Wow," Griffin said, echoing Bailey's thoughts. "That's awesome. I was doing the same thing, and I found a bunch of the same stuff. A lot of those are just dummy corporations to funnel money through." He nudged her shoulder. "Great job. Remind me to call you next time I need an extra hand in an investigation."

"Thanks," she said, ducking her chin. "We learned about this stuff in school last year. I noticed a lot of them were created by an attorney as the agent, so I checked for other businesses listed by him."

"Good thinking. I'm impressed," Griffin told her.

"I sure wasn't impressed with this Werner guy. So many of his business names were stupid or cheesy. Did you see that one that was under Modest Mountain Inc.? I couldn't say for sure, but that sounded too much like Humble Hills to not be one of his."

"Yeah, that's what I thought too."

"I didn't know how to dig much deeper, but I know there's more out there."

"You're right," Griffin said. "There is." He looked down at his boots, then up at Bailey as if weighing his next words.

She knew him well enough to see when he was worried. "Just tell us," she said. "We're all in this together."

He gave her a curt nod, then turned to the other women in the room. "I'm sorry to say that I did find evidence of checks from a few women in this room too."

Aster's shoulders sank, then she raised her hand. "I know. One of them was mine. I gave him a thousand dollars last month."

"Aster Grace," Marigold said after a shocked gasp.

"I know. I know. *Now*. But I didn't know any of this stuff *then*. And he told me the money was to help *kids*." She bristled at her sister's stern look. "Besides, it's *my* money, and I can spend it if I want to."

"You mean *waste* it," Marigold muttered.

"I thought it was to help kids," Aster insisted again, then turned back to Griffin. "Are you sure *some* of it didn't go to help some kids?"

"No, I'm sorry," he told her. Then he looked over at Dot.

She rolled her eyes. "Yes. I know. I'm right in Aster's boat with her, tossing money over the side. I just wish it was *only* a thousand dollars."

"Oh no," Evie said softly, resting a hand reassuringly on Dot's arm. "How much did you give him?"

Dottie looked at Griffin then down into her lap where she was twisting the hem of her blouse between her fingers. "A lot," she said, her voice so soft they almost couldn't hear her.

"It's okay," Aster said, putting an arm around her friend. "I fell for it too. Did you think you were helping kids?"

Dottie shook her head, looking miserable. Bailey was worried she might cry. "No, I thought the majority of mine was going to help animals. I made a considerable donation to the shelter where I found Leopold years ago. And he's been the best friend I've ever had. I just wanted to help other cats like him find good homes." She looked at Griffin, her tear-filled eyes begging him to tell her some of her money had gone to the shelter.

He held her gaze for a second then dropped his chin. "Don't worry. He must have wanted it to look real, so he did donate a sizable portion of your checks to the shelter. Your money *is* helping animals."

She choked out a small sob and pressed her hand to her lips. "Thank you," she whispered.

Evie patted her shoulder then handed her a glass of lemonade.

"Don't beat yourselves up," Griffin told both women. "There were a lot of others who fell for the same kind of scams. Most of the time it looked like they thought they were donating to the betterment of Humble Hills."

Bailey caught Evie's eye, knowing they were both thinking about what Helen had told them the day before. "Then surely some of that money went to help the town?"

"You'd think so. But he had a pretty elaborate scheme set up. It looks like he's been embezzling from the city for years. It started small. I almost missed it, but there was this one withdrawal for an odd amount, eleven hundred and sixteen dollars, that came out, then went back in a few months later, only for just a little more, like someone had borrowed it then replaced it *with interest*."

She and Evie looked at each other again. They'd both heard that exact number recently. *Susan's mortgage payment.* Her words about Werner taking advantage of people when they were at their lowest came back to her. "When did that first withdrawal come out?"

He twisted his mouth to the side, the expression he made when he was thinking, then said, "It was five years ago, in the summer. I can't remember if it was June or July."

That matched up with the time Susan had told them she'd lost her husband. And summer would have been just long enough for their savings to run out and just shy of when his life insurance money would have arrived. She was just guessing, but the numbers added up, and from the knowing look Evie was giving her, she was obviously thinking the same thing.

Desperate times call for desperate measures.

"But whoever took that money paid it back."

"Yeah, the first few times," Griffin agreed. "Then not ever again. Then it just turned into straight out embezzling from the city funds. It's all there—if someone takes the time to really look." He glanced down at his watch. "Listen, I've got a call I need to be on, so I need to get back to the motel. But I'll check in with you later tonight."

"I'll walk you out," Bailey told him, then waited as everyone said their goodbyes. "Don't talk about anything good while I'm gone," she called over her shoulder as they stepped out onto the porch.

The scents of freshly mown hay and lavender filled the warm summer air. The bees loved the purple flowered bushes, so Granny planted tons of them all over the ranch.

"I've got a question for you," Griffin said as they walked toward his truck. "Why are all the women in your family named after flowers and you're named after an Irish Cream liqueur?"

Bailey laughed. "For your information, I *am* named after a flower. Just not a very common one. My mom loved roses, and I'm named after one of her favorites, the Bailey Red."

"Are you sure that wasn't a story she came up with later? Because I imagine you much more as being named for a bottle of fancy whiskey than an uncommon rose." He nudged her side as he teased her.

"So says the guy named after a mythical creature."

"Touché."

Griffin opened his car door, but Bailey stopped him before he got in. "Hey, I've got a question for you too."

"Yeah?"

"None of Dottie's money went to the shelter, did it?"

He let out a breath, all joking aside as his expression turned serious, and he shook his head.

Bailey's eyes pricked with tears. "You're a good man, Griff."

He wrapped an arm around her shoulder and gave her a side hug. Leaning down, he spoke into her ear. "Don't let it get around. It'll ruin my reputation."

"As what? A curmudgeon?"

He barked out a laugh. "I was thinking more along the lines of a bad ass detective."

"Oh yeah," she said, grinning as she watched him slide into the driver's seat and crank the engine. "That's what I was thinking too."

Everyone had moved into the kitchen, and Granny was setting out food for lunch when Bailey walked back in. "Okay, ladies, we need to get busy and really dig in today. Griff has given us a great place to start, but there's got to be more. We've got to find something to get the spotlight off Granny and onto another suspect."

* * *

Late that night, Bailey waited for Evie as she stood in the shadows of Werner's house. She'd put on black jeans, a black T-shirt, and black tennis shoes, and there was barely any moon tonight, so she was hoping for the combination of the darkness, the black clothes, and the thick trees on the side of the house to camouflage her.

She'd charged her watch that afternoon, and checked it now, holding her hand over her wrist to block the light. It was twelve minutes past ten, and they'd agreed to meet at a quarter after. It was her idea to each park their cars a few blocks away and walk in from different directions, but now she was wishing they'd just come over together.

Every sound made her jump—the crunch of tires on gravel of a car going down the street in front of the house, the soft hoot of an owl, the tiny skitters in the dried leaves next to the house that could be a mouse or a bug or a very large spider. Bailey shivered and jumped as more leaves crunched directly in front of her. She squinted into the darkness, her heart in her throat, then laughed at herself as she made out the long ears and furry body of a bunny.

"Hey," a voice said quietly from beside her.

Chapter Eighteen

Bailey jumped about a mile into the air and let out a tiny squeak of a shriek at the dark shadow of a figure.

"Shhhh!" the shadow said. "Geez Louise. It's me."

Bailey clapped her hand over her mouth, willing her heart to slow down as she recognized her friend. "Holy crap! You just about scared the gumption out of me," she finally said, using one of Granny's favorite expressions as she reached out to slap at Evie's arm.

"I hope not," Evie said. "Because we're gonna need all the gumption we can muster to break into this house."

"You mean this *crime scene*," Bailey said, pointing to the yellow tape across the front of the porch. She'd come into the yard from the back, somehow feeling like maybe this wasn't so bad if they didn't actually cross or duck under the tape.

"How do you suggest we get in?" Evie asked, stepping out of the shadows to peer at the house.

Bailey's mouth dropped open. "What the heck are you wearing?"

Evie had on black yoga pants, a black shirt, and black boots, similar to what Bailey had chosen, but where she'd grabbed a black stocking cap to pull down over her head, Evie wore a long, full, platinum blond wig.

Evie smoothed the hair of the wig. "What? It's a disguise."

"What kind of disguise is that?" She pointed to the hair, now looking silver as it caught the thin rays of moonlight.

"One that protects me if anyone says they witnessed a blond woman breaking into the mayor's house."

Bailey planted a hand on her hip. "But that's *me* they'd be describing. *I'm* a blond woman breaking into the mayor's house."

"Don't get your panties in a twist. I already thought of that," she said, digging into the black messenger bag she wore across her shoulder and pulling out a tangled bright red wig. "*Voilà*—not anymore you're not. Now you're a redhead."

"Seriously? I am *not* wearing that."

"Yes, you are. We need to be disguised. Did you forget the whole reason we're going into the house? To find the cameras he's got hidden. Do you think it's a good idea for the cameras to record *us* breaking in? Or two bombshells with blond and red hair?"

She made a certain kind of sense, Bailey thought as she grabbed the wig. "More like two hookers. Where did you even find these things?" Her hair was already pulled back into a braid, so she tugged off her stocking cap and twisted the braid under the wig as she wrenched it on her head.

Evie pulled the wig around so the fringe of bangs cut across Bailey's forehead, then leaned back to check how it looked. She made a face like she'd just caught a whiff of dog poo. "I borrowed them from my nieces' Halloween stuff. This one was a little mashed. And I think they may have practiced cutting hair with it. Give me the cap." She tugged the cap over the wig and tucked the sides behind Bailey's ears. "That will have to do. But I don't think anyone's going to mistake you for a hooker. At least not a very good one."

"Great. I've been downgraded from bombshell to hooker to vagrant. Let's go break into someone's house. Maybe I can try for an upgrade to cat burglar."

"Or jailbird if we're not careful," Evie said, sidling closer to the house. "Seriously. How are we supposed to get in there? What if there's an alarm?"

"I really don't think there is. I didn't see one, and nothing went off when Sawyer and I broke into the house the other day when we found him."

"Thank heavens for small favors."

"I'm sure the front door is locked, and the back one is too. I already checked while I was waiting for you. But I found a small window that looks like it's opened a crack. Maybe it's a mudroom or a laundry room." She motioned for Evie to follow her, then stopped under a window about fifteen feet from the back of the house.

The window *was* open a few inches, but the bottom sills of all the windows were about five feet off the ground.

"How the heck are we supposed to get up there?" Evie whispered, reaching up to touch the sill. "I do a little yoga and Pilates, but there isn't a move in the world that could get me to pull my body up and over that windowsill."

Bailey laughed. "You do *not* do Pilates. *Or* yoga."

Evie planted a hand on her hip. "Well, I wear *yoga pants*."

"Oh, pardon me. I stand corrected. That *is* practically the same thing. Next time I put on my favorite concert T-shirt, I'll be sure to tell everyone I'm part of the band."

"Shut up and give me a boost."

"How?"

"I don't know. Cup your hands together, and I'll stand up in them. Or get down on your hands and knees, and I'll stand on your back and boost myself in."

Bailey stared at her. "You're joking, right?"

"Dang. Why didn't we go out for cheerleading? Those girls knew how to make a pyramid."

Bailey looked around. "Where's a time machine when we need one? Going back to high school to try out for the cheer squad sounds like the perfect solution to our current predicament."

"Oh, hush up and look around for something for us to stand on." Evie's gaze traveled around the yard then she snapped her fingers. "I've got it. I saw some lawn furniture on the patio when I was sneaking through the back yard. I'll be right back."

She bent low and scurried around the back of the house, disappearing into the darkness, then returned a few minutes later hauling a patio chair. She planted it in the dirt under the window. "That should work." She started to step up on it, but Bailey put out a hand to stop her.

"I should go first. This was my stupid idea."

Evie took a step back. "If you insist. But we're in this together, so I'm right behind you."

Bailey tested the sturdiness of the chair then stepped up on it. The windowsill was about chest high now, and she put her hands on the sash and carefully pushed the window up and leaned her head inside. She almost screamed and fell backward when a ghostly white hand blew out and brushed against her cheek.

Okay, it was just the end of a sheer white curtain. But it *felt* like a ghostly white hand.

"You okay?" Evie whispered, her arms wrapped around Bailey's shins.

"Yes, the curtain blew out and scared the pee out of me."

"I hope not, 'cause I'm down here holding your legs."

"Well, you can let go of them because I'm going to try to haul myself over the sill." She planted both hands on the windowsill, the peeling paint cracking and stabbing into her palms.

Here goes nothing.

She jumped up, pushing with her legs and her forearms, trying to catapult herself through the open window. She landed with a thud on her stomach, her arms in, her legs dangling over the side. "I'm stuck," she whimpered.

She could feel Evie pushing at one of her legs and hear her voice whisper-shouting up to her. "Swing your leg over."

"I'm trying," she shout-whispered back. "I'm high-centered." She heard what sounded like a snort and kicked toward her friend. "You better not be laughing."

"I'm not," Evie said, obviously trying to catch her breath. She let out another snort laugh. "Okay, not anymore. I'm not laughing anymore."

Swinging her hips as much as she could, she tried, and failed, to fling one leg up onto the windowsill.

"You almost had it," Evie said, her voice still breathless as she grappled for her foot. "Try again."

"Stop laughing."

"I'm not."

Bailey tried again, flinging her leg with all her might as Evie pushed up, one hand on her shin and one on her rear end. Her toe got a foothold, and she pulled herself forward with her foot.

"You got it," Evie said, pushing harder. "Keep pulling."

"Keep your hand out of my crack." She scooted on her stomach, holding on with her hands while she continued to propel her leg forward until she was halfway in. She put her hand on the wall and reached her foot out and down, trying to find something to stand on or to steady herself against.

Her foot hit something solid, a table maybe, and she pushed more of her body through the window. But then the sole of her shoe slid off the side of whatever she was trying to stand on, and her foot landed with a splash in cold water.

"Crapola," she whisper-yelled, then prayed that wasn't what she'd just landed in.

"What happened?" Evie called, her voice still a whisper, but her head was closer to the window, so she must have stood up on the chair.

"Nothing." She tried to pull her foot back out of the bowl, but her shoe was wedged in sideways. "Dang it," she whisper-swore, but now she at least had her bearings. She'd obviously climbed into a bathroom window, and she knew the relative shape of most toilets, so she let the rest of her body slide over the windowsill and twisted around to get her other foot on the floor.

"Are you okay?" Evie asked, her head popping into the window. She'd launched herself up and was now halfway in the room. The sound of her feet could be heard scrambling for purchase against the outer wall.

"Dang. You really have been doing yoga."

"I told you." She paused, halfway through the window and squinted into the dark room. "Where are we?"

"Must be the guest bathroom. The toilet's right below you."

"Gotcha." She wiggled further in and put her hand down on the back of the tank. "Okay, I'm just going to keep pulling myself forward. I can basically crawl in if you get out of the way."

"I can't."

"Why not?"

"I'm stuck."

"What?"

"My foot. It's stuck. In the toilet."

They had still been whispering and trying not to make any more noise than they had to, but Evie barked out a laugh at her predicament.

"Shhh!" Bailey pulled at her arm, hauling her the rest of the way in.

She came forward through the window, stepping her hands from the tank to the rim to the floor. Landing on the floor with a thud, she did a half somersault forward, her feet tumbling in after her. She lay sprawled out on the floor, her wig twisted sideways, so the bangs pushed down across one of her eyelids.

"Are you okay?" Bailey whispered, worried that she'd pulled her too hard. It was dark in the room, but she could see her on the floor and could feel Evie's body shaking next to her leg. "Evie?"

Her friend rolled over and pressed her face against Bailey's leg as she let out another snort of laughter.

"I thought you were hurt." She pushed at Evie's shoulder. "Stop laughing and stand up and help me get my dang foot out of the toilet."

Evie curled into a ball, the giggles bubbling out of her. "I can't," she whispered, laughing so hard now she was barely able to take a breath. "Your foot. It's stuck in the toilet."

"I know," Bailey said. She yanked at her foot again, and her shoe gave way with a squelchy belch followed by a bubble from the bowels of the bowl as Bailey fell backward and landed hard on her bottom.

"Oof," she said, rubbing her sore fanny. But at least she was free.

*   *   *

She looked over at Evie, who had her hand pressed hard against her mouth trying to control her giggles.

Then the hilarity of the situation hit Bailey too, and a bubble of laughter erupted out of her. Then she was bent forward, holding her stomach, as the giggles overtook her and the two of them were whisper-laughing hysterically like a couple of loons.

Their laughter died on their lips as the sound of a heavy thud and footsteps walked across the floor above them.

Chapter Nineteen

Bailey grabbed for Evie's hand, squeezing it as all the moisture dried up in her mouth. Their eyes had adjusted to the dark by now and they looked at each other, both their eyes wide.

Evie pointed to the window. "Should we go back out?" she mouthed.

Bailey looked from the window to her friend then back to the window. She had no idea what to do. She'd never been in a situation even remotely similar to this.

But her characters had. And she would never have her heroine or hero run away from a situation. They were always barreling headfirst into whatever trouble she threw at them. But that was the difference—she could control what happened to them.

The footsteps sounded again, followed by another door shutting. The door to the bathroom was shut, but a sliver of moonlight shone along the crack at the bottom. Evie slid silently across the floor, putting her ear close to the crack, her body tense as she listened.

Bailey carefully crawled over to her and bent her head to listen too. They both jumped at the sound of another door shutting, then the steady rhythmic thumps of footfalls running down the stairs. She knew enough of the layout from the day of Werner's death to know that a set of stairs came out at the rear of the kitchen near the back door. So they had to be in the small powder room next to the pantry.

Depending on which way the intruder . . . the *other* intruder . . . besides the two of them . . . decided to go, they would either exit the house out the back or pass right by this door.

She held her breath as the footfalls hit the bottom steps then changed to a soft squeak as they crossed the kitchen tile. Evie was squeezing her hand, and she squeezed back as they both held otherwise perfectly still, every nerve of their bodies concentrating on the sound of those steps.

A loud creak made them both jump. Bailey wasn't sure if it was *her* hand that was shaking or Evie's, as they heard the back door creak open, then seconds later creak shut again and close with a solid thud.

Both women let out their breath as they released each other's hands. Bailey sagged against the bathroom door, but Evie scrambled across the floor and slowly raised her head to see out the window, as if she might catch a glimpse of the other intruder.

"See anything?" Bailey whispered, crawling over to peer out on the window's other side. The yard was dark and quiet, but then they heard a car engine starting and driving away from what sounded like the next block over.

"All I saw was the back of a dark figure running out of the back yard." Evie straightened her wig and adjusted her T-shirt. "But I think we need to go find those cameras and get the H-E-double hockey sticks out of here."

"I agree."

They pushed up off the floor and carefully opened the bathroom door, sticking their heads slowly out to make sure they didn't see, or *hear*, anyone else in the house.

"Where should we start looking?" Evie asked.

Apparently, they really stunk at this sneaking in to search someone's house idea. They hadn't even come up with a plan of action for how they were going to search or where they would look first.

Bailey pointed her finger toward the ceiling. "I say we go up there and see if we can figure out what the other guy was looking for."

Evie nodded then followed her up the back stairs. They tried to be quiet, but Evie snorted at every other step when Bailey's wet shoe squelched against the hard wood.

At the top of the stairs, they found themselves at the back of a hallway. Looking down the hallway, they could see four closed doors, two on each side, then a landing area with a reading nook area that led down the front set of stairs. On the other side of the landing, an identical hallway led to the far side of the house. Even in the moonlight, Bailey recognized the same chintz chair she'd spotted at the top of the stairs when she'd been standing at the bottom in the foyer inside the door.

"I guess we start opening doors," she whispered.

"Wait." Evie pulled another two sets of plastic disposable gloves from her bag, the kind they used to make and serve food at the bakery, and the same kind they'd worn in Werner's office, and passed a pair to Bailey. "So we don't leave fingerprints."

Bailey nodded and pulled a pair on, the plastic crinkling and sticking to her sweaty hands so she had to jam her fingers into the slots. "Why didn't you give us these before we climbed into the window and put our hands onto the toilet tank."

"I forgot. I'm kind of new to this breaking and entering game."

"Thankfully we've only entered so far and haven't broken anything."

"Unless you broke the toilet when you landed in it."

She was never going to live this down. Right now, she just prayed that her wet footprints wouldn't leave visible marks on the floor after they'd found what they were looking for and skedaddled.

She reached for the knob of the door closest to her. The plastic glove crinkled against the steel knob as she turned it and pulled the door open and peered inside. "Another bathroom," she told Evie, who had opened the door opposite hers.

"Linen closet," Evie whispered, then moved to the next one. "Guest bedroom," she said after peering inside.

"This one's looks like a study," Bailey said, glancing into the next room. "I think this is the room directly above the bathroom. Seems like a good place to start."

"Agreed." Evie followed her in and peered around at the bookshelves lining the walls and the heavy desk facing the center of the room. She pointed at a large volume that was on the floor in front of the window. "Do you think that was the thud we heard?"

Bailey shrugged. "It could have been. But I swear I heard the sound of *two* doors closing directly above us. And there's no other doors in this room." She shook her foot as a breeze blew over her wet ankle. "Dang. My foot is freezing." She leaned over the desk, pulling open drawers and squinting at their contents.

"Here, this should help," Evie said, handing her a small penlight. "Just try not to use it too much in case someone outside sees the light moving in the room."

"Thanks." Bailey clicked it on, cupping her hand around the beam. *Wait.* She clicked the light off again. "Evie, I said my foot is freezing."

"I know, I heard you." Her back was to her as she skimmed the bookshelves, presumably looking for anything odd or out of place, or that looked like video recording equipment disguised as books.

"No, I mean my foot is freezing because there's like a breeze or something that just blew over my ankle and made me shiver."

"Where would a breeze come from in this room? The window's shut. I already checked."

Bailey dropped to her knees, holding her hand out in front of the bookcases. "There. I can feel it." She pointed to the bookshelf. "I think this is one of those secret doors."

"Seriously?"

"Yes. Why not? All the creepy rich guys who blackmail people in the movies always have a secret door to a hidden room. Why should our creepy rich guy be any different?"

"You're right. So how do we get in there?"

"I don't know. The books maybe." Bailey started on one side of the middle shelf, pulling at each book, hoping for it to be a lever to release a secret door. No luck on the first shelf. Or the second, or the third.

Evie wasn't having much luck with the books in the next case over either. "Are you sure about this?" she said, yanking on the top of a marble book end in the shape of a horse's head.

The bookend tipped forward, and a shiver raced across Bailey's spine at the quiet whisper of a latch releasing. And then the bookcase in front of her swung forward.

"I can't believe that worked." Evie crowded in next to her, trying to see what was in the room. A long counter ran the length of one wall, six black and white screens flickered above it, each one revealing a different area of the house. She gasped. "Olive was right. He does have hidden cameras in here."

"You know that's what we're here looking for, right?"

"Well, yes, but I just wasn't sure we were actually going to find them. It sounded so out there." She stepped into the room and bent down to peer into one of the screens. "Who would do this?"

"Our humble mayor, apparently." On the other side of the room stood two file cabinets, and Bailey pulled open one of the drawers, revealing a neat row of files inside. The screens provided enough light for them to see to move around, but not to read the small print on the files. She turned on the flashlight and pointed it at the tabs.

They each held one word, presumably a last name, in neat handwritten block letters. Her fingers played over the files, trying to read the names, and recognizing some of the more prominent members of Humble Hills society.

A shiver ran up Bailey's spine as she realized these files had to contain the dirty little secrets of half the town. She pulled out Helen Dobbs's file and the one for Werner's secretary. She couldn't bring herself to look in them, at least not yet anyway. It felt too creepy, too invasive.

She sucked in a breath as her flashlight spanned over the name *Briggs*. Bailey pulled the folder out, her mind reeling. There had been a lot of Briggses in this town during Werner's life—her great-grandfather, her grandmother, her aunts, her mother, even her. The file seemed awfully thin for the secrets of all those people.

She added it to the stack.

"Check this out," Evie said, peering into one of the drawers in the other file cabinet.

Bailey looked into the drawer with her. It was full of video-tapes, clearly labeled with a date, and some again had just a last name.

"Holy time warp. Welcome back to the seventies," Evie said. "Are you sure we didn't travel back in time after all? Who the heck still uses videotapes? How old is this guy? Hasn't he heard of Bluetooth?"

Bailey checked both drawers below it. "These go back for years."

"So does all this stuff. The folders, the tapes, this is all the stuff our esteemed mayor was using to blackmail people." Evie made a gagging noise with her throat. "This is disgusting. People have a right to their secrets. I don't even want to know what's in this stuff."

Bailey pointed to the cabinet with the folders. "What if there's a folder marked Delgado in there?" She hadn't had a chance to check. "Do you want me to look?"

"Heck no. He didn't have anything on me, and if he had something on Abuelita, then that's her business, not mine."

"These are all arranged in numerical order, with a few extras with the names on them thrown in the mix," Bailey said, study-ing the tapes in the drawers. She pointed to several gaps in the tapes. "It looks like some are missing."

"What about the one for the night of the murder? That's the one we really want to see. Where is that one?"

They shuffled through the tapes together, searching for the most recent. "It isn't here." Bailey slapped at the file cabinet in front of the newest tapes. "The tape from the night of Werner's death is missing."

"That had to be what the guy who was in here before us took. Which totally makes sense."

Bailey sucked in a breath. "You realize that means we were in the same house as the murderer? What if he would have found us?" She sagged against the counter. "We could have been his next victims."

Evie rubbed her arms, knowing Bailey's tendency to hyperventilate when her anxiety took over. "Breathe, girl. We're okay. Nothing happened. The guy who was here, whether he killed Werner or not, he didn't get us. He didn't even know we were in the house. We're okay."

"You're right." She sucked in a deep calming breath then let it out slowly. "We're okay." She turned in a circle, trying to take in the details of the room. She stepped closer to the screens then peered down at the black boxes below each of them. "I think these are separate units for each camera." She pointed up at the screens. There were six altogether, but one was a bit bigger. "See, each one displays a different room or place in the house. There's the living room, the master bedroom, *ewww*, that's kind of sick," she said with another shiver. "This one looks like another bedroom, maybe a guest room, and this one goes back and forth between the dining room and kitchen."

"Same with this one," Evie said, pointing to one that was currently showing the front porch area. "Except it flips back and forth between the front porch and the back."

Bailey watched the last one, the bigger setup, for a few seconds. "This one is different. It looks like it cycles through *all* the areas."

"This dude was weird. What was he recording in his own house?"

"Maybe he was getting people to reveal their secrets then tapping their conversations and that's how he was blackmailing them.

It makes sense he would want to know who was coming and going from his house, since there were probably a lot of people who weren't too happy with him." She touched the screen for the guest room. "I don't even want to know what was happening here. Was this some kind of peeping tom thing?"

Evie shook her head. "I don't know. But this guy was all sorts of messed up. I can tell you one thing—Olive was right about the cameras. Werner *would* have seen her if she'd been stealing."

"But how did she *know* about the cameras? It's not like this room is easy to find."

"She could have accidentally hit the lever and opened the door when she was cleaning," Evie offered. "Or maybe she *didn't* see them. Werner could have just tried to keep her in check with the *threat* that there were cameras all over the house."

"Or maybe she didn't see this stuff, but she saw the actual cameras in the rooms."

"I think we need to talk to Olive Green again." Evie pointed to one of the screens. "But first, I think we need to get out of here. And now."

Bailey inhaled a sharp breath at the image Evie had pointed to. It was on the screen with the front porch and the steps and sidewalk leading up to it were clearly displayed. And so was the man walking up those steps. A man they both recognized.

Sawyer was still in uniform, and as he approached the front door he pulled his service weapon and held it out in front of him.

Evie knocked the file cabinet drawer closed with her hip then raced for the door.

Bailey grabbed for the stack of folders, then couldn't help herself and quickly rifled through the Ds. Sure enough, there was a folder labeled "Delgado." Evie didn't have to look inside it, but at least she could keep anyone else from seeing it. She pulled it out, then blinked as her gaze caught on the next folder and the neatly printed word "Dunn."

"Come on," Evie said, leaning her head back through the door. "We've got to go."

Evie had set her bag on the floor while they were searching through the tapes, and Bailey grabbed it and shoved all the folders inside, then raced out of the room after her friend.

They sprinted down the back stairs, Bailey almost tripping as her wet shoe skidded on the last step. The kitchen was dark, but Bailey could see the open door of the powder room, and she ran toward it, thinking they'd go back out the same way they came in.

She assumed Evie was right behind her, but when she turned to help her out the window, her friend was gone. She froze at the sound of the telltale creak of the back door, sounding extra loud in the quiet house, telling Bailey that either Evie had escaped out the back door or someone had just come in through it.

She prayed that was the way Evie had gotten out as she stepped onto the rim of the toilet and reached for the edge of the windowsill.

Her stupid wet shoe foiled her again, the sole slipping on the slick rim, and her foot landed back in the toilet with a splash.

She pressed her lips together to hold back the squeal as the cold water seeped through her already damp sock.

Then she heard a noise behind her as the bathroom door swung open and Sawyer's stern voice commanded, "Hold it right there."

Chapter Twenty

Bailey shot her hands into the air. "Don't shoot, Sawyer. It's me."

"*Bailey?*" His voice held a note of incredulousness to it. "Turn around. *Slowly.*"

Shoot. Shoot. Double shoot. Seriously?

"I can't," she whimpered, keeping her hands in the air as she tried to turn her upper body.

"Why not?"

"Because my stupid foot is stuck in the toilet." *Again.*

She kept that last part to herself.

"What are you talking about?"

She heard the flip of the switch, then squinted against the sudden harsh light filling the room.

Sawyer barked out one hard laugh. "Holy crap, your foot really *is* stuck in the toilet."

"I know. That's what I just said. Now stop laughing and help me." This felt like a repeat of the conversation she'd had twenty minutes ago with Evie. Dang. She hoped this embarrassing moment with the sheriff and the commode was at least giving her friend a chance to get the heck out of there.

Sawyer holstered his gun then slid an arm around her waist, giving her something to hold on to as he grabbed her leg and wrenched her foot free.

She stood up with a splat as her wet shoe hit the tiled floor. He let her go when he was sure she was steady, and she straightened her clothes, pulling her T-shirt down where it had ridden up her back.

"Bailey Briggs," Sawyer said, staring down at her. "What in the Sam Hill are you doing here? And why in the world are you wearing that wig? I could have shot you. You look like . . . well, never mind."

She looked like . . . *who*? Was he going to say Olive Green? She was the only one in town who Bailey knew had long red hair, although she was sure Olive's was styled much better.

"What?" She pressed him. "Who were you going to say? Olive Green? The housekeeper who loves frogs and recently got fired for stealing?"

"Loves frogs? What are you talking about?"

"What are *you* talking about?"

"I was going to say you looked like one of the Weasleys. Or Carrot Top on a bad night."

"Ouch. That hurts." She turned and gasped as she caught a look at herself in the bathroom mirror.

She was going to *kill* Evie.

One side of the wig hung in wavy ringlets while the other was chopped into some kind of bad mullet, not that there was any kind of a *good* mullet, but this one was beyond awful. Forget Carrot Top, she looked Chuckie's deranged sister. She jerked the wig from her head, crying out as the cheap rubber band around it pulled several strands of her real hair, and then let it dangle from her hand like a dead squirrel. Which wasn't too far off for a description. The thing could now pass for roadkill.

"Sorry," Sawyer said, holding his hand out as if to ward off the glare of her stare. "It didn't look *that* bad."

"Nice try."

He pulled his shoulders back. "Wait a minute. I'm the one who's supposed to be mad here. What are you doing in this house? You know this is a crime scene."

"I know. And we weren't ever in the dining room where the body was. I swear."

"Is that really supposed to make me feel better? Or make this okay?"

"No. I'm sorry. Olive Green told us that Werner had cameras hidden all over his house. So we . . . I mean I, absolutely me, alone, all by myself, just wanted to see if that was true."

"Hidden cameras?"

She nodded. "Yes. You didn't know?"

"Not a clue." He scrubbed his hand through his hair. "So what? You thought you'd just sneak in here . . . all alone, you said . . . *repeatedly* . . . and see if you could find these cameras. Then what? You were going to watch them? To see if your grandmother was on them?"

She offered him the smallest shrug.

"Dang it, Bailey. When are you going to trust me? I do *not* have it in for Granny Bee. I just want to find out the truth about what really happened. I don't understand why you wouldn't just tell me. I've got a guy down at the station who specializes in this kind of thing. He could have hacked into Werner's cameras in an hour and saved us both the trouble of having to come to this dang house in the middle of the night."

She smiled. "Your guy wouldn't have been able to hack into this system."

"You don't know my guy."

"You don't know Werner's system. It's videotapes."

"Videotapes? Like analog?"

She nodded.

"So you already found the tapes?"

She nodded again.

"Did you watch them?"

"No. Well, not much of them. You showed up before we . . . I mean I could. But I did search the dates, and the tape for the night of the murder is missing. We think the guy who broke in here before us must have taken it."

"The guy who broke in *before* you?" He let out a heavy sigh. "You'd better show me."

She filled him in on the other intruder as she took him upstairs to Werner's den and showed him the lever, even though the door to the hidden room was still standing open. Pointing to the screens, she told him everything they'd figured out so far.

He let out a heavy breath, his brow furrowed, as he looked around the room.

She gestured to the file cabinets. "These are where it looks like he keeps all the evidence on the people he's been blackmailing. One has all the tapes." She pointed to the file drawer she'd left pulled open. "And this one has folders on half the people in town, and I'm sure they contain all kinds of incriminating evidence."

He narrowed his eyes. "Did you look at them?"

She shook her head. "No, it felt too weird." She hesitated, then figured he'd find out anyway. "Sawyer, um, he's got one on you."

Sawyer shrugged, seemingly nonplussed. "I'm sure he does."

"Has he come after you for money?"

"Nah. The guy was pretty full of himself, but I don't know if he's *that* bold."

Bailey still had on the stupid plastic gloves, so she dug through the file cabinet and pointed to the folder marked "Dunn" in neat block letters. "Don't you want to look at it?"

His gaze bounced from Bailey's face to the files, then back to her face before he shook his head again.

"Well, I do." She would have already checked the one with "Briggs" on it if she hadn't sent it with Evie. She pulled the Dunn file from the drawer, held it up, and then looked at him, waiting for his permission.

"Go ahead," he said with a sigh. "I know you're dying to look in there."

She opened the folder. There were three items inside. The first was a receipt for a towing company with notes about towing a tractor from a lake. Stapled to the corner of the receipt was a canceled check. It was written by Werner and covered the damages. Underneath the receipt were two Polaroid photos, and Bailey gasped as she recognized the teenage boy in the pictures, but just barely.

She knew it was Sawyer, even recognized the same jeans and blue flannel he'd been wearing the last night she had seen him, but he'd been fine when she'd seen him last. He'd even winked and offered her one of his roguish grins as the sheriff had put him into the back of the squad car to take him home.

But this boy in the picture, she'd never seen him. His face was bruised and battered, one eye completely swollen shut and the other almost as bad. Blood smeared from a cut above his eyebrow down the edge of his face and along his cheek. The white under-shirt he wore was smudged with dirt and more blood. A thick purple bruise circled his forearm and another blossomed along his jaw. His lip was split and swollen. In the first picture, taken in his house, he was cradling his arm. The other was taken in another house, and he wore a sling made from a tea towel, a bright blue and yellow flower embroidered on one edge.

Chapter
Twenty-One

"Sawyer," Bailey whispered, unable to get any other words through her raw and swollen throat. Her hand fluttered to her mouth as she blinked back tears. "What happened to you?"

He stared down at the photos, his expression blank, as if he were looking at a piece of evidence. "I don't remember them taking pictures. But I was pretty out of it. I think I was barely conscious in that first one. Those were taken our senior year, the night we'd stolen the tractor and driven it into the lake and the sheriff had taken me home. One of the best nights of my life that ended up turning into the worst."

Her breath hitched in her chest. How could she not have known? "Who did this to you?"

He huffed out a sardonic laugh. "My dear old dad. He'd barely waited for the sheriff's car to get out of our driveway before he started whaling on me. He'd already been drinking, and losing our tractor was bad enough, I knew I'd get whipped for that, but having the police bring me home, that was something else entirely. He was so mad he could barely see straight. And I couldn't see anything at all, not after his fists started flying. It was like he was in a blind rage, and I'm pretty sure he would have killed me that night."

He swallowed, not looking at her, but still staring at the pictures. "The only thing that saved me was that the sheriff decided to come back to tell him they'd arranged to get the tractor towed out of the lake. I was on the floor by that time, trying to curl myself into a ball, praying for it to be over. He was on top of me, just pulverizing my ribs. He didn't usually hit me in the face—that way no one would know when he'd beat me—but that night he must not have been able to help himself. One of my eyes was already swollen shut, but I could still kind of see out of the other one. I remember seeing our front door being kicked in and then the sheriff running toward us and hauling my dad off me and throwing him across the room."

Sawyer's gaze had gone blank, as if lost in the memory of the night, almost forgetting that she was there. "He told me to go get in the car while he dealt with my dad. And I wanted to go, but I couldn't get up. I couldn't move. We found out later he'd broken one of my ribs. My dad tried to fight him, but Sheriff Dale was having none of it. He punched my dad hard, just one time in the face, before he had him on the floor and his hands cuffed behind his back.

"Then he used our kitchen phone to make a call before coming back to me. He was a big man, tough as hell, but he was gentle as he lifted me up off the floor, like I was just a little bird with a broken wing, and he helped me to the couch. I think I must have passed out because that looks like where that picture was taken. I came to as he was helping me out to the squad car. Three garbage bags were already in the back seat, holding just about everything I owned. He'd packed all my clothes, most of my books, some of the knickknacks and mementos he'd found on my shelves and in my drawers. Another car was driving up as he was loading me into the back seat. I was still pretty out of it, and I don't remember much else, except that it was a fancy car, and after it got there I left with the sheriff."

"Where did you go? Did he take you to the hospital?" A million questions swirled through her head. But the one she most wanted to ask was, why hadn't he called her? She would've been by his side in a minute.

"No. He never took me to the hospital. He took me to his house. His wife was there. I learned later that she used to be a nurse, and they took care of me. They cleaned me up and put ice on my face and gave me some Advil. Mrs. Dale made me a sandwich and a cup of hot tea that I'm pretty sure had a little whiskey in it. I knew the smell, and even though I hated everything about it, I still took a few sips. They put me to bed in their guest room, and I passed out for the rest of the night. When I woke up in the morning all my clothes had been washed and neatly packed into two duffel bags, and the sheriff told me I was going to live with my uncle. He said it was all arranged with my dad, then he put me on a bus to Montana less than an hour later."

"Why didn't you call me? Why didn't you tell me any of this?" she whispered, barely able to get the question out.

He finally looked at her. And her heart broke at the pain in his eyes. "I don't know. I should have. But I was ashamed. I figured my dad had gotten arrested and the whole town would have found out our dirty little secret, that he regularly beat up his son. I didn't know what you'd heard or what you thought of me."

"I never heard anything. I never *knew* anything. I just thought you left me behind because you didn't care enough."

He reached out his hand and tenderly touched her cheek. "You were the only thing that I *ever* cared about. And I guess I cared too much. Don't you get it? I was ashamed. Back then, I thought all of it was my fault, that I wasn't good enough. And I was worried you'd think the same thing. I figured once you found out, you were probably glad to get rid of me."

"Glad to get rid of you?" She pushed his hand away, trying to calm the ire that rose in her throat. The anger warred with the absolute horror and sadness she felt for the teenage boy who'd already suffered so much. "I wasn't *glad*. I was heartbroken. I *loved* you. With everything in my soul. If I had known, I could have been there for you. Like you'd always been there for me. Like I thought we were there for each other. But apparently you didn't trust me enough to tell me what was going on."

"Yeah, maybe that was part of it too. Not that I didn't trust *you*, but maybe I didn't trust that all that wouldn't change how you felt about me. I'd already lost *everything*. Maybe it was easier to believe you still cared about me than know the truth." He scrubbed a hand through his hair. "I don't know, Bailey. I was a stupid kid. And I was beat to hell. It took weeks for me to fully recover, so I don't know that I was thinking straight anyway. Remember, we were only a few months away from graduation? Someone must have worked out a deal with the school because they sent me homework and tests and then a diploma. As soon as I got it, I enlisted and threw myself into being a soldier. Sheriff Dale had made an impact on my life that night. He saved my life, and I wanted to be just like him, so after my tour was up, I went into the police academy. I'd kept in touch with him and his wife—not all the time, but I called once or twice a year."

Sawyer glanced at her, then hung his head. "I know. I should've called you too, but after so long, I didn't know how. I didn't know what to say, how to explain. Those first five or six years, I still had a lot of shame. I blamed myself, all the usual bullshit. I know that's not an excuse. I should've called, I knew where you were, eventually. I couldn't bring myself to ever ask Granny Bee about you, I figured she probably hated my guts. But once I got out of the military, I tracked you down. You were living in Denver by then."

"You tracked me down? *Years* ago?" She blinked up at him, barely able to comprehend what he was telling her. He'd wanted to find her? She couldn't bear to let herself think about all those wasted years that they could have been together. "Then why didn't you ever come to me? Or pick up the phone and call me?"

"It seemed to me like you'd moved on. You were with someone else, you had a little girl, seemed like you were better off without having a loser like me come back in to destroy your life."

"With someone else? What are you talking about?"

"You were living with some guy. I actually came up to the door, had some stupid flowers and everything. Like a handful of grocery store roses would make up for what I'd done. I know it was dumb. But then this guy answered the door, and when I asked for you, he called into the house for you. And this adorable little girl was hanging on to his leg. She grinned at me, and I knew she was yours. Her eyes do that same thing yours do when you smile. I thought my heart was going to break. So I told him to never mind, to forget it, and I high-tailed it out of there and tried to forget about you."

Her chest felt heavy. She couldn't believe he'd come to see her. "For such a smart guy, you're kind of an idiot. It doesn't seem like you learned much at the police academy. If you had asked some questions, or stayed and talked to me, you would have found out *that guy* and I were just friends."

"It didn't seem like it to me. He called you 'honey' when he shouted into the house for you. And the little girl acted like he was her dad."

She rolled her eyes. "He calls *everyone* honey, and Daisy absolutely adored him. That *guy* was Evie's cousin, and the reason we lived there was because we'd worked out this great deal with him and *his husband* that I would cook and clean the house and they would help me with childcare so I could write and go to school. We moved in with them after we left the ranch. And it worked out great, for years in fact, until one of them got a great job offer and they had to move to California."

"Oh." Sawyer let out a long, heavy breath. "I guess I *am* an idiot."

Bailey wasn't sure she could process everything he'd just told her. She needed time to think, to mull it all over. Easier to move on. For now. "So, after all that, why did you come back here?"

"I didn't think I ever would. Especially after my dad died. But like I said, I'd kept in touch with the sheriff, and when he was getting ready to retire last year, he put me up for his job. I'd only had a few years' experience on the force and taking the role of sheriff seemed like a big step, but he assured me I was ready and that I could handle a small town with low crime like Humble Hills. My dad was gone, but he'd left me the farm. I had a little money saved, just enough to fix the house up a bit, buy some cattle. Figured it was time to face the demons and see if I could carve out a life for myself here. Thought I'd give it a year or so, and I reckoned I owed the sheriff." He looked down at the photos again. "This folder wasn't for me. It was for my dad. I guess that man in the fancy car was Werner, and he must've blackmailed my dad, made some kind of deal to keep him out of jail if he agreed to send me to my uncle's. I don't know why he would have done it, other than maybe as a favor to the sheriff, but that deal saved me from my dad ever pounding on me again."

He picked up the folder and snapped it shut. "I guess I owe Werner one. So I should probably get back to trying to figure out who killed him."

Bailey nodded, trying to shift gears and not think about how her, and Daisy's, life might have been different if she'd only known, closing her mind to their past the same way he'd shut that folder. She turned back to the drawer with the tapes. "We looked . . . I mean, *I* looked, and the tape from that night isn't here. There's a tape from the day before, but the newest one is missing."

"But it wouldn't be in the drawer because there's no way Werner would have been able to file it after he died. It has to still be in the machine."

She slapped her hand to her forehead. "Oh duh, why didn't we . . . I mean *I* think of that? Of course it's in the machine."

He looked closer at the recording device below the camera. "It looks like there's a tape in each one."

She pulled one of the plastic gloves from her hand and passed it to him. "Here. Use this. You don't want your fingerprints on it."

He glanced down at the glove then back up at her, and even though she hadn't seen him in years, she still knew his expressions. And this was not one of his happy ones. "Remember that part of the story where I went to the police academy and became the sheriff?"

She pulled the glove back. "Sorry."

He drew a ballpoint pen from his pocket and used it to push the levered flap open and peer inside. "You're right, though. The tape from the dining room and kitchen is gone."

At least I was right about something, she thought, still smarting over not figuring out that the tape would have been in the machine. She put the glove back on her hand—not a pleasant experience since it was damp and sticky from her previously sweating hands, but she knew she didn't want her fingerprints anywhere in this room. Pulling out the tape with the most recent date on it, the day before Werner had been murdered, she pushed it into the empty machine and hit play before Sawyer had a chance to stop her.

The screen was just static, so she rewound a few seconds then let the tape go. "Check it out," she said, pointing toward the bottom corner of the screen. "There's a time stamp. This was recorded just after eight. And see the windows. It isn't quite dark yet."

They watched and Bailey sucked in a breath as a dark smudge fell across the wall. She pointed to the screen, trying to contain her excitement. It felt like this was a clue. A real clue. "There's a shadow. And look in the mirror behind the dishes in the china hutch. You can see someone come in, set something down, and walk out again."

She squinted at the screen. "Dang it. I can't see their face. That stupid plate obscures their whole head, but you can see some of their body, enough to tell . . . oh my gosh, look, they're wearing a black and white maid's uniform." She waggled her eyebrows as she grinned up at Sawyer. "So it *wasn't* the butler, but the *maid* who did it."

"Hold on now. We don't know that anyone *did* anything. All we can see is that someone set the table. That could've been hours before Werner even got home."

"Okay, maybe. But this tape should be enough to put Granny in the clear. Or at least give you another person of interest to investigate."

He didn't say anything.

He was watching the rest of the tape on the screen. The picture cycled through as she was talking, filming an empty kitchen and then an empty living room and then flicking to the front porch . . . which was *not* empty.

Oh no. Bailey clapped her hand over mouth as she watched a woman stomp across the porch, raise her hand, and hammer the front door with several hard knocks. The woman looked mad as a hornet.

Thankfully, it wasn't her grandmother. But that fact was little consolation to Bailey, since the woman on the tape who was pounding furiously at Werner's door was the next closest thing.

It was her aunt.

Chapter
Twenty-Two

I t didn't matter that the picture was black and white, or even that it was a little grainy. Bailey would recognize her aunt's severe stance and stern scowl anywhere.

But what the heck was her Aunt Marigold doing at Werner's house?

"Well, that's new," Sawyer said, scratching the back of his neck. "Maybe your Aunt Aster wasn't the only one who had a side thing going with Werner."

"*Eww.* Gross. And no way. My Aunt Marigold would never. But she *would* show up to kick some major mayor ass for messing around with her sisters."

Before they could say anything more, a movement on the live feed caught their attention as a woman with long platinum blond hair snuck onto the front porch, rang the doorbell, and then ran away.

Oh crud. She'd told Evie to take off. Leave it to her bestie to come back and try to rescue her. And leave it to Evie to use the old ding-dong-ditch method to do it.

Sawyer cocked an eyebrow at Bailey.

She lifted her shoulders in what she hoped looked like an innocent shrug. "I have no idea who that woman is. Or even if it was a woman. Maybe that was a man. Or just a weird kid playing a prank."

Sawyer turned and strode through the office and down the back stairs.

Bailey was right on his heels. "You're going the wrong way. That crazy woman/man/person was at the *front* door."

"Uh huh," was all he said before striding through the kitchen and yanking open the back door to a startled platinum blond.

Bailey had always thought Evie should have been an actress, but her skills were a tad lacking tonight as she stared wide-eyed at Sawyer.

Then she collected herself as she pushed her shoulders back and rearranged her expression into a stern scowl as she addressed Bailey as if scolding a child. "There you are, Bailey. I thought I might find you here. I can't believe you'd try something so stupid on your own." She jerked a thumb toward Bailey as she nodded conspiratorially at Sawyer. "I thought this one might try something crazy like this. But don't you worry. I'll get her out of here right now, and I'll be sure to give her a stern talking to. And you can bet she'll never do anything like this again." She waved Bailey forward. "Come on, Bailes. I'll take you home."

Bailey tried to scoot around Sawyer, not even bothered that Evie was fake-scolding her. She'd let her fake-lecture her the entire ride home if it meant that she got her out of here.

Sawyer put a hand up between them. "Hold it right there. You two aren't going anywhere." His gaze bounced back and forth between them. "I'm not sure how you thought you'd get away with this Lucy and Ethel routine, but I know you were in this together."

"Who? *Us?*" Bailey tried once more, although she already knew they'd been made.

"Just please tell me that you *both* wore gloves the whole time you were in this house," Sawyer said.

"Of course we did," Evie said, apparently giving up on their ruse. Geez, she was an easy nut to crack. "What do we look like? A couple of idiots?"

Sawyer wisely kept his mouth shut, but his gaze did flick up to Evie's wig, then down to Bailey's sopping shoe.

"We did wear gloves *almost* the whole time," Bailey corrected. "But not when we first climbed slash fell into the window. So our fingerprints might be on the sill."

"*And* the toilet tank," Evie added.

"*And* on the doorknob," Bailey said. "But once we went upstairs, that's when we wore the gloves the whole time."

Sawyer sighed then pulled out his notebook. "Okay, we'll deal with the bathroom in a minute. But right now, since I've got you here, Evie, I need you to fill me in on the other intruder you two heard. Bailey told me her version, but I need to hear yours as well."

Bailey kept silent as Evie told him everything she remembered.

"It happened so fast," Evie said. "And we never actually *saw* anything. We just heard them. And beyond some thuds and footsteps and doors creaking, we didn't hear that much. Maybe we should have jumped out and tried to tackle them." She looked at Bailey. "With the two of us, we probably could have managed."

"Yeah, we should have. Except we were too scared," Bailey said.

Sawyer closed his notebook and stuffed it back into his pocket. "No, you did absolutely the right thing. When someone's breaking in somewhere, they're already on edge, and this person could have been armed or hopped up on drugs."

"I didn't think about that," Bailey said, her stomach doing a queasy flip.

"We can't be sure that this intruder even had anything to do with Werner's death. They could have just been taking advantage of the empty house and looking for stuff to steal," Sawyer explained.

Evie didn't look convinced. "No way. If they were just some rando thief, they would have just grabbed expensive stuff on this level and ran. They wouldn't have been upstairs in the room with the hidden door, and they wouldn't have taken the tape from the night of the murder."

Bailey nodded at her friend. "She makes a convincing argument."

"I'm just saying sometimes things aren't always what they seem."

"Like with my Aunt Marigold," Bailey said. "Who we need to talk to now to figure out what she was doing here the night Werner was killed."

"No, *I* need to talk to her," Sawyer said. "*I'm* the sheriff."

Bailey huffed. "I know."

"Do you? It seems maybe you and your blond coconspirator here might need reminding." He gestured toward Evie.

"Why do you need to talk to Aunt Marigold?" the blond coconspirator asked, looking confused.

Bailey filled her in on what they'd seen on the tape.

"Oh, shi . . . izzle, that seems bad," Evie said. She really was doing better with her swearing. Bailey was proud of her.

197

"It isn't good," Sawyer agreed.

"You can probably talk to her now," Evie said. "If you want."

"Now?" Bailey flipped her wrist to glance at her watch. "It's almost eleven."

"I'm guessing she's still up. She's probably just sitting in the kitchen having a snack and reading a book." Evie leaned close to Bailey and lowered her voice. "I may have just seen her through the window when I was hiding in their yard."

"Makes sense. She's always been a night owl." She held her phone up to Sawyer. "I can text her to make sure she's still up if you want to just talk to her now."

"I'm gonna have to call this in. Then I'll need to stay here and wait for a team. I have a feeling we're going to be processing that room all night."

"We can stand on her porch to talk, and you'll be able to see the house from there," Bailey suggested. "You know I'm too curious to wait until tomorrow to find out what she knows, so I'm going up there tonight anyway. You might as well come along. Two birds, one stone, and all that."

He gave a reluctant nod. "Fine. I won't be able to talk to her once the team gets here, so let's get this over with now."

Bailey shot her aunt a text, and Marigold was dressed in a purple velour jogging set and waiting on the porch with a pot of tea and four mugs by the time they got there.

She poured some into a cup and held it out to Sawyer. "You want a little something extra in yours, Sheriff?"

"No, not tonight. I think I'd better keep my wits about me. Long night ahead."

Marigold checked her watch. "By my calculations, the night's already half over."

"Not my night."

Bailey and Sawyer had talked on the walk up about what she could share with Marigold, and he'd given her permission to mention the cameras. "Apparently Werner had hidden cameras that we just discovered all over his house."

"Hidden cameras?" Marigold pressed a hand to her chest.

Bailey studied her aunt, watching for any signs of guilt. But Marigold seemed genuinely surprised by the revelation.

"That's actually why we're here," Sawyer said. "Because we saw *you*. On the cameras. At the front door. On the night of the murder."

Marigold heaved a resigned sigh as she sank into one of the wicker rockers. "I figured someone would eventually figure that out."

"Well, if that's what you thought," Sawyer said, "then dang it, why didn't you just come to me and tell me about it first?"

"You know, like a preemptive strike?" Evie added.

"What does she look like? A colonel?" Bailey muttered to her friend.

Marigold ignored them both. "Because nothing happened. I knocked on the door, no one answered, I left. End of story."

"That's a pretty short story," Evie said.

Bailey shushed her. "But *why* did you go to Werner's that night?"

Marigold pursed her lips as she stared at the porch floor. Then she lifted her chin and looked directly at Sawyer. "I was angry. That . . . that . . . gigolo . . . had been dating my sister *and* one of my dear friends and then had the absolute nerve to make a pass at my *other* sister. Of course I went to his house. I was going to give him a piece of my mind and possibly a piece of my sensible size nine shoe up his behind. Pardon my French, Sheriff, but I was hopping mad."

"So you killed him?" Evie asked.

Marigold turned and gave her one of her aunty evil-eye stares. "No, Evie Marie, I did *not* kill him. I wanted to maim the man, but I wasn't planning to kill anyone. And it doesn't matter anyway. Like I said, I marched up to the door and knocked. *Repeatedly.* But no one answered, so I left."

She pursed her lips again, then folded her arms across her chest. "I *will* admit to kicking over one of his stupid garden gnomes on my way out, though. There's a solid chance the head might've broken off. If you want to arrest me for that, go ahead. I'll pay the fine or spend the night in jail. How long is the sentence for knocking out a gnome anyway?" She waved her hand through the air. "Doesn't matter. I'll pay. It was worth it."

She stuck her hands out in front of her. "Do you want to arrest me now or in the morning? I wouldn't mind finishing tonight in my own bed before you throw me in the slammer."

Sawyer rolled his eyes and gestured for her to lower her hands. "I'm not going to arrest you. Not *yet* at least. But only for the sole reason that I hate those garden gnomes too. They creep me out." He gave a little shudder. "I do believe you that no one was home, but walk me through it anyway. You might've seen something you didn't realize was important at the time."

She nodded. "All right. I don't think there was anything noteworthy, but I'm happy to try. I arrived around eight, I think, or maybe it was nine. We'd gone out to dinner after we dropped everyone off from high tea, and Aster went up to her room to rest. Which I'm sure had something to do with all the 'tea' she'd drunk, both at Bee's and at the restaurant." She winked at Bailey, who still couldn't believe her aunts were drinking beer at high tea. "I was driving, so I hadn't had any 'tea' at all, which was probably also contributing to my foul mood. I tried to forget about it and just watch television, but the longer I sat there, the more I stewed on it, until finally I couldn't stand it, and I just had to do something."

Sawyer looked confused and Bailey nudged his arm. "I'll explain later," she told him.

"I don't remember any other cars on the street or any neighbors out, but I wasn't paying much attention to that. I was pretty set on getting to Werner's and giving him a piece of my mind. Then he wasn't even home." She paused. "Although, knowing what we know now, maybe he *was* home, and just couldn't come to the door."

"Anything else you can remember?" Sawyer asked. "Did you hear anything funny or see anyone else around?"

Marigold shook her head. "No. Not that I recall. Although I thought I saw the maid in there when I walked up to the house. Does that count?"

"As seeing someone else in the house?" Sawyer asked then let out a sigh. "*Yes*, Miss Marigold, that would count."

"Oh, well, then, I guess I did see someone. But I didn't actually see *them*, I just thought I saw the back of that little black and white outfit he made his maid wear. And that's what made me even more angry. That I was causing a holy racket pounding my fists off, and she didn't even come to the door. Hence the assault on the garden elf."

"See," Bailey said. "You *did* remember more than you thought."

Marigold shrugged. "I guess. I don't know if any of that was helpful."

"Everything helps," Sawyer said.

Marigold yawned and slumped back against the chair. "I hate to break up a good party, but I think it's time for me to go to bed."

Sawyer and Evie waited on the porch while Bailey helped take the tea and her aunt inside.

"Well, this night feels like a big waste of time and one perfectly good tennis shoe," Evie said, pointing to Bailey's foot as the three of them walked and squelched their way back toward Werner's house.

"Waste of a shoe, yes," Bailey agreed. "But waste of time? No way."

"Really? I'm more confused than before we went into that house. And we already knew going in that there were hidden cameras inside. So what did we even learn? Besides that I'm still a knockout as a blond and you should never, ever color your hair red and get a mullet."

"Thanks for that," Bailey said. "Now I have to change my cut and color appointment next week with my hairdresser."

"Maybe I'm just tired and grouchy," Evie said. "I guess I was hoping we would find something that would break the case wide open, and we'd reveal the killer and be heroes, and then the town would throw us a parade."

"No wonder you're grouchy," Sawyer said. "Rarely do you find a clue that breaks a case wide open and helps you solve it in one night. And no one's thrown me a parade yet."

"Have you solved a murder case?" Evie asked.

"No, but I did help rescue three pigs that had locked themselves in Ray Finlayson's pickup last week in the parking lot of the Price Mart."

"That's pretty heroic," Evie agreed. "But I'm not sure it's parade-worthy."

"Could we get back to the case at hand, please?" Bailey asked. "We may not have uncovered the single case-solving clue, but I think we still learned some important things." She held up her fingers and ticked off the items as she relayed them. "We learned that Werner has incriminating files on half the people in this town, which widens the circle of suspects exponentially. We learned that someone else broke into Werner's house tonight. And we learned that someone was at the house the night of the murder wearing a maid's uniform, which means something doesn't track with Olive's story."

"True," Evie said. "Which means either Olive lied about being fired, or she snuck back into the house to kill Werner for firing her."

"Or . . . someone else could have been wearing a maid's outfit," Bailey chimed in.

"Or . . ." Sawyer said. "The maid's outfit has nothing to do with the murder at all."

Bailey and Evie looked at each other for a moment, as if considering his idea, then both shook their heads.

"Nah, it's connected somehow," Evie said.

"Absolutely," Bailey concurred, then held up another finger. "Oh, and we also learned that someone else knew about the hidden cameras and the files and the tapes *and* that whatever was on those tapes was important enough to risk breaking into a crime scene for . . ." She paused for dramatic effect. "And maybe important enough to *kill* for."

Chapter
Twenty-Three

Bailey dropped Evie off at her car ten minutes later. Sawyer had insisted on walking them both to her car and only went back to Werner's house after she promised to drive Evie to her car and make sure she got in safely.

"Thanks for rescuing me tonight," Bailey told her friend before she got out of the car.

"Any time." Evie wrinkled her nose. "Although I had thought that ding-dong-ditch plan was going to go a lot smoother."

Bailey chuckled and then pointed to the messenger bag at Evie's hip. "I am feeling a little guilty for stealing those files."

"Don't," Evie said. "You did it to help your grandmother, and whatever we find, we know we'll keep to ourselves. Besides, some of them are *our* family's secrets."

"True. So, do you think we should look at them now?"

Evie looked down at the bag. "I don't know. We could take a quick peek, just so we know what's in them and then we can warn them if it's too bad."

Bailey chewed her lip, weighing the decision. "No. I say we wait. The Hive's supposed to come over for lunch anyway tomorrow, so let's give them the files then and let them decide what to do with them."

"Good idea. Do you want to hold on to them tonight or should I?"

"You. I'm afraid I'll be too tempted to peek."

Evie grinned. "Oh, I'll be tempted too, but the risk of Rosa Delgado finding out I snooped into her dirty laundry will keep my nose out of them."

* * *

For such a late night out, Bailey was still up early the next morning. Her buzzing brain wouldn't let her sleep—too many thoughts and ideas running through her mind of what all they'd discovered over the last few days could mean.

The clues were like a puzzle, except she couldn't figure out how to put them together. How did the blackmail piece fit into the embezzlement piece, and where did the honey piece and the maid's outfit piece go, and was the maid's outfit even a piece of the puzzle at all?

She ran her hand through her hair, her scalp still itchy from the suffocating wig, as she got out of bed and padded to the window. Speaking of buzzing, she smiled as she looked into the field in front of the farmhouse and saw two figures encased in white bee suits at the hives. She loved that Daisy was helping Granny Bee harvest honey and learning about the hives. Her daughter had always been fascinated by the bees and their incredibly intricate system of producing honey, pollinating flowers, and working for and protecting their queen.

Daisy was holding the smoker and gently wafting smoke over an open hive box as Granny carefully lifted a frame from its interior. Even from this far away, Bailey could see it was covered with a dark mass of bees. She cringed as she knew what was coming.

Granny knocked the frame against the box a couple of times and shook the majority of the bees free before lowering the frame into one of the five-gallon buckets she had secured in the yellow and black painted wagon she used to haul her equipment to and from the hives.

The knocking didn't hurt the bees, and most of them were subdued, the smoke calming them by masking their sense of smell and preventing the transfer of intruder alarm signals. Granny had taught her a long time ago that the smoke fooled the bees into thinking their home was on fire, so they would gorge themselves on honey thinking they'd need the energy to find a new home and the honey stored in their abdomens to build it.

Gran used to tell her the smoke made the bees get drunk on honey so they wouldn't sting her. She'd taught Bailey about the hives when she was about her daughter's age. In fact, Daisy was probably wearing her old bee suit.

Seeing them from this angle, it made her heart hurt a little that Daisy was almost as tall as Granny Bee. How was she growing up so fast? She wasn't worried about Daisy with the bees—the suit protected her, and she trusted her grandmother and her beekeeping skills.

However, her doofus dog was another story. Cooper had just leaped into the air as if trying to catch a bee in his mouth. That was an accomplishment he'd only achieve once. She hoped. Her golden retriever was the sweetest, most loyal dog, who would do anything to please her and Daisy, but he wasn't always the brightest when it came to learning lessons.

Secure in the knowledge that her daughter and grandmother were safe and occupied, she grabbed a pair of shorts and a T-shirt that read "I love the smell of writing in the morning," and headed for the bathroom. By the time she'd showered and dressed and grabbed coffee and a thick slice of Granny Bee's honey vanilla banana bread, the honey harvesters had left the hives.

An enthusiastic Cooper ran around her—probably more interested in the banana bread than her—as she made her way across the driveway and headed toward Busy Bee, the cute nickname Granny had for her workshop, which was housed in a large building next to the barn. Designed by Gran and her sisters, the building was separated into five spaces, each used for a specific part of the business.

The front area was an adorable shop that carried all the various products they created, from gorgeous beeswax candles and lip balm to herbal remedies and the jars of flavored honeys. They carried a few things from local artisans, like bee-inspired jewelry, pottery, and yard art, as well as some crafty things they'd made on their own. Aster and Marigold had crocheted the most adorable beehive potholders and bumblebee trivets. She and Daisy still used the hand-crafted honey jar she'd purchased there years before.

The shop was normally open for a few hours on weekdays and most of the day on weekends, but Lyle had posted a sign at the end of the driveway stating the shop would be closed until further notice. He and Granny had figured the murder investigation would bring out all sorts of lookie-loos to the ranch but doubted they'd buy much.

A few townspeople had already tried to come out that first day, but Granny had said it was mostly to gossip and gawk. Bailey made a mental note to get their names and add them to their list of suspects in case one of them had been responsible for leaving the scarf in the barn.

Behind the shop was an office and two rooms set up with workstations, one for making products like the candles and lip balms, the other for assembly and production. Daisy had told her she'd spent several hours there the day before helping Granny put labels on honey jars, tie raffia bows around scented candles, and package online orders in preparation for shipping.

At the back of the building was the honey harvest room, with stainless steel machines, a long workbench and sink, and linoleum floors with a drain in the center that could be hosed down. It was quite a setup, and Bailey was proud of the work her grandmother and aunts had done with the shop.

The back room was where Bailey found her grandmother and daughter after giving her last bite of bread to Cooper and meandering through the shop to scope out the changes they'd made and the new products they carried. She had her eye on a gorgeous pair of earrings that had a sterling silver bee sitting on an amber topaz drop of honey.

Bailey inhaled the intoxicating fragrance of the room. Extracting the honey always gave off the most delicious scent. "How's the honey harvest going?" she asked, giving her daughter a side hug as she peered into the honey spinner, the machine they used to extract the honey from the frames.

"Great," Daisy said, pushing her bangs away from her forehead. "Gran said the bees had capped their honey in one of her hives, so she said I could help her harvest it. She even let me use the scratcher to clean off the wax she missed with the knife when she was uncapping the honey." She pointed to a forked tool that looked like a large hair pick. "But you don't really *scratch*, it's more like you use the scratcher to *lift* off the wax." Her voice went high and breathy as she said the word "lift," and Bailey could hear her grandmother's voice in her head as she'd explained the process to her when she'd been about Daisy's age.

"That's awesome," Bailey told her as she peered into the strainer holding the wax they'd uncapped from the frames. "Looks like you did a great job."

"And Gran said we'll use that wax to make candles and lotion and even lip balm."

"That's right." Bailey smiled at her grandmother, who gave her a wink. "Anything I can do to help?"

"We can always use an extra hand," Granny said. "And I can't think of a better way to spend a morning than making honey with my two favorite honeys."

Cooper had followed Bailey in and was circling the room, his tail wagging as he sniffed the machines and occasionally licked a spare drop of honey. He let out a quick woof.

"Sorry," Granny said. "I meant to say my *three* favorite honeys."

* * *

Working together, Bailey, Daisy, and Granny Bee finished just in time to get cleaned up and set out the lunch fixings Granny had put together the night before. Chicken salad, croissants, hearty kettle chips, and a veggie tray with a creamy dill dip. The aunts were bringing a jar of their canned pickles, and Rosa and Evie had promised to bring something sinful from the coffeeshop for dessert. Poor Dottie was stuck working at the library today and couldn't get away for lunch.

Bailey had just poured the iced tea when the women arrived, and they must have all been hungry because it didn't take them long to sit down and devour their lunch. Lyle had come in at one point and made a plate, but he took it back out to the barn with him, claiming he didn't want to interrupt them.

Working with the honey had gotten Bailey's brain buzzing again, and while they ate, she asked them all to think about where the killer could have gotten the spiced honey.

"It's for sale in over half the shops in town," Marigold told her.

"We sell it in the bakery," Evie said. "And they carry it in the grocery store."

"They've got a little display of it at the truck stop by the highway," Aster added. "And Bee's given tons of it away. It's her favorite gift."

"Yeah, it is," Marigold muttered. "Would it kill her to just once maybe include an Amazon gift card, or a tennis bracelet, with the jar?"

"You don't even play tennis," Aster whispered. "But a gift card *would* be nice."

"We did a deal with the Convention of Visitors Bureau last year to include a jar of it in every welcome basket they pass out to new residents," Granny explained, ignoring her sisters.

Rosa snapped her fingers. "Since he's the mayor, maybe he had a few of those welcome baskets at his house. And it was just a weapon of convenience."

Granny shook her head. "No way Werner would have it in his house. He wouldn't get within ten feet of a jar of honey."

"And this doesn't feel like a weapon of convenience. The killer would have *had* to have known about Werner's bee allergy," Marigold said.

"*Everyone* knew about his bee allergy," Granny said. "I swear there was a sign in his office that read 'Beware—a bee could kill me.' I think it was a point of pride with him—although it beats me what's to be proud about—but he told *everyone* he met that he was allergic to bees, honey, pollen, beeswax, bee movies, spelling bees . . ." Granny rolled her eyes. "Okay, I may be reaching with those last two, but I swear that man was annoying the way he constantly talked about my sweethearts as if they were killer bees out to get him."

"Apparently they were," Evie muttered.

"Is there any kind of code on your labels or packaging that might tell us when the honey was harvested, or where or who you sold it to?" Bailey asked, ignoring her friend.

Granny shook her head. "No, I'm not that sophisticated an operation."

"It doesn't matter anyway," Marigold pointed out. "Because we don't have access to the jar. I'm sure it's locked up somewhere with the evidence from the case."

"Maybe we could find a way to break into the evidence room . . ." Bailey started to say but was cut off as Evie and Granny both spoke at the same time.

"*No.*"

She held up her hands in surrender. "Okay, okay, it was just an idea."

"A bad one," Granny said. "You girls need to keep your noses clean. I don't want you breaking the law or getting yourselves into trouble on my account."

Bailey and Evie looked at each other. "Well then, you're probably not going to like what we have to tell you," Bailey said.

They filled the group in on what had happened the night before and the things they'd discovered, including the folders filled with incriminating information. After dessert, Bailey cleared away the dishes as Evie pulled out the folders they'd taken.

"We haven't looked at any of these yet," Evie told them as she spread the four folders out on the table. "We took the ones with our family's names on them and also the ones for the mayor's admin, Susan, and for Helen Dobbs. We talked to both of those women and figured we could use the files to check if their stories were true and then decide if we want to turn these over to the police or return them to the ladies."

"Are you sure we want to look into their files?" Aster asked. "It seems like we're crossing a line, invading their privacy. And this isn't just information like their name and Social Security number. Whatever's in there is bad enough that they've been willing to pay to keep it a secret."

Bailey nodded. "We know. And we've been wrestling with that as well. But a man's been murdered, and there may be something in these files that could help lead us to the identity of his killer." She paused with her hand on the folders as she peered around at the other women. "We won't look unless we all agree."

Marigold spoke first. "I say we look in the files, but first we all swear to keep whatever we find just between us. These women deserve to keep their secrets. And not have to pay some dirtbag man for his silence."

"Agreed," Rosa said. "Unless they're the killer."

Her comment started a round of nervous laughter.

"I really like both these women," Evie said. "Is it wrong that I hope neither of them killed him?"

"No, I like them too." Bailey took a deep breath, then picked up Susan's folder. "We already suspect that Susan borrowed money from the county to pay her mortgage after her husband died, then paid it back later. Hopefully that's what we find in here. Here goes nothing." The folder contained several photocopied pages of county ledgers showing where eleven hundred and sixteen dollars had been taken out and then replaced several months later. The line item was listed as *Petty Cash for Winter Carnival*. And there was a copy of her mortgage statement and several overdue notices as well.

Evie glanced through the pages. "There's nothing in here we didn't already know."

"Then I say we give this folder and everything in it back to Susan," Bailey said.

All the women nodded or murmured their agreement.

"I'll go over there with you this afternoon," Evie said then pulled out Helen's folder. "Helen said that whatever Werner had on her happened a long time ago and wasn't that bad by today's standards. She told him a few weeks ago that she wasn't going to pay him anymore." She opened the folder to reveal several photographs clipped inside along with copies of what looked like love letters written to Helen.

"This *was* a long time ago," Bailey said, glancing through the pictures. "Look how young Helen was. She was so pretty." She picked up one that looked like it was Helen with her parents and turned the picture over. "This says 'College—Freshman Year—Parents Weekend,' so she was probably around eighteen or nineteen."

Granny picked up a school picture of a man quite a bit older. "This guy isn't. He's got to be in his forties. Pretty handsome, though. Says here that he's a professor of liberal arts."

"Wowza," Bailey said, skimming one of the love letters. "He's liberal in this letter all right, but I'm not sure you would call this art. They were obviously sleeping together. He's describing their . . . um . . . time together . . . in great detail." She winced as she read a particularly graphic line. "Oh. My goodness."

"Let me see," Daisy said, reaching for the letter.

Bailey snatched it away. "Not on your life, missy."

"I don't get it," Aster said. "This all points to a secret tryst between a student and a professor. But that's hardly scandalous nowadays. And personally, I think it makes Helen Dobbs seem more interesting. I don't know why she'd pay to keep this quiet. Unless he was married."

"This might have something to do with it," Granny said, holding up a picture of the professor with his arm around Helen's dad. "It looks like the guy was good friends with her father. I'm sure he wouldn't take kindly to his best friend boinking his daughter."

"Especially if it started while she was still in high school," Evie pointed out.

"Gross," Daisy said. "Why would a high school girl want to be with that old guy?"

"That's a great point," Bailey said, collecting all the pictures and papers and clipping them back into the folder. "And the perfect time to put all this away. There's nothing in here that makes me think Helen would want to murder someone over. This all happened so long ago."

"I think you're right," Granny said. "And if our theory is correct, maybe Helen decided to stop paying Werner because one or both of her parents had recently passed away and the information could no longer hurt them. Whatever the case, I think you should give this all back to Helen. Might give her some peace of mind to know that whatever happened will be kept her secret."

"Speaking of secrets," Evie said, tapping the last two folders. "Are you sure you want to open these here? On the one hand, it doesn't seem like they could have anything *too* bad in them, because if they did, Werner would have already been using the information to blackmail you. But on the other hand, there could be something super incriminating inside that he's just been holding onto until he needed to use it for leverage against you. Either way, we'd all understand if you want to take them somewhere private to look first."

"*Ay, dios mio*," Rosa said, grabbing her folder and jerking it open. A collective gasp went up from the group as Rosa held it by the corner and shook it. "There's nothing here." She narrowed her eyes at her niece. "Are you pranking me?"

Evie shook her head. "No, Abeulita, I swear."

"Then I'm not the least bit surprised," Rosa said, nonchalantly tossing the empty folder onto the table.

"Why not?" Daisy asked. "Because you've never done anything that was blackmail worthy?"

Rosa offered her an impish grin. "Oh no, *tesoro*, I've done plenty of blackmail worthy things in my life, just none that Werner Humble would ever have had a way to find out about."

"On that note," Granny Bee said, picking up the Briggs folder and effectively changing the subject. Her sisters leaned forward as she addressed them. "This one has just our last name on it, so it could have information on any of us. You sure you want me to open this here?"

Aster gave a quick nod, her eyes wide and her hands clasped tightly in her lap.

Marigold shrugged. "It's fine by me. I've got nothin' to hide. I'm more concerned about finding out something awful about Daddy than I am about finding something concerning me." She turned to Aster. "And I don't think you've done a single appalling thing in your whole life." She shifted her gaze to Granny. "You, on the other hand, I'm surprised that file isn't stuffed with information."

Granny stuck her tongue out at her sister, then regarded the folder again. "It is awfully thin. Surely our family has stirred up more trouble than this."

Bailey had a sudden queasy feeling in her stomach. All this talk about secrets and blackmail—she'd only been thinking about her grandmother and her aunts. She hadn't considered that the folder could contain damning information about her mother.

Or about her.

She reached for the folder just as her aunt whacked the top of the table.

"Just open it already," Marigold snapped.

Granny lifted the corner of the folder and peeked inside, then she huffed out her disappointment as she flipped it all the way open. "Well, that was anticlimactic. Ours is empty too."

Bailey let out the breath she hadn't realized she'd been holding.

Her Aunt Aster let out a nervous giggle. "I knew it would be nothing."

"But what does this mean?" Evie asked. "Why the empty envelopes? Does that mean Werner had nothing on you and just made a file in case he dug something up for you in the future?"

"Or," Bailey asked, "did someone *take* the information Werner compiled on our families and is planning to use it against us later?"

Chapter Twenty-Four

An hour later, Bailey and Evie had snuck up to the third floor of the courthouse again. This time, Susan was at her desk, a pencil stuck behind her ear and growling at her computer.

"Son of a basset hound," she said, as she repeatedly clicked the mouse.

Evie grinned at Bailey. "I'll have to use that one. I like it."

"Can we help?" Bailey asked, knocking then stepping into the office.

"Gah!" Susan yelped as she pressed her hand to her chest. "Good lima beans, you scared the ship out of me."

"Sorry," Bailey told her. "We tried to knock."

Susan waved their concerns away. "You just startled me."

"Whatever you're working on seems to be frustrating you," Evie said. "Although I applaud your creative cuss words. Can we give you a hand?"

"I've got a little experience with irritating computers," Bailey told her.

"Do you know anything about newsletters?"

"Enough to get by," Bailey said. "I send out a monthly one to my readers."

Susan pushed her chair back. "Great. Have at it. I'm trying to create an email list to send out a notice about Werner's memorial service tomorrow."

"Werner's funeral is tomorrow?" Evie asked. "I wouldn't think they'd have released the body yet."

"They haven't," Susan said, slumping back in her chair and massaging her temples. "That's why Edward's just doing a memorial service at the funeral home. No body. Personally, I think he's just pushing the service so he can get to the reading of the will."

"He seems to be chomping at the bit to move into Werner's house," Bailey said. She'd pulled a chair around to the other side of the desk and was maneuvering the mouse across the screen. She was glad to help but was also taking advantage of the chance to peruse the guest list for the service *and* add her own email to it.

"Oh, he's chomping at the bit to get *everything* of Werner's," Susan told them. "I don't know anything for sure, but I think he's going to be in for one big fat giant disappointment. I'd bet my silver soup tureen that Werner has that house mortgaged to the hilt and all Eddie's going to inherit is a heaping pile of debt."

"I'm not taking that bet," Evie said. She pulled a small pink bakery box from the bag she was carrying and set it on Susan's desk. "We brought you some churros."

Susan's face lit up as she reached for the box. "Oh, bless you. I skipped breakfast, and I'm starving." She pointed to the coffee bar area set up against the wall in her office. "Can I get either of you some coffee? The pot's fresh. I just made it thirty minutes ago."

"Sure, that would be nice," Evie said, already crossing the room. "But let me get it. You sit. Sounds like you've had a rough day."

Bailey took the cup Evie brought her and spent another ten minutes at the computer before declaring it was all set up.

"I can't believe it," Susan told her, wiping churro sugar from the corner of her mouth. "You have no idea how much aggravation this has saved me."

"We're glad we could help," Bailey said. "And I'm happy you like the churros. We just hope *you're* still happy we're here after we give you the other thing we brought." She nodded to Evie, who pulled the manila folder from her bag and set it on Susan's desk. "We'll talk about this now, then we'll never speak of it again. Okay?"

"Okayyy," Susan said, hesitating as she reached for the folder. "Do I want to know what's inside this?"

"You already know," Evie said. "And your secret is safe with us."

"Without going into too much detail," Bailey said. "We found Werner's stash of incriminating files that he was using to . . . shall we say . . . *coerce* people into offering him money."

Susan sucked in a quick breath of air, then grabbed the file and held it to her chest. "And this is mine?"

Bailey and Evie nodded.

"Did you look at it?"

Bailey kept her tone even, not wanting Susan to feel threatened by them. "Yes, but we already knew what was in it too."

"How?"

"You sort of told us the night we brought you home. When we were talking about your husband and your house and you selling your soul to the devil to keep it. We've seen the county's records, the real ones, with the embezzlement, and it wasn't hard to put together the dates and the amounts of that first withdrawal after what you'd told us."

Tears filled Susan's eyes. "It was only the one time, I swear. And I wouldn't have done it if I wasn't desperate."

"We believe you," Evie told her.

"I still don't know how Werner found out, but once he had, he *made* me tell him how I'd done it. I've got too much wrapped up in this job to lose it. After twenty-five years with the county, I get free health care *for life*. You have no idea how important that is to a single woman on her own."

Oh, she got it, all right. "I'm a single mom, so I totally understand. And we're not here to throw you under the bus. We talked about it, and we don't want you to have to suffer because your boss was a dipstick. That's why we took your folder and are giving it to you."

She let out a shuddering breath and clutched the folder tighter. "Thank you. I owe you."

"No, you don't," Evie said. "We're just women looking out for each other."

"That's right," Bailey said. "No strings. But if you *do* happen to think of anything that might help my grandmother, or help us to figure out who killed Werner, we'd still appreciate you passing it on."

"Sure. Yes. Of course." Susan closed her eyes and inhaled a deep breath. "I can't believe this is really over."

Bailey and Evie stood to leave. "You take care now," Bailey said as Evie cleaned up their empty cups. "And no more fighting with your computer." She turned to go but stopped at the sudden pensive look on Susan's face. "What? Did you think of something?"

The receptionist shrugged. "I don't know. Maybe. When you just said fighting, it reminded about a man who was here in

Werner's office a few weeks before he was killed. They were fighting." She tapped her finger against her lips. "I've been so focused on replaying the days right *before* the murder, trying to think if I heard or saw anything, that I totally forgot about this man."

"Who was he?" Bailey asked.

Susan shook her head. "I don't know. I didn't recognize him."

"Why were they fighting?" Bailey asked.

Susan stared down at the carpet. "Let me think. I'm not sure what they were fighting about, but they were definitely angry. He was already in Werner's office when I came back from lunch, and I could hear them shouting at each other. I think it was about a woman."

"Why do you think that?"

"I don't know. A feeling? Or maybe something they said?" She knocked her knuckles against her forehead. "Dang menopause brain. I swear, I can't remember anything anymore. When I stop thinking about it, I know it will come to me."

"Maybe one of Werner's lady friends was married, and it was a jealous husband coming in to threaten to kick the mayor's butt," Evie offered.

"I like that theory," Bailey said. "That would give us one more suspect, at least. Can you remember what he looked like?"

"No, I'm sorry. I remember he was tall and had on a blue shirt and jeans. And he was older, like closer to Werner's age."

"That would fall in line with my theory," Evie said. "The mayor liked to prey on older women."

"But not usually ones who were married," Susan said.

"Maybe he didn't know she was married," Bailey offered.

Susan shrugged. "I don't know. I'm sorry. That's all I remember."

"That was a lot. Thank you." Bailey scribbled her number on a Post-it note on the desk. "We appreciate it. Really. And if you think of any other details about this man, or anything else, please give me a call."

"Thanks again, Susan," Evie said, giving her a wave. "Hang in there. And we'll see you at the bakery soon."

"And at the memorial service tomorrow," Bailey muttered quietly to Evie as they made their way to the elevator.

"Really? I wouldn't think our names would have made it onto the invite list."

"They weren't," Bailey said, offering her friend a conspiratorial wink. "But they are now."

* * *

The stop at Helen's house lasted less than ten minutes. This time there was no offer of drinks or delicious soft cheese. A different woman, younger, with blond hair instead of dark, answered the door today, but she also wore the traditional black and white maid outfit like the one before.

"What is it with the rich olds in this town and their housekeeping getups?" Evie whispered as the maid led them into the foyer. "I half expect Lurch to come out of the kitchen wearing his bowtie and carrying a silver tray."

"Sorry, gals, no time to chat today," Helen said as she swept in from the hallway in an off-white Chanel business suit and nude kitten heels. She wore a black shell underneath and a strand of neat white pearls around her neck. Her tone was more formal, her posture stiff and imposing, nothing like the chatty lonely widow they'd met a few days before who seemed to only want to visit and stuff them with expensive crackers and fancy cheese.

"That's okay. We can't stay anyway," Bailey told her, holding out the folder with her name printed on its side. "We just wanted to bring you this."

"It's the incriminating evidence Werner had against you," Evie explained. "We found a whole cabinet full of files at his house. It looked like he had something on half the town. We took yours before the police got there."

"Did you?" Helen marveled at the folder as she took it from Bailey. Her eyes were bright, almost calculating, as her mouth curved into a grin. "I knew you would do it. That was almost too easy," she muttered, more to herself than to them.

"Pardon me?" Bailey asked. "You knew we would do what?"

"Why, get the evidence on me, of course," Helen said. "You just needed a firm hand to steer you in the right direction."

"Steer us?" Evie asked.

But Helen's attention was on the contents of the folder as she quickly flipped through the pictures and photocopied pages, then snapped the file shut. "I assume you looked at this."

Bailey nodded. "But your secrets are safe with us." By us, she meant her, Evie, and the rest of the members of The Hive, but she didn't think now was the right moment to mention that to Helen. "We aren't planning to tell anyone what we saw."

"It's really not *that* bad, though," Evie said.

"No, I'm sure it wouldn't seem that way to you. But it would have been life-altering to my family if my father had found out. He and Charles had been best friends since they were boys; they were like brothers. It was a stupid act of rebellion on my part, but it would have destroyed my father." Helen's voice turned wistful. "My mother's been gone ten years now, but I just recently lost my father. Thankfully, he never found out."

"I'm sorry for your loss," Bailey told her.

"Thank you. So am I. I miss him every day. But after his death, I decided I was tired of Werner holding this secret over my head and extorting money from me, which is what I told him when I laid into him at that party."

"Good for you," Evie said.

"No, none of this was good. But I'm thankful for the folder. And now I've got to run," Helen said, dismissing them with her tone and a wave of her hand. "I've got an afternoon meeting. Thanks for bringing this by. I won't forget what you did for me."

They mumbled quick goodbyes as she shooed them out the front door.

"Why do I get the feeling we've just been successfully played?" Evie asked once they were back in the car.

"I don't know," Bailey answered. "But I've got the same feeling. And I think our sweet new friend Helen Dobbs is a heck of a lot craftier than we gave her credit for."

Chapter Twenty-Five

L ater that night, Bailey sat out on the front porch with Griffin, sharing one last glass of iced tea before he headed back to the motel. It was close to nine, but the sky held just the faintest bit of light still, and the scent of lavender and pine trees wafted through the warm summer night air.

"This is a really cool place," Griff said, peering out at the bee-hives and the fields beyond.

"I know," Bailey said. "I love it here."

"Then why has it taken you so long to come back?"

She shrugged. "I don't know. Lot of memories here. Maybe a few demons I haven't quite faced."

"Would one of those demons happen to own the farm up the road and wear a gold star on his chest?"

"Maybe."

"So have you talked to your grandmother yet? About moving back here?"

She shook her head and lowered her voice. Granny Bee had told them goodnight and turned in twenty minutes ago, but her grandmother had a way of hearing things, sometimes from a county away, it seemed.

"Why not?" Griff asked, lowering his voice to a whisper. "Don't you have to be out of your rental by the end of the month?"

"Don't remind me." Maybe the reason she hadn't told her grandmother that she and Daisy were about to be homeless and were hoping to come live at the farm was because she hadn't quite faced the facts of it yet herself.

They'd rented the same three-bedroom tri-level for the past five years, ever since they'd left Evie's cousin's house. It had been a perfect house for them, in a great neighborhood, with good schools and shopping nearby, with just enough lawn to keep Cooper happy but not too much for her to take care of. Unfortunately for all of them, their landlords were getting a divorce and the wife needed the house to move back into. They'd given them two months to move out.

Bailey had been on deadline for the first of those two months, and then suddenly the last two weeks had snuck up on them and they'd barely even begun to pack. They'd looked for something else in the neighborhood, but rental prices had increased so much in the past five years and with the recent issues Daisy had been experiencing in school—why were some middle school girls so cruel?—it just seemed like the right time to come home to Humble Hills.

"Having second thoughts about coming back to the nest . . . er, maybe *hive* would be more appropriate in this case," Griff said, grinning at his own joke.

"Maybe. No. Not really. I don't know. I've just worked so hard to make a life for myself and my daughter, I don't want to feel like I'm taking a step backward instead of forward."

"All kinds of steps," Griff said, in his trademark matter-of-fact voice. He was often a man of few words, but the ones he did choose to dispense were usually wise ones.

The screen door opened, and Cooper and Daisy came out onto the porch, the golden racing over to Bailey then to Griffin, nudging their legs for a head scratch, his tail wagging in a happy circle like it had been ages since he'd seen them instead of less than an hour ago.

"Hey, guys," Daisy said, her voice carrying a slight tone of reluctance. "Can you come up to my room? I think I found something."

"Yeah, sure, honey," Bailey said, pushing up from her chair.

"The thing is," she said, hesitating at the door. "It's something on my laptop, and I don't really want to tell Granny about it yet."

A nervous quiver tickled up Bailey's spine. This didn't sound good. "Okay."

"I know she's already in bed, but her wall is next to mine. And you know she can hear a fly land on the counter from two rooms away."

Bailey smiled. "Yeah, I know. Why don't you get your laptop, and we'll meet in my room?"

She'd been about Daisy's age when her grandmother had decided to convert a section of the attic into a large bedroom suite for her. Granny would have done anything to bring back her granddaughter's smile after what had happened with her mom, so she'd hired a couple of local guys to do the work, putting in a bathroom with a claw-foot tub and a huge closet with a built-in vanity and makeup mirror. One side of the room held her bed and nightstand while the other was set up with a desk and a small sofa and wingback chair. Bailey's favorite part was the corner reading nook Granny had designed, with its tall bookcases and thick-cushioned window seat that looked out over the whole farm.

It was the perfect room for a girl who loved to spend hours reading books and writing stories.

This was a great place to grow up, Bailey thought, praying it would be the same for her daughter.

"You and Evie have so much history here," Daisy said a few minutes later when they'd all assembled in the attic room. "I got to thinking about that and the fact that Werner has lived here all his life, so he probably has a lot of history here too."

"I'm sure he does," Bailey said, urging her to go on.

"So I started digging into his past, thinking maybe he'd made enemies when he was younger, like maybe his murder had been planned for a long time. But I didn't really know how to do that or who had been in this town a long time besides our family and his, so I thought I'd look up the yearbooks for their high school. Most of them are online now, and I wasn't sure if theirs would be since their school was so small, but I found them through the school's website."

"Good thinking," Griff said, smiling down at her as if she were his protégée.

Ugh. Just what Bailey needed. Her daughter romanticizing the life of the private investigator. At some point, she'd have to get Griffin to share some stories with her daughter about all the tedious research his job involved and the boring stakeouts with bad junk food and having to pee so bad it hurt but not being able to leave in case he missed a shot of the person he was following. She'd been on a few of those with him, for research for one of her books, and what had seemed exciting at first quickly became monotonous.

"I thought Granny and Werner were close to the same age, so I started with her class. Turns out he was a few years older, but I still found him in one of her yearbooks." Daisy opened her laptop and clicked the keys to bring up grainy pictures of the yearbook pages. Blocks of pictures formed rows on the page, and she pointed out the pictures of Granny and Werner. "Granny Bee was so pretty, but you can tell by the pictures of her sprinkled throughout the yearbook that she was kind of a troublemaker, even back then. There's one of her and Aunt Aster and like six other kids all trying to squish themselves into a phone booth."

"I'm surprised you know what a phone booth is," Griff said.

"Why? They have them in Harry Potter," Daisy informed him. "Anyway, I found a few pictures of Werner too. He was in the chess club and the debate team, and there was one of him with this woman at a dance." She brought each picture up on the laptop screen.

Werner had been quite a looker, his hair once dark and slicked back in thick waves. The woman in the dancing picture, a brunette with a short cap of hair and pin curls at her temples, smiled up at him from the circle of his arms. But he looked at her with pure reverence. His was the face of a man obviously in love. The caption said her name was June Kilpatrick.

"Is that his wife?" Griff asked.

Bailey shook her head. "No, his wife's name was Lydia."

"It's interesting that you ask that question, though," Daisy said, tapping at the keys again to bring up more pictures. "Because there are more pictures of her in the next year's yearbook, but they're not with *just* Werner."

She pointed to a picture of two guys with a girl in the middle of them, their arms wrapped around each other's shoulders. There was no caption, but two of them were obviously Werner and June. Bailey didn't recognize the boy on the other side. Although something about him seemed familiar. He was tall and wore horn-rimmed glasses. His dark hair was cut short, with one side slicked back with pomade. "I found a few pictures of these three. Seemed like they were total besties. But then I got to the pictures of the spring dance, and in the background of this one you can see Werner's been replaced."

The picture was of a guy dipping his partner, both laughing, but off to one side was another couple, seemingly swaying to their own music and oblivious to anyone else around them. Their gazes were locked on each other, and the depth of their adoration practically leaped off the page. The woman was June, but her new boyfriend was the other guy in the previous picture, and as smiley as she'd been in the photo with Werner, she was positively glowing in this one.

"So who is this new guy?" Griff asked.

"That's what I wanted to know," Daisy said. "I thought he looked familiar, which was totally weird, like how would I know anyone from that long ago, but then I turned the page and saw this picture."

Bailey gasped.

The new photo was of the same three—Werner, June, and the new guy—they were laughing as the two guys held up a trophy. This time there was a caption. It read: *Heck of a team! Humble Hills High debate team takes first place at State tournament thanks to top forensics partners Werner Humble and Lyle Ambrose.*

"I didn't know Lyle went to high school here," Bailey said. "Or that he knew the mayor."

Daisy grimaced. "Not just knew him, but was like best friends with him. See why I didn't want Granny to hear?"

"Yes, but I'm not sure what this all means."

"It means we need to do some more digging into this Lyle Ambrose guy," Griff said. "My laptop's in the truck. Let me go grab it, and we'll see what we can find out about him."

* * *

Two hours later, Bailey was astounded at all the information they'd found. She'd pulled out her computer too, and the three of them had been working together to uncover the history of the threesome, Werner, June, and Lyle.

With Griffin's guidance, they'd all searched different records and come up with a pretty clear picture of Lyle's life. He and June had gotten married the summer they graduated and moved to Fort Collins to attend Colorado State University. June had gone into teaching, and Lyle had majored in agriculture studies. He'd worked as a hand for a couple of farming operations before the couple had purchased a ranch of their own in nearby northern Weld County and set to raising cattle and corn. They'd never had children, but from the bits of social media and local news they'd pieced together, it seemed like the couple was happy and part of their community. Until about five years ago.

That was when June died. Griffin found her obituary in the local paper. It took some more digging, but it looked like Lyle's life fell apart after the death of his wife. His corn and beef yields had dropped considerably from years past, and he must have fallen behind in his payments, because he'd been forced to declare bankruptcy and eventually lost his ranch. It had gone to auction, and a corporation had swept in and bought it at a considerable loss.

That corporation was Modest Mountain Inc.

They may have been friends at one time, but nothing ruins a friendship quicker than falling for the same girl. And apparently

Werner Humble held a grudge. He'd waited until June died, but after that, he'd swooped in like a vulture to a carrion feast.

Werner had essentially ruined what remained of Lyle's life—taking whatever he had left of value.

They'd spent the last several hours digging into Granny Bee's new boyfriend's life, but the main thing they'd uncovered was a big fat motive for murder.

Chapter
Twenty-Six

B ailey was fidgety the next morning as she finished getting dressed for the memorial service. She hadn't slept well, her mind too busy jumping around to too many worries, the most pressing being that her grandmother might be spending "quality time" with a murderer.

Then all she could think about was how on this green earth she was going to tell her. Griffin offered to break the news, figuring he had less skin in the game, and Bailey was considering taking him up on his offer.

But first they needed to talk to Sawyer. They'd agreed the night before that they wouldn't do anything until they had brought their findings to the sheriff, and then they'd let him take the lead. This was too important for them to get it wrong.

She straightened the bodice of her dress, thankful she'd thought to throw in her favorite navy one, but already missing the comfort of her normal "writing outfit" of yoga pants and flip-flops or sneakers. Not that she'd needed much of an outfit lately. She'd barely written a word since she'd been here. She'd done some journaling, of course, jotted down a few new ideas and some plot bunnies that had come to her for the new book. And she knew she'd be adding in a wild-haired, joke-cracking coroner as a new character to the series.

But how could she focus on creating a new murder scenario when she had a *real* murder to solve?

She checked her phone again before dumping it into her purse and heading downstairs. Still no word from Sawyer. She'd texted him first thing this morning to say she needed to talk to him—that they discovered something she thought might "help the case."

Maybe she should've left that part off. He hadn't seemed too excited about her offers to help so far.

Is that why he hadn't texted her back?

"Wow, you look great, Gran," she said, stopping at the kitchen table to stare at her grandmother.

Granny Bee had on a black western dress and black leather cowboy boots. Instead of her normal braid, she wore her long hair loose, and it fell in soft waves around her shoulders.

"What? This old thing?" Granny tsked. But Bailey swore she saw a tinge of pink rise to her cheeks.

She blinked—not sure she'd ever seen her grandmother blush.

A sinking feeling filled the pit of her stomach. Was she all dressed up because Lyle was going to be at the memorial service? Surely she wouldn't put this much effort into looking nice for a man she despised as much as Werner. She'd forgotten until now that Granny had said she was going to ride into town with the farm manager. It hadn't seemed like that big of a deal the night before. But then, that was before they discovered Lyle's motive for murder.

She shivered. Why was Lyle even attending the memorial service? He had to have hated Werner as well.

234

Although, on the crime shows she watched on television, the murderer was *always* showing up to the funeral, laughing at all the oblivious people who had no idea he was actually the killer.

Stop it. This wasn't television. And they didn't know that Lyle was a murderer. Or even dangerous.

Still. This was her *grandmother*. She wasn't taking any chances with Granny's life.

"Are you sure you don't want to ride in with us?" Bailey asked.

"No, honey, I'll be fine with Lyle," Granny said. Bailey prayed that was true. "You and Daisy go on and ride with Griffin. I'll meet you there."

Susan, the mayor's secretary, had reached out to Evie the afternoon before and asked if the bakery would be able to provide the refreshments for the memorial service. There was no way Evie was turning down a paying customer who also let her attend the service and eavesdrop on the attendees. Evie had told her she'd be amazed at what people say in front of the catering staff, talking to one another as if they were invisible.

Hopefully that worked today and either Evie or Rosa would hear something useful. Something that would let her granny's new *boo* off the hook for murder.

* * *

There was a surprisingly large turnout for Werner's memorial service, what with only one day's notice. But it seemed like half the town was already at the church by the time Bailey, Daisy, and Griffin showed up. Her aunts and Dottie were seated near the back and had saved room for them in their pew.

"Quite a crowd," Aster said as Bailey slid in next to her.

"From what we know about Werner, most of them are probably here just to make sure he's really dead," Marigold whispered.

But apparently not quietly enough. A woman in the row ahead of them turned around and offered her a "shush."

"Oh . . . shush yourself," Marigold said. "The service hasn't even started."

"We've been working on compiling a list of everyone who's here," Aster told her, keeping her voice softer than her sister's. "You know, on television, the murderer often shows up at the service, so we thought we'd just create a list of possible suspects."

"I was just thinking about that this morning," Bailey said.

"We figured we'd give it to Sawyer after the reception," Marigold said. "I hope they have those little pinwheels with the pickles inside at the reception. I just love those."

"Rosa and Evie are catering the reception, so I doubt it," Bailey said.

"Oh shoot."

Aster poked her sister's side. "How can you say, 'oh shoot'? The food will be a million times better with Rosa and Evie in charge."

"True," Marigold grudgingly agreed. "I was just really hoping for some of those little pinwheels."

"Oh, for heaven's sake," Aster said. "I'll make you some when we get home. They'll take me all of five minutes."

"Would you?" Marigold said. "That would be so nice." She winked at Bailey, and she had to wonder if that had been her aunt's plan all along.

"I think your list seems like a good idea," Bailey told them. "I'm just not sure Sawyer will agree. He doesn't seem to appreciate our assistance at the moment. I texted him this morning to tell him about some new information and still haven't heard back from him."

Aster sighed. "We just want to be able to do something to help. Bee is our sister, and she's got herself into sticky situations before, but nothing like this."

Speaking of Bee, a hush fell over the room as her grandmother and Lyle walked into the room. Granny ignored the tittering and made a beeline for them. Dottie had kept the two seats on her other side open and they slipped into them.

"What new information?" Marigold asked, ignoring her sister's arrival.

Bailey's phone buzzed, just a single time, indicating it was a text message. "I'll tell you about it later," she said, as she dug her phone out of her bag, her heart already beating triple-time at the hope that it would be from Sawyer.

It wasn't.

It was from Evie, asking her how the service was going.

"Hasn't started yet," she typed back, surprised at the deep feeling of disappointment at not hearing from Sawyer sinking into her gut like a stone.

"Come find me after," Evie's next message read, followed by a heart then a magnifying glass emoji.

She shoved her phone back in her purse, not sure if Evie's emoji was to convey she'd *found* a clue or that she would be searching for one.

Griffin nudged her and nodded to the front of the room where Helen Dobbs and Alice Crawford, who must've just returned from her vacation, were vying for the seat of honor in the front row pew. Why would Helen even *want* to sit up there? Although she'd proven to be more cunning than Bailey and Evie had originally thought, so maybe she really *liked* the attention and power being with the mayor gave her. Either that, or those business contacts she made must have been important enough to keep up the ruse. And dating Werner was probably much easier for her to stomach now that he was dead.

Before either of the women could get their fanny planted in the pew, the door at the back of the church pushed open, and Bailey turned to see a woman wearing a tight black dress, a fur stole, and a large black hat walk in. Through the closing door behind her, she caught a glimpse of a fancy car sitting at the curb. She was terrible with makes and models, but it was something silver and expensive.

Another hush fell over the room as what seemed like half the congregation were craning their necks to see who the newcomer was. Wearing stiletto heels, not the most appropriate footwear for a funeral, the woman sashayed to the front of the room as if she owned the place. She looked to be in her late sixties or early seventies, although from what Bailey could see from under the big hat, her hair was still blond . . . ish.

She stopped in front of the two women arguing over the front pew and spoke in a voice loud enough for all to hear. "Excuse me, ladies, but I believe you're blocking my seat." Her voice had the slightly southern tone that somehow managed to sound polite and catty at the same time.

"I beg your pardon," Helen said.

"Why on earth would this seat belong to you?" Alice lifted her chin. "Just who do you think you are?"

The room held their collective breath as the woman paused, almost as if she were waiting to make sure she had the full attention of her captive audience before she let the truth bomb drop. "Me? Why, I'm Werner's wife."

Chapter Twenty-Seven

The sanctuary exploded into gasps and hushed whispers. Bailey turned to look at her aunts and her grandmother. Dottie had gone ashen between them. "*Wife?*" she mouthed.

As if one body, the three Briggs sisters shrugged their shoulders in unison while Dottie's mouth opened then closed again.

Griffin nudged her again, and she returned her attention to the front of the room where Alice was sputtering out something that possibly resembled words, while Helen, who had at first looked shocked, quickly recovered and now just glared at the woman.

Edward was sitting in the pew on the opposite side of the aisle, and his reaction was just as priceless. His eyes had just about popped out of his head, and he started to stand, then slumped back into the pew, shaking his head, as a furrow grew between his eyebrows. His face morphed from perplexed and bewildered to astonished, then angry, then changed into pure rage.

The ostensible Mrs. Humble sat down in the front pew's seat of honor and pulled a white handkerchief from her purse and proceeded to dramatically dab the corners of her eyes. "I'm here for you, baby," she said toward the front of the altar.

Was she speaking to his spirit or thinking he was up there somewhere or just commenting for the benefit of her rapt audience? If she really was his spouse, it would seem she would have been told that the body would not be present at the service.

Thunder clouds had been looming as Bailey and Griff had driven into town, and the air in the church was warm and muggy as a typical mountain storm rumbled its way into town. A flash of lightning lit the stained glass, followed by a loud clap of thunder as the preacher approached the altar.

"On that note . . . ," he said with a kind smile. "If you would all take your seats, I think we should get started."

Helen and Alice jostled each other for places in the next row. Helen may have even thrown an elbow in Alice's side as they shooed the current occupants, Lon Bracken, the new acting mayor, and two city council members, down the pew and squished in next to them.

Daisy was seated on the other side of Griffin, and she pulled a book from her purse, the only reason she carried one, and settled back against the pew to read. She hadn't brought a dress, but they'd found a skirt that would work for her in Granny Bee's closet, a simple black one with an elastic waist they had cinched up with a safety pin. She'd had a dark maroon top that was a somber enough color for the occasion, and Bailey had swallowed at how grown up she'd looked when she'd come downstairs that morning. But seeing her tucked against Griffin's side, her finger twisting absently around a curl of her hair as she read, reminded Bailey she still had her book-loving little girl around for a while.

The storm had started in earnest by the time the service ended, and it was either the heavy rain or the curiosity about the mysterious Mrs. Humble that had the majority of the attendees filing downstairs to the reception in the church basement.

Bailey's row followed suit and fell in line behind them. She hadn't realized she was hungry until they started down the stairs, and her stomach growled at the delicious scents wafting through the air.

She waved to Rosa, who was in the kitchen, then her gaze traveled around the room in search of her bestie. It wasn't hard to spot her. Even in black pants and a simple white shirt, Evie stood out. Her smile was as big as her personality, and people naturally gravitated to her. It also helped that she was holding a tray of grilled garlic shrimp and some kind of stuffed mushrooms.

There wasn't a cream cheese and pickle pinwheel in sight. Instead, they'd set up what looked like a fajita bar. The long tables were draped in navy blue cloths and lined with silver warming trays filled with seasoned chicken strips, carne asada, grilled peppers and onions, and warm homemade tortillas. Bowls of cheese, sour cream, and four types of salsas followed the trays. It smelled heavenly.

Bailey was surprised to see Olive Green, her red hair pulled up into a ponytail and wearing an outfit similar to Evie's, manning the buffet table. Evie's brother, Mateo, came out of the kitchen carrying a fresh bowl of tortilla chips. He said something to Olive as he set the new bowl down and grabbed the empty one, that had her laughing and a pink tinge rising to her cheeks.

Mateo had that effect on people, especially people of the female persuasion. Like his sister, he made the black pants and white button-up shirt look good, and Olive wasn't the only woman in the room to notice.

"What's the deal with Olive?" Bailey asked Evie when she finally made her way across the room to her.

"She went into the bakery yesterday and filled out an application about ten minutes after we got the call to do the memorial service. My abuela interviewed her and liked her. She told her we'd hire her for this event as a trial run, and depending on how well she does, we'll decide if we want to hire her on at the café."

"Good thinking. How's she doing?" Bailey picked up a mushroom and popped it into her mouth. Her taste buds exploded with flavor. She held back a groan as she snuck another.

"Seems to be doing well," Evie said, nodding toward the redhead. "She showed up early and helped us get everything set up and seems to be a hard worker. But we've yet to see how she handles the hordes of hungry people when there are homemade fajitas on the line."

Bailey surveyed the crowd. "I didn't think there'd be this many. I hope you have enough food."

Evie huffed. "Have you *met* my abuela? 'Not enough food' are three words that are not even in her vocabulary. But you're right. There's more people here than I thought there would be too."

Bailey had already called her that morning to tell her what they'd found out about Lyle, so she quickly filled her in on her theories about the people at the service and the arrival of the mayor's mysterious new wife.

"Where is she?" Evie asked, scanning the assembled gathering. Her eyebrows rose as she jerked her head back to Bailey. "Never mind. I think I've spotted her . . . small dress, big hat, weird animal fur around her neck."

"You got it."

"What is that thing? A ferret pelt?"

"I think it's a fox."

Evie wrinkled her nose then shivered. "Creepy." She lifted her tray and winked at Bailey. "I'm going in. I'll ply her with a stuffed mushroom, then use my charming personality to get her talking and see what kind of dirt I can find out from her."

"You got this." She pointed toward the buffet tables. "I'm starving so I'm going to grab a plate. Come find me when you're done with your interrogation."

"Will do." Evie paused before walking away. "Hey, have you heard from Sawyer yet?"

"Not yet," she answered, shaking her head then reaching into her bag to check again. But there was nothing to check. Her phone wasn't in her bag. She thought back to the last time she'd used it. "Oh shoot. I think I left my phone upstairs in the pew. You go try to ply info from the mayor's wife while I run back upstairs. I'll be right back."

"Roger that." Evie squared her shoulders as she lifted her tray and made a beeline for the new widow.

Bailey hurried up the stairs and found her phone tucked in between the velvet cushion and the wood back of the pew. She plucked it up, checking the screen as she did—*drat*, still nothing from Sawyer—and pushed it back into her purse.

Heading back toward the stairs, she paused at the sound of raised voices coming from the hallway that led to the church offices. The sound of her steps was muffled on the thick carpet as she crept closer to try to hear what the argument was about, and more importantly, *who* was having it.

It wasn't hard to recognize Edward's voice, but it took Bailey a minute to place the second man.

"You said once we got things wrapped up, you'd be able to read the will. So now we've had the service, I don't get why you're stalling," Edward was saying, his voice rising in anger. "Just what kind of game are you playing, Carl?"

That was the other voice. Carl Hathaway. One of Humble Hills' five lawyers. She remembered him coming out to the ranch and working with Granny Bee on business and estate stuff. She also remembered thinking he looked kind of like Colonel Sanders with his glasses and thick white beard and moustache.

She could see he hadn't changed much as she got close enough to peer through the crack of the open door. The lawyer's suit jacket pulled tight across his ample belly as he ran a hand through his hair, maybe not quite as thick as she remembered.

"Nobody's playing any games, Edward," Carl said, the exasperation evident in his voice. "When I said we needed to get things wrapped up, I didn't *just* mean the service. There are other things involved. For gosh sakes, son, they haven't even released the body."

Edward's face was red, and his hands were gripped into tight fists. "You're just putting off the reading, and I don't get why you can't just do it. Are you trying to keep all the money for yourself or something?"

Carl let out an exasperated laugh. "No, son. I'm not trying to keep any money, because there *isn't* any money. I know that's why you're so gosh-darned fired up to get to the reading of the will, but you're just setting yourself up for disappointment. I *can't* do the reading, but I *can* tell you that Werner left you a few things, but if you're expecting a big payout, you're in for a big letdown."

"What are you talking about? My uncle was one of the most influential and wealthiest men in this town."

Bailey could see Carl shake his head. "He may have been influential, but he hasn't been wealthy in a long time."

"You're crazy. What about that big house?"

"It's mortgaged to the hilt."

"But he wore expensive clothes and had a sweet ride. There's no way he could afford all that if he didn't have a pile of money."

"Looks can be deceiving. The car was leased, and it's my guess that a lot of those things were gifts. He had a lot of friends with money, but his own coffers were empty."

"That can't be." Some of the bluster had gone out of Edward's voice, and he sagged against the side of the desk. "I *need* that money."

"I'm sorry. Your uncle hasn't always made the best business decisions or been the wisest at financial planning. I know this isn't what you want to hear, but I figured I should let you know that part at least, since you seem to be in such a rush to get to the reading of the will."

Bailey's phone chimed out the tone for a text message, and Edward's head whipped up to meet her gaze through the wide crack in the door. She took a step back, hoping he hadn't recognized her, then hurried toward the stairs.

Stupid phone. Of course it picked the worst time in the world to ding. And she'd sworn it had been on silent. Maybe Daisy had been watching a video on it or something.

Edward burst into the reception seconds after she did. He must have run after her. She shrank back into the crowd, looking for Evie, but instead ran into the hard, muscled chest of Mateo.

"Hey Bailes, you look great in that dress," he said, grinning down at her. Then his smile fell as he took in her expression of worry. "What's wrong?"

"Edward's looking for me," she whispered, scurrying around to stand behind him. She hoped his tall body would block the other man's view.

"Why is he looking for you?" Mateo asked quietly, not turning around. He widened his stance and stuck his elbows out to hide her.

"Because he just caught me spying on him."

"Of course he did." His shoulders shook with his light chuckle. "I think you're safe now, though. It looks like he's found a new target."

Staying behind Mateo, she peeked her head around the side of his broad shoulder.

Edward was marching toward the new Mrs. Humble, fire flashing in his eyes. She was standing with Lon Bracken and one of the city council members, and by the way she was twirling her hair and jutting one hip toward Lon, it appeared she was looking to catch the new mayor as well.

"Look, lady," Edward said, his voice too high as he shook his finger in her face. "I don't know who you think you are, but if you're here to get a piece of my uncle's fortune, you can forget it."

She pressed a hand to her neck, appearing to be offended, but not coming off quite as genuine as she should have. "What do you mean? Are you doubting my relationship with your . . . *father*? *Grandfather*?" she asked, obviously guessing at the relationship.

"My *uncle*," he fumed. "It doesn't matter. I'm telling you that you're not getting any of his money."

"But I told you, I'm his wife," she sputtered.

"I don't care who that old fart was married to. I'm saying you're not getting any money because there *is no money*. The guy was flat broke."

"What are you talking about? Werner was loaded. Did you see the car he drove?"

"Not his. Leased. And I'll bet someone in this room leased it for him." He scanned the room, and his gaze caught on Alice Crawford, who was doing everything she could to avoid it. He turned back to the grieving widow. "All he left was a mountain of debt. Which you might have to pay off if you signed anything with him."

The woman's face paled, and she gripped the body of her stole. Bailey almost expected the animal's eyes to pop out, she was holding it so tightly. "Well, I mean, that is to say, we had more of a *common law* type marriage. There was never actually a ceremony."

Edward's eyes narrowed as he glared at her, and she seemed to shrink in from of him.

"Okay. Okay," she said, all the southern gentility gone from her voice. "We really just spent a long weekend in Vegas together. And it was two years ago. Maybe three." Her eyes narrowed almost as tightly as Edward's. "Which, come to think of it, that whole weekend was mostly expensed on *my* credit card. He kept saying he'd get the next meal or the next round, but he never did. That rat! Grr. I'm out of here." She made a growling sound in her throat, then swung the end of her stole across her shoulder and flounced up the stairs and out of the basement.

Edward let her go and stomped off toward the kitchen, hopefully not to yell at Rosa. Although Matteo's abuela could handle a guy like Edward without batting an eye. And if he was in the kitchen, at least he wouldn't be looking for her.

"Thanks, Mattie," Bailey told Mateo, leaning against his solid shoulder. "I owe you one."

"No problem. I *am* here to serve." He flashed her a grin that caused a small flutter in her stomach. The man had an amazing smile. "How about you let me take you out to dinner tomorrow, and we'll call it even."

"Oh shoot, I can't. I mean, I've got plans," she said, backpedaling as she wracked her brain to think of a plausible excuse. "Rain check, though." She slipped away, turning to push through the crowd of people. Why were so many of them still here? Didn't any of them have places to be?

Bailey pulled at the collar of her dress. The basement was too crowded and too stuffy. She needed a minute alone.

Ducking down the hall, she found the ladies' and stepped inside. The restroom had a small chair next to the vanity, and she dropped into it, her bones suddenly feeling too heavy to hold up. It wasn't that she didn't like Mateo. He was gorgeous, and sweet, and so funny. And did she mention gorgeous? But they'd tried that route before, back in high school, after Sawyer had left, and it hadn't worked. Mainly because she hadn't been over the tractor-stealing bad boy.

And she still wasn't sure she was over him yet.

She pulled out her phone, finally able to check who had dinged her earlier and given away her position to Edward.

Speaking of the bad boy, now apparently turned good man, she was surprised, and relieved, to see the message was from Sawyer. It was about dang time.

"Sorry for the delay," the message read, as if she were a client he was getting back to. "Heck of a day. Interested to hear what you found. I have to make an appearance at the memorial service then will head to the farm to see you."

"I'm at the memorial. Find me here," she typed, then hit send just as a loud clap of thunder shook the building and the lights flickered. *Great.* That's just what they needed, to lose power and have the minuscule amount of air conditioning in the church basement give out.

She wet a paper towel and pressed it to her cheeks then her neck. The lights flickered again, and she tossed the towel and reached for the door. The electricity went out just as she stepped into the deserted hallway.

Except it wasn't deserted. Someone else was there.

She heard his footsteps seconds before a man grabbed Bailey roughly from behind, wrapping his arm around her shoulders and pulling his forearm tightly against her throat.

His breath was hot as he whispered against her ear, "You'd better stop snooping around this town and pay attention to your own family." He paused for just a beat, then tightened his grip. "I'd hate for something bad to happen to one of them because you couldn't mind your own business."

Chapter Twenty-Eight

Bailey couldn't move, couldn't breathe. She wanted to scream, to fight, but instead, her worst nightmare came true, and she stood frozen in fear, unable to do anything to help herself.

Then he let her go and shoved her hard, pitching her forward into the darkness.

She stumbled, her feet tangling with each other, and stuck her hands out in front of her to break her fall. Too late, she remembered a stack of folding chairs that she'd swerved around on her way to the bathroom.

She heard his footsteps running away, down the hallway, seconds before she crashed into the chairs, sending them flying into the reception area. The lights came back on just as her head hit the corner of one chair.

She thought she saw Mateo running toward her as a fuzzy grayness crowded her vision. Then everything went black again.

* * *

"Bailey? Bailes? Can you hear me?"

Bailey came to, blinking her eyes and disoriented as she felt herself being cradled in a strong set of arms. "Sawyer?" she said, the word coming out in a bleary rush.

"I'm here, Bailey."

She heard his voice, but it was coming from the dark shape kneeling in front of her.

Then who . . . ?

"I've got you, *carina*." A hand pushed her bangs from her forehead and cupped her cheek. "Can you hear me?"

"Yes, I can hear you. What happened?" She tried to sit up, her mind fuzzy as she reached for the details of why she was on the floor. Her head hurt, and she raised her hand to her forehead, then pulled it back at the tender lump she found next to her eyebrow.

"Stay still," the voice said, cradling her closer to his chest. She knew that voice, knew it well enough to instinctively feel that she was safe in his arms. Her brain clicked. *Mateo.* Who else would call her *honey* in Spanish? "The power went out and you fell," he told her. "You must've tripped on these chairs in the dark."

Fell? That wasn't right.

"No. I didn't fall," she said. "I was pushed."

"Pushed?" Sawyer asked. "By who?"

She tried to shake her head but winced at the pain shooting through it. "I don't know. A man. He threatened me, then pushed me and ran off."

"Which way?" Sawyer asked, already rising to his feet.

She lifted her hand, hoping she was pointing the right direction. "Back down the hallway."

"Stay with her," Sawyer told Mateo, then took off down the hall.

"I'm not going anywhere," Mattie said, pulling her closer.

*　*　*

The Hive had been alerted that one of their bees had been hurt, and it sprang into action. Someone had righted another chair and by the time Sawyer came back, Mateo had helped Bailey into it, and Dottie had brought her a glass of water.

Daisy was holding her hand and looking worried, and Granny Bee and the aunts were buzzing around, taking turns rubbing her shoulder or touching her arm. Rosa disappeared, then arrived back seconds later with a churro on a plate. Evie was pacing behind Mateo, smacking her hand into her palm and uttering words that were not acceptable terms for use in a church basement.

Rosa pushed the plate toward her. "Here. Eat this. You need your strength and sugar will help."

Although Bailey wholly believed in the healing power of sugar, as evidenced by the many cartons of ice cream in her freezer, a churro wasn't what she needed. Right now, all she needed were answers.

"Did you find him?" she asked, grabbing for Sawyer's hand and clinging to it like a lifeline.

He squeezed her hand back then didn't let go. "Sorry. No sign of him. He could've gone out the back door or up the back stairs into the sanctuary. Or he could have cut through the store-room and come out the other side and be mingling among everyone still here at the reception." He scanned the crowded room of chatting people, most of them seemingly unaware that anything had happened. "Why are there so many blasted people here?" he asked. "I didn't think this many people even *liked* Werner."

"Oh, they didn't," Granny Bee said. "But they all like drama."

"And they *love* Rosa and Evie's cooking," Marigold pointed out. "If we'd had our normal fare of pinwheels and ham and butter sandwiches with chips, I'm sure they would've cleared out by now."

"Oh, for goodness sakes," Aster said, nudging her sister. "Would you stop going on about the dang pinwheels."

"I didn't see anything either," Griffin said from behind her. "I checked the parking lot and around the sanctuary but didn't find anything."

She tried to turn to see him, but the motion hurt her head.

"Bailey, what can you tell us about the man who shoved you?" Sawyer asked, squeezing her hand again. "Was it someone you knew?"

"No, I don't think so." She tried to concentrate on the details of the man but couldn't bring much to mind. "It was so dark. Once the lights went out, it was pitch black in the hallway. He grabbed me from behind and held his arm across my throat. I could smell starch on his sleeve and the fabric was stiff."

"That's good. What else?" Sawyer urged her on.

She closed her eyes and tried to go back to that moment, thankful Sawyer still had hold of her hand. "He had on aftershave or cologne. It smelled familiar, like I should know what it was, but I couldn't place it."

"Was he taller than you? Shorter? About the same height? And are you sure it was a man?"

She nodded. "Taller, I guess, since he had his arm around my throat. And yes, I'm sure it was a man. His body. His voice. He whispered into my ear, but I'm sure it was a man." She shivered at the memory of his hot breath on her skin.

"You're doing amazing," Sawyer said. "This is all helpful. Did you see his shoes or what clothes he was wearing?"

"No. I'm sorry. It was totally dark. And it happened so fast."

"It's okay. You're doing great," he told her again. "You said earlier that he threatened you. What did he say? Did you recognize his voice?"

"No, I didn't recognize his voice. He whispered, like he was trying to disguise it maybe. He told me to stop snooping around and then he threatened . . ." She looked from Sawyer to Daisy then back to him again. "Um . . . me. He threatened me."

Sawyer nodded, just the slightest motion as his lips pressed together in a tight line, and she knew he understood her veiled message. "Don't worry. I won't let anything happen to you . . . *or* anyone else," he assured her, squeezing her hand again.

Yeah, he got it.

"Why don't we clear out of here and get you back to the ranch," Griffin suggested.

"Good idea," Granny Bee said. "I'll find Lyle and get him to bring the car around. We'll take you back, honey. Just as soon as you're steady enough to stand."

"I'm fine," she said, pushing to her feet, then sitting right back down as a wave of dizziness overtook her.

"The only place you're going is to the hospital to get checked out," Sawyer told her.

"I agree," Granny said.

"Should we call an ambulance?" Daisy asked, her voice soft and small.

"No, honey, I'm fine. Really," Bailey said, squeezing her daughter's hand. It somehow felt right to be holding both her daughter's and Sawyer's hands at the same time.

Ohhhh no. Definitely *not* the time to be thinking about *that*.

Five minutes later, after consuming half a glass of water and the whole churro, Bailey felt strong enough to try standing again. This time she was a little more steady on her feet, but she still leaned on Sawyer as he led her up the stairs. The Hive followed behind them, as if they were in a weird sort of parade, stopping just outside the doors of the church.

Bailey had enough of her wits about her to notice the absence of the expensive silver car. It hadn't taken the "widow Humble" long to make her escape. She was probably halfway down the mountain by now.

"I'll stay here and get things cleaned up," Rosa told them. "Mattie and Evie can help me." She raised her hand to ward off their protests. "We've still got Olive downstairs manning the buffet, so between the four of us, we can make quick work of it and get this place cleared out and cleaned up in no time."

"Make that between the *five* of us," Griffin said. "I can stay and help. I hate hospitals."

"*Gracias*," Rosa said, although the knowing look she gave him said she knew he was staying more out of his *like* for her granddaughter than his *dislike* of hospitals. "We'll meet you back at the ranch in an hour."

Griffin held the door, and Rosa, Evie, Mateo, and he disappeared back into the church.

"I need to call this in," Sawyer told her, giving her arm a squeeze. "But I'll meet you at the hospital, okay?"

"Yes, I'm fine, really. The hospital is like four minutes away. I could walk there," she told him. "And I'm feeling better already, so I could just go home."

"No way. You need to get checked out. Promise me?"

The look of concern on his face had warmth spreading through her chest. "Yes, fine. I promise."

He nodded then passed her arm to Granny Bee. "I'm leaving her in your care. I'll meet you at the hospital in a few."

"We're fine," Granny told him.

Between her, Daisy, Dottie, and the aunts, she was covered for anything she could possibly need.

"Where's your purse?" Marigold asked, always the most observant one.

Bailey looked down at herself as if she might be holding it and just didn't realize it. Nope. No purse. No phone either. "Oh shoot, I must have dropped it and my phone when I got attacked." She turned back toward the door, but Granny stopped her.

"You stay here. I'll run downstairs and grab your things." She passed Bailey's arm to Marigold. She was starting to feel like a hot potato, the way she was getting passed from one person to the next. "I'll be back in a jiff."

Several people were still milling around the church yard and had gathered on the sidewalk, including Susan Dodd, the mayor's admin, who came over to their group, concern etched on her face. "Bailey, are you all right?"

"Yes, I'm fine. I just . . . fell . . . and hit my head when the lights went out."

"Oh no."

"I'll be fine," Bailey assured her. "We're heading over to the hospital to get me checked out."

"That's good. Do you need a ride? I've got my car here."

"No, thank you. You're sweet to offer, but I'm covered." She nodded to the farm manager, who had pulled up as they were speaking and gotten out of the truck. He'd had to park several spaces down, so he crossed the lawn as he walked toward them.

Susan turned then inhaled a quick intake of breath. She grabbed Bailey's arm, lowering her voice as she pointed to Lyle. "Bailey, that's the man. The one I was telling you about. The one who was in the office arguing with Werner."

Chapter
Twenty-Nine

B ailey peered down at Susan. "Are you sure?"

"I'm positive."

Hmm. Apparently, they *had* been arguing over a woman. And it seemed like that argument had started back in high school. Bailey looked up and saw that Lyle had turned away and was hurrying back in the direction of his truck.

What the heck? Why was he leaving? And why was he in such a doggone hurry? Had he just heard Susan identify him?

"We have to stop him," Susan said. "He's getting away."

Maybe she did have a concussion, or she just wasn't thinking straight, or maybe their new farm manager had something to hide. Whatever it was, Bailey knew they didn't want him to get away without talking to him first.

Her aunts had been telling her they wanted to help. Now was their chance. She pointed to Lyle. "Stop that man."

Marigold looked up at her like she'd lost her marbles. "You mean Lyle?"

She nodded, adding urgency to her voice. "Yes. Lyle. He may be involved in the murder. Grab him."

"In the *murder*?" Marigold gasped, then turned to Dottie and her sister. "Let's get him."

Bailey's idea had been that the aunts would flag the farm manager down or holler for him to stop. She was not prepared for Marigold, Aster, and Dottie to take off in a sprint across the lawn—well, as much as three women in their seventies wearing dresses, pantyhose, and swinging handbags from their arms could sprint. But there was something to be said for sensible shoes because they caught up to him just at the edge of the lawn.

And they *really* caught him. Marigold grabbed him by the arm and yanked him back just as Aster piled into him like a mini geriatric defensive linebacker.

The man went down in a heap, and Aster threw herself onto his back as Dottie made a grab for his legs. Marigold nudged in next to her sister, grabbing one of Lyle's flailing arms and pulling it up behind his back.

"Stay where you are, slimeball," Marigold growled down at him then hollered back to Bailey. "We got him."

Yes, she could see that. And so could everyone standing out on the church lawn. Most of them just stood there with their mouths open, gaping at the spectacle. But Harvey McCormack, the proprietor of Harv's House of Pizza, was the only one who ran to the older women's aid.

"Anything I can do to help?" he asked, standing over Lyle's prone body. Harvey had played football in high school and still had the muscles from it.

"Thanks, honey," Marigold told him. "But we've got him covered."

"What is going on?" Lyle called out, his voice muffled since his face was pressed into the grass.

Bailey and Daisy hurried across the lawn.

"Slow down, Mom," Daisy said, trying to steady her. "Don't hurt yourself."

"I'm fine," Bailey told her. "I'm better than Lyle," she said, holding back a laugh. She peered down at Dottie and her aunts, who were all sprawled across Lyle's back and legs. Maybe not what she'd meant when she said to grab him, but still effective. "Looks like you got him all right."

"What in the blue devil is going on out here?" Granny Bee came flying across the lawn, Bailey's purse tucked under her arm.

"That's what I'd like to know," Lyle said with another *oomph*.

"That's what I'd like to know too," Sawyer said, coming up from behind them.

"I thought you left," Bailey said.

"I did. I went to my truck to call in your assault and was pulling out to head to the hospital when I saw your aunts take Lyle down like they were the defensive line for the Denver Broncos."

"Get off him." Granny was circling Lyle, swinging Bailey's purse toward her sisters. "Why in the Sam Hill are you lying on top of him?"

"Bailey told us to get him," Marigold said, putting her arm up to avoid the swinging handbag.

Granny jerked her head toward her granddaughter. "Why?"

"She said he was the murderer," Aster said.

Bailey held up her hand. "No, I didn't. I said he might *know* something about the murder. I told you to grab him, not tackle him."

"I didn't murder anyone," Lyle said. "But you're murdering my back by sitting on my sciatic nerve."

Sawyer held out his hand to Aster. "You all can let him up now. I've got it from here." Aster took his hand, and he pulled her gently to her feet, then helped Dottie up as well.

"You sure?" Marigold asked, still holding Lyle's arm. "I've got a pretty good hold on him. I learned this move in self-defense class. Pretty excited that I got a chance to try it out on a real perp."

"Yes, I'm sure. You can let him go. And no one's saying Lyle is a *perp*," Sawyer said, mainly to the few people standing behind them. "You all can go on home now. Nothing to see here."

"I'm here if you need me, Sheriff," Harvey told Sawyer, as the rest of the townsfolk headed toward their cars.

"Thanks, Harv, but we're good. I've got it from here."

Harvey waved as he got into his truck and took off, leaving just Sawyer, Lyle, and the women behind.

Granny had dropped to her knees and was fretting over Lyle, helping him to sit up as she glared at her sisters.

Sawyer turned to Bailey. "Why do you think Lyle has something to do with the murder?"

"Because Werner ruined his life. He stole his farm and bankrupted him. They knew each other in high school and were in love with the same woman, but Lyle was the one who married her. I'm sure Lyle came here looking for revenge."

"Werner didn't ruin my life," Lyle said, sighing as he brushed his hair back from his forehead and replaced his hat that had fallen off in the scuffle. "Losing my wife ruined my life."

"But then Werner took everything from you. We saw the county records," Bailey said. "His corporation is the one that bought your farm for far less than it was worth."

Sawyer raised an eyebrow in her direction. "Wow. Looks like somebody still fancies themselves a detective. Even though you told me you were going to *stop* digging into my case. Did you google all this?"

"No, it wasn't that easy. It took a lot of digging. And I never said I was going to stop. I said I was going to share what I found out with you. And I tried. I called and texted you to tell you what we'd, I mean what *I'd* found." Sawyer already wasn't looking too happy, no need to get Daisy and Griffin in trouble with him too.

"This is the new information you wanted to tell me about?" Sawyer asked.

She nodded.

"Well, you're too late. I already knew all of this."

"You did? How?"

"Because Lyle came to my office the day after Werner was killed and told me everything."

Lyle nodded. "I wanted him to have the information so he didn't waste the time and energy of his department digging into me."

"That's convenient," Dottie said, still looking skeptical. Her blouse had come untucked from her skirt, and she had a grass stain on her knee, but she'd held her own in the takedown.

"He also had an alibi," Sawyer said.

"My history with Werner goes back a long way," Lyle said, pushing to his feet and brushing bits of grass from his jeans. "I'm not gonna lie to you. I did come back to Humble Hills to exact some kind of revenge against him. I hated the man. I was grieving and angry and had my sights set on making him as miserable as I felt."

"Dead is pretty miserable," Marigold pointed out.

"True. But I hadn't even considered killing him. That would have been too easy, and too good for him. I wanted him to suffer like I had. But then I started working for Bee." He smiled down at Granny Bee as he put an arm around her shoulder. "And suddenly all that revenge stuff didn't seem to matter so much anymore. I enjoyed my work on the ranch, and Bee made me laugh, something I wasn't sure I'd ever be able to do again. And the longer I was here, the more I came to realize that Werner Humble's life was already pretty miserable. And my vendetta, or whatever you want to call it, against him just didn't seem to matter anymore."

"You don't seem too surprised by any of this, Bee," Aster said to her sister.

"I'm not," Granny said, still fussing over Lyle. "He told me all this stuff months ago."

Bailey gaped at her grandmother. "*Months ago?* Well, that would have been a good thing to share with the rest of us, don't you think?"

Granny bristled. "It was none of your business. None of anyone's business. Losing a spouse is hard, and this was Lyle's story to share. Or *not* to share, as he saw fit." She narrowed her eyes at Bailey. "And you didn't share any of this with me, either. How was I supposed to know you were going to dig into my new man's history and then have my sisters tackle him on the church lawn."

"Hey, I helped," Dottie muttered.

Bailey looked down at her feet, feeling like she had when Granny had scolded her as a child. She peered back up at Lyle. "Sorry. I didn't mean anything against you. But she's my grandmother. I was just trying to protect her. And I really didn't mean for The Hive to tackle you."

Lyle tried to hold a stern stare, but the corners of his lips tugged up. "I understand. And no real harm done. This is the most attention I've had from a group of women in a long time. I can't wait to tell the guys down at the Elks Lodge that I was wrestling on the ground with three women at once."

Granny swatted his arm. "Don't you dare tell anyone that."

Marigold huffed. "There wasn't any wrestling. We just took you down."

"In their defense, they were just trying to catch you," Bailey said. One thing still bothered her. "Why did you run when Susan pointed you out?"

Lyle looked confused. "I don't know who Susan is. I just forgot to set the parking brake so I was hurrying back to do it."

Bailey caught Sawyer trying not to laugh. He'd turned his face away and covered his mouth, but she saw the twinkle of amusement there when he caught her eye. Then he rearranged his expression and lowered his voice into his more commanding sheriff tone. "I think we've all learned a valuable lesson here today. Mainly that we all need to leave the police work to the actual police." He peered over at Marigold. "*And* that those self-defense classes they've been offering over at the community center really work."

* * *

Two hours later, Bailey pushed away from Granny Bee's table with a yawn. She'd been checked out and released from the hospital with instructions for her grandmother to keep an eye out for signs of a concussion. But other than a few bumps and bruises, including the lovely purple one that had blossomed over her eyebrow, she was no worse for wear.

Her body ached, though, and mentally she felt drained. "I'm going to go upstairs and lie down for a bit," she told her grandmother and aunts.

Everyone else had left by then. It had been a busy day. After leaving the hospital, they'd all met back at the ranch, and they'd filled Rosa, Mateo, Evie, and Griffin in on all the excitement they'd missed while cleaning up. Granny had served a honey vanilla pound cake she'd put together that morning, and they'd gone through three pots of tea before calling it a day.

"A nap sounds wonderful," Aster said. "Come on, sister, let's go home and take one of those ourselves." She gave Bailey a hug. "You take care of yourself. Get some rest. We'll be by in the morning."

"Call us if you need us, though," Marigold said, giving Bailey a hug too. She turned to her sister. "You too. Do you want us to bring something out for supper?"

Granny Bee shook her head. "No, we're fine. I've got some of that leftover chili I made the other night and plenty of sandwich fixin's. We'll make do. You two go home and enjoy a night in. Put your feet up. You've had a busy day too. What with all that police backup you gave and all."

The sisters laughed. Bailey loved the sound of their warm laughter. She hadn't realized how much she'd missed it. That and the comforting feeling of family, of being with people who've known you and loved you forever. She wanted that for her daughter.

It was time to come home. She'd talk to Granny tonight.

Right after her nap.

* * *

Bailey came downstairs a few hours later to find Granny Bee sacked out on the couch. Her short nap had turned into an hour, then she'd soaked in the tub for a bit to ease her sore muscles. Dressed in yoga pants, sneakers, and a comfortable T-shirt, she felt more like herself.

She tiptoed into the kitchen and poured a glass of iced tea, noting the absence of her daughter and the golden retriever under her feet.

"How was your nap?" Granny asked, rubbing her cheeks as she came into the kitchen.

"Good. How was yours?"

"Oh, I didn't sleep. I just closed my eyes for a minute."

"Uh huh. That's why I heard you snoring."

Granny chuckled. "A lady does *not* snore. Those were just gentle murmurs of breath."

"Right," Bailey said, laughing with her.

"You hungry for dinner?" Granny asked, glancing up at the clock. "I can't believe it's already past five."

"Sure. If you are. Where's Daisy?"

Granny looked around the room as if she might be under a chair cushion. "Oh, I don't know. She spends so much time reading, I just assumed she was tucked into a chair somewhere with a book. She was going to ride that old bike of yours up to the gas station to get an ice cream, but I'm sure she's back by now. She must be in her room or maybe out in the barn with Lyle."

A knock sounded on the front screen door, then Lyle walked into the kitchen carrying a small basket. "Brought you a few eggs," he said, putting the basket on the counter.

"Thanks, honey," Granny said, beaming up at him. "Hey, have you seen Daisy? We thought she might be in the barn with you."

He shook his head. "No. Last I saw her, she was heading to the gas station. Asked me if I wanted anything. She said she was taking her mom's old bike and the dog." He frowned as he checked his watch. "But that had to have been a couple of hours ago. They should have been back long before now."

Chapter Thirty

The first tendrils of panic slithered through Bailey's chest. "Did you say a couple of *hours* ago?"

The ride to the gas station should have taken five minutes. She could walk there in less than ten. Even if Daisy milled around and looked at magazines or ate her ice cream there, it wouldn't take more than *one* hour.

"All right, don't panic now," Lyle said, as if he could pick up on the fear already flying through her. "I'm sure she's fine. She's a smart girl."

"I know she is," Bailey said. "It's not that. There's something I didn't tell you. About what happened today. With that man." She fought to keep her breathing normal, already feeling the tingling in her cheeks that told her she was starting to hyperventilate.

With everything that had happened in the last several days—discovering a dead body, breaking into a crime scene, being assaulted—she had been able to keep her anxiety, and her breathing, in check. But not this time. Not when it came to her daughter.

Granny must have recognized the signs, the clenching and unclenching of her fists as her fingers pulled into themselves, the way she rubbed her face to fight the numbness. Hyperventilating was her body's way of showing anxiety, had been since she was a teenager, and her grandmother was already grabbing a paper lunch sack from the drawer and shaking it open. "Here ya go, honey," she said, passing the bag to Bailey. "Just breathe."

Bailey shook her head. "We have to find Daisy."

Her grandmother pushed the bag up to her mouth. "We will. But I need you to breathe first." She rubbed a comforting hand on her back.

This was ridiculous. Why did her body fail her when she needed it the most? She needed to be running to her car and driving around town, not leaning on the counter, drawing long breaths in and out through a freakin' paper bag.

"Knock, knock," a male voice said from the front door before Sawyer walked in. "Sorry I'm late. I just wanted to check on Bailey." He came around the corner and his eyes widened for just a second, then he went into action, grabbing a stool and pulling it up behind her. "Hey now, take it easy. Have a seat. Sounds like you're doing good, nice long slow breaths."

He'd been here before with her, knew the signs, knew her.

The first time it had happened, he'd freaked out, worried she was going to pass out if she breathed in the paper bag for too long. But after that time, he'd studied up on what to do if it happened again and made sure she kept a paper bag in her backpack, and one time she'd found a new one in the spare pocket of his.

He picked up her hand and gently massaged her fingers, loosening the tendons that were tightening there. "Hey, Lyle, why don't you grab Bailey a drink of water?"

The farm manager grabbed a glass from the cupboard and filled it with water, seemingly thankful to have a task to do, and quickly passed it to Sawyer.

He held it out to her. "Take a small sip of this."

She reached to take the glass, but her hand was shaking too much to grasp it. He put his hand over hers to steady it as she drew the glass to her lips. The water was cool on her parched throat and within a few sips she could feel the numbness in her face start to subside. She hated this. But she knew she had to get herself under control before she could help her daughter.

"I'm okay," she said, taking another long breath, then slowly breathing it out. "I'm really glad you're here, though," she told Sawyer. "Daisy is missing."

"Missing?"

Bailey noted the way his hand automatically went to his service weapon.

"Hold on now. We don't know that she's *missing*," Lyle said. "But she rode her bike to the service station a few hours ago and she hasn't come home."

"But that's what I was trying to tell you before," Bailey said. "That man, the one that grabbed me this morning. He didn't threaten *me*. He basically told me to mind my own business, or he'd come after my *family*." She grabbed Sawyer's hand and crushed it in hers. "What if he's got Daisy?"

"Okay, it's okay," Sawyer said. "We're going to find her. Have you called her cell phone?"

She shook her head, fumbling to pull her phone from her pocket. Why hadn't she thought of that? Her brain must have been really muddled. She *had* to calm down. Panicking wouldn't help anything. Her hands shook as she tapped the screen and found Daisy's number in her favorites.

She listened as the phone rang four times, then went to voice mail. "No answer."

"What about one of those 'find my phone' apps? Do you have one of those parent things on her phone?"

"Yes. Oh my gosh, why didn't I think of that? I can't seem to get my brain to think straight." She scrolled to the app and tapped the screen to open it.

"Because you're her mother," Sawyer said. "Your brain's not gonna think straight when your child's involved."

The app opened to a map with a stationary red dot. Bailey poked at the screen then squinted at the map around the dot. "There she is." She held the phone out to Sawyer. "Where is that?"

It only took him a second to read the map. "It's okay. It looks like she's still at the gas station." He took her elbow. "Come on, I'll run you up there, and you can see she's all right." He nodded to Lyle and Granny Bee. "We'll be right back. I'm sure she's fine. She's probably sitting on the stoop lost in a book."

Bailey prayed he was right as she followed him to the car. But this didn't feel right. Something felt very wrong.

She fought the panic seeping back in and was thankful Sawyer had grabbed the paper bag and shoved it in his pocket as they'd left the kitchen. And even more thankful that he'd floored it and made it down the highway and to the gas station in less than three minutes.

"Hey, kid," Sawyer said to the teenage cashier as they entered the convenience store area. "You happen to see a young girl in here recently? About twelve years old?"

He pointed toward the book section, and Bailey's body sagged with relief. She raced down the aisle expecting to see her daughter turning around and rolling her eyes at her mother for getting all worked up. She wouldn't believe it when she told her she'd actually hyperventilated.

A girl *was* standing by the young adult books, and she *was* probably around twelve, but she *wasn't* Daisy.

Bailey's breath caught in her throat. She swallowed at the burning there. "Hi, um, I'm sorry to bug you, but did you see another girl here?" Bailey pointed to the book the girl was holding. "She loves that series too."

The girl shook her head. "No, sorry."

"Have you been standing here long?"

She shrugged. "I don't know. Maybe ten minutes. I've read two chapters already."

"Okay, thanks. If you do see another girl, will you tell her to call her mom."

The girl rolled her eyes, reminding Bailey so much of her own daughter that it made her chest ache. "Sure."

"Thanks," she said before turning around and bumping into Sawyer's chest. "It's not her."

"I already checked the rest of the store. She's not here," he said. "Do you have a picture of her on your phone? We can ask the cashier if he's seen her."

"Yes, of course." She pulled up a picture she'd taken a few days ago. Daisy had been curled in the corner of Granny's couch reading a book and Cooper had been sprawled across her legs, staring at her with his normal devotion. She passed the phone to Sawyer.

He showed it to the clerk. "This is the girl we're looking for," he told him. "She would have come in maybe an hour or two ago. And she would have had this dog with her."

"Oh yeah," the teenage boy said, pointing at the screen. "I saw her. He was a cool dog. I told her she could bring him in, and I gave him some water while she looked around."

"Why didn't you say that before?" Bailey kept her voice calm, but she wanted to scream.

He shrugged. "You asked about a girl. Not a dog."

"Do you know when she left or which direction she went?" Sawyer prodded.

The kid shook his head. "Nah. One of those camp buses stopped, and it was full of kids, so I got real busy. I don't know where she went. Last I saw her, I think she was headed to the bathroom." He shrugged again. "Sorry, man."

"It's okay," Sawyer told him.

Sawyer's shoulder mic squawked as they headed toward the back of the store. "Hey, Sheriff, this is dispatch," Linda Johnson's voice came through the speaker. "We got a disturbance call about a barking dog. It was from old man Ferguson, um, sorry, I mean *Clem* Ferguson, and it's the second time he's called in about it."

He shook his head at Bailey. "Sorry. You remember old man Ferguson? He makes a disturbance call every other week. Someone's always disturbing something with him—music's too loud, somebody's weeds are too long, or he's got raccoons in his trash." Sawyer pressed the button and spoke into the mic. "Thanks, Linda. Let Clem know I'll deal with it later. I've got a more pressing situation right now."

Bailey heard the last part as she was already hurrying toward the back of the store. She slammed the door of the bathroom open, and it banged against the wall harder than she'd planned. She jumped at the sound of it whacking into the drywall. "Daisy? Are you in here? Are you hurt? Baby?"

But no one answered. The bathroom was empty.

She checked both stalls anyway, pushing the doors all the way open. Praying to find some kind of clue as to where her daughter had gone, she went all the way into the first one then the second. A flash of color caught her eye as she entered the second stall, and her heart jumped to her throat as she recognized Daisy's pink backpack hanging on the back of the door.

She yanked it off, already unzipping it as she pushed out of the stall. "This is her backpack," she told Sawyer, who stood in the open doorway of the bathroom.

Fumbling through the contents of the bag, she pushed aside a paperback novel, a bag of Cheetos, a Ziploc with Cooper's favorite dog treats, and a thin cotton jacket.

A harsh cry escaped her throat as her fingers touched cool glass, and she pulled Daisy's cell phone from the bottom of the bag.

The tingling in her cheeks started again, and she slid to the bathroom floor, clutching the pink backpack to her chest.

Chapter Thirty-One

"Bailey." He'd only spoken her name, but Sawyer's voice was as strong and solid as the hand on her arm pulling her up. "We're going to find her, but we need to go. And I need you clearheaded so you can think."

She drew on his strength, reaching for his hand as she followed him back into the store. Focusing on her breathing, she tried to calm down and concentrate. Daisy needed her.

Sawyer was ready this time, pulling the paper bag from his pocket and handing it to her, then grabbing a Gatorade from the case on the way back to the cashier. He twisted the top off and passed it to her. "Drink this."

She did as he said, trying to sip the sweet orange drink as she hurried along behind him.

"She's not back there," he told the kid behind the counter as he tossed a few dollars on the counter to cover the drink. "I need to take a look at your security camera footage for the store and the parking lot."

The teenager leaned closer. "There is no footage. The owner's been having kind of a tough time and stopped spending the money on the security service, so those cameras don't actually work."

Sawyer swore, not quite under his breath. He was somehow holding Bailey's hand again, and he gave it a gentle squeeze. "Don't worry."

The door to the gas station opened, and Evie and Griffin walked in. Evie was laughing at something Griff had said and her face lit up when she saw them, her gaze going first to their joined hands. "Hey guys, what are you up to?" Her expression changed as she must have caught the alarm on Bailey's face, and she hurried toward her. "Hey. Oh no. What's going on?"

The words stuck in her throat as she tried to choke them out. "Daisy's missing," was all she could manage to say.

"What can we do?" Evie asked as Griffin stepped in behind her.

"We can help," Griff said without hesitation. He looked to Sawyer, waiting for his instruction. "Whatever you need."

Sawyer turned to Bailey and Evie. "Griffin and I are going to check around outside, see if we can find bike tracks or any other clues." He didn't say any signs that she had been abducted or taken, but Bailey knew that's what he meant, and she fought the panic threatening to rise in her again. He squeezed her hand once more. "I need you and Evie to get on the phone. Call your grandmas, call your aunts, see if anyone has seen her. Don't panic. There's a chance she rode into town and is sipping tea at your aunts' house right now."

"Or she could have gone to the library to find a new book," Evie added.

Bailey shook her head. "No. I appreciate what you're trying to do, but she wouldn't take off without letting me know where she was going. She's not like that. Something's wrong. I can feel it."

"Stay calm. We're going to find her," Griffin said before turning and heading out the front door.

"Get on the phone. Tell your grandma to stay put in case she comes home. We'll be back," Sawyer said, following Griff.

Evie already had her phone in her hand and had tapped the screen. "I'll call my abuela, you call yours."

Bailey fumbled her phone from her pocket, almost dropping it, but catching it before it fell. Her hands were shaking, but it felt good to have an action, something to do.

Granny Bee picked up on the first ring. "Did you find her?"

"No. She and Cooper were here but she's gone now. She left her backpack and her phone hanging on the back of the door of the bathroom stall."

"That's weird. And not like her to forget her stuff."

"I know, Gran. I'm terrified."

"Just breathe, honey. What can we do?"

"Can you call the aunts? See if they've seen her?"

"I already did. And I called Dottie to see if she'd shown up at the library. None of them have seen or heard from her. Dottie said she'd get on the phone and start calling any place she could think of to see if they've seen her, and I've already sent my sisters out driving around town to look for her, just in case."

"Bless you. But how did you know to call them?"

"I don't know. Instinct. Grandma sense. This isn't like her. And something just feels off, so I figured it couldn't hurt to get a jump on the search."

Bailey understood what she meant. "I'm glad you did. Evie's here, and she's on the phone with Rosa." She looked up at her friend, who shook her head.

"She hasn't been in the bakery," Evie told her. "Mattie's there, and they're going to go look for her. They're going to check the park in case she decided to take Cooper over there."

"I heard her," Granny said. "Should we go look too?"

"No, Sawyer wants you to stay put in case she comes home."

"Okay. We'll be here. Text or call me if you hear anything, and I'll do the same."

"Love you, Gran."

"You too, honey."

She shoved her phone back into her pocket as Sawyer waved her and Evie outside. They hurried out to where he and Griffin were standing by his SUV.

"We found tracks, from the bike and the dog, coming into the station from the direction of the farm and leaving the station in the direction of town. Do you have any idea where she would go?"

Bailey shook her head. "No, I don't. We've only been in town less than a week. It's not like she's made a bunch of friends here or has places she would want to go." She filled them in on what they'd found out from Granny and Rosa.

"I'm glad everyone's looking, and the town's not that big," Sawyer said. "We're gonna find her. But we need a plan. We don't want to waste time having people all searching in the same spots."

"I've brought a map of the town up on my phone and divided it into quadrants," Griffin said, holding it up for Sawyer to see. "I think we could split up and each take a different area."

"I was thinking the same thing," Sawyer said. "And I'll get a couple of my deputies to start looking too and put my dispatch on alert for anything suspicious or any sightings of her or Cooper."

They spent a few minutes putting together a plan and calling everyone to assign them a section of town to search. Evie and Griffin were going to take downtown, and Sawyer and Bailey were going to check out the west side.

Every time they saw a bicycle or a young girl, Bailey's pulse jumped in her throat. She'd never prayed harder for anything in her life. All she wanted was to find her and have Daisy be okay. She kept hoping she'd just lost track of time, or heck, she'd be okay if she was hanging out with a boy, as long as she was safe.

But Bailey knew there was something more going on. Even if Daisy had forgotten her backpack and phone, she would have gone back to the store to get it by now.

She wrung her hands in her lap as she stared out the window of Sawyer's truck. The hyperventilation had passed now that she had something to do, something to focus on. And something about this man kept her calm. That and her mom instincts had finally kicked in and now she was all action—running in and out of stores and restaurants—driving from one place to the next, methodically looking for her daughter.

The town wasn't that big, and it felt like they'd driven up and down every street, more than once. They'd passed her aunts and Evie and Griff several times. How could no one have spotted her yet?

Sawyer pulled the truck over in front of the park. He banged his fist against the steering wheel. "We've got to think. Where else could she be?"

His phone rang before she could answer. Not that she had an answer anyway. She was completely out of ideas. He yanked it from his pocket and checked the screen. It was an unknown number. "Sheriff Dunn here," he answered, then held the phone away from his ear as the caller yelled through it.

The man's voice on the other end was hollering so loud, Bailey could hear him clearly and recognized old man Ferguson.

"Sheriff, this is Clem Ferguson. I called down to the station already, and I don't think they're taking me seriously. But you've got to do something. That damn dog's been yapping for over an hour now and running around the yard like his tail is on fire. I swear he's going to tear up the begonias I just put in."

Sawyer blew out a breath. "Listen, Clem, I don't have the time right now—"

"No, you listen, Sheriff. You need to *make* the time. I'm a tax-paying citizen of this town, and I've got rights. If you don't send somebody over here to shut that dang golden retriever up, I swear there's going to be hell to pay . . ."

"I understand, Clem. I do. But I've got a situation—" Sawyer started to say, then Bailey stopped him by grabbing his arm.

"Wait. Did he say golden retriever? What if it's Cooper? Where does this guy live?"

Something in Sawyer's expression clicked, and he cranked the engine. "Right next door to Werner."

Bailey's throat threatened to close as her mouth went dry, but this was the first solid lead they'd had. "Let's go."

"All right, Clem. I'm on my way," Sawyer said into the phone. "Don't do anything. I'll be there in less than five minutes."

"Now that's more like it," they heard him say before Sawyer clicked off and threw the truck in gear.

*　*　*

Werner's house looked silent and empty when they pulled up. The yellow caution tape had come loose from one side of the porch railing, and it fluttered in the light breeze.

Bailey was out of the truck and running toward the house before Sawyer even had a chance to park.

"Bailey." His voice, low and commanding, stopped her in her tracks. She looked back at him and was surprised to see his hand on his holster. "You need to hold up. If someone's inside, we don't want to spook them."

She dropped to a crouch next to the half-dead lilac bush that looked like it hadn't been watered in weeks. Sawyer was right. They had to be smart about this. If someone was holding Daisy in the house, they needed to stop and make a plan, not go charging in and getting someone hurt.

Before they could talk anything out, they heard a loud woof and Cooper came charging around the side of the house, racing toward her and practically climbing into her lap. She almost wept at the sight of him. "You're a good boy," she told him, burying her face in his furry neck. "Where's Daisy?"

He gave another woof then took off around the side of the house. She and Sawyer stayed low as they ran after him. Coming around the back corner, Bailey spotted her old bicycle half-buried in a bush. She pointed it out to Sawyer. "There's the bike."

But he'd already spotted it and was moving along the house, checking locks and cautiously peering inside. "She's here," he said, dropping to the ground next to one of the basement windows.

Bailey ran to him, almost tripping over the dog as she crouched down next to him. The window was open about an inch and at the top of the basement wall. Inside was a storeroom of sorts, filled with trunks and boxes and holiday decorations. Her gaze raced over the contents, desperately searching for any sign of her daughter, but all she saw were boxes and old furniture.

"There." Sawyer pointed to a spot next to the far wall where some storage tubs were stacked up next to an old dresser. Daisy was sitting on the floor behind them, her knees pulled up to her chest, her arms wrapped around them.

"I see her." Bailey wanted to break the window, to climb in to get her, but Sawyer held her arm. He tapped gently on the window, but it must have been loud enough for Daisy to hear.

She lifted her head, and Bailey saw her shoulders sag in relief. She ran across the storage room and climbed up on something—Bailey couldn't see what—to reach the window. She pushed her fingers through as she pressed her forehead to the glass. "Mom. I'm so glad you're here. I've been stuck down here forever."

Bailey took her fingers, squeezing them and never wanting to let go. Another frisson of fear tore through her as she realized Daisey's hand was crusted with dried blood. "You're bleeding. Are you okay? Where are you hurt?" She had a million questions but mostly she wanted to get her daughter out of that basement.

Cooper lay on the ground next to her, pushing his head as close to the crack in the window as possible and trying to lick Daisy's hand.

"I'm okay. I scraped my leg, but it's fine now." She'd already been talking softly, now her voice dipped even lower and fat tears filled her eyes. "I'm so sorry, Mom. You must have been so scared. I messed everything up, *and* I lost my phone."

"Don't worry about that now," Bailey told her, wishing she could pull her into her lap.

"Did someone lock you in there?" Sawyer asked.

"No, I climbed in, then the window shut behind me. And I couldn't get out. I was calling for help, but no one was around. Then I just heard someone walking around in the house again, and I freaked out thinking it might be the killer. I didn't know what to do, so I just hid." She wiped at her cheek with the back of her arm, catching the one tear that had escaped. "Unless that was you."

"No, we haven't been inside."

Daisy's eyes widened, and she pointed at the ceiling as she whispered. "Well, someone's up there right now."

Chapter
Thirty-Two

Bailey pushed up from the ground, ready to charge in and protect her baby from whoever was inside.

"Stay hidden," Sawyer told Daisy. "We're coming around to get you. We'll tell you when it's safe to come out."

Bailey instructed Cooper to stay, then keeping low, they reversed the way they'd come, running along the edge of the house then tiptoeing up the porch steps.

"Stay behind me," Sawyer said, pulling his gun from the holster as he carefully approached the door. It stood open an inch, and he carefully pushed it wider before tentatively stepping inside.

Bailey followed closely on his heels. There were noises coming from the kitchen, what sounded like drawers being yanked open then slammed shut, as if someone was searching for something.

They eased around the wall and peered into the kitchen. "Hold it right there," Sawyer said, his tone even and controlled.

Olive Green looked up at them, panic in her eyes. But not from seeing them or from Sawyer's charge.

She seemed frenzied as she yanked at another drawer then rifled through the contents inside. "You've got to help me! There's someone in the basement. I heard them calling for help. I think it's a child."

"It is," Bailey said, stepping into the kitchen. "It's my child."

"Oh no. Is she hurt? How did she get down there? She must be so scared." She pointed to a door in the hallway. "The door is locked, but I know there's a spare key to it around here somewhere. I've only been down there once, to bring up some boxes for the mayor, but I'm sure the key was in one of these drawers." She pulled open a small one next to the refrigerator. "Yes! Here it is." She grabbed a lone key hanging from a ring and passed it to Sawyer. "Can you do it? My hands are shaking too much. Hurry! I heard her calling for help. She sounded scared."

Sawyer stared at her for a moment, as if assessing her sincerity, then holstered his weapon and took the key. He fit it into the lock and turned the knob, then cautiously pushed the door open. "Daisy?" he called down. "It's okay. You can come up now."

The sound of sneakers came clambering up the stairs, and Daisy burst into the kitchen and ran into Bailey's open arms. "I'm so sorry, Mom."

"I was so scared. If anything would have happened to you, I don't know what I would have done." Bailey held her tightly against her chest, and she wasn't sure if one of them was shaking or both.

"I know. I'm sorry. I was so stupid."

"It's okay. I'm just glad you're safe." Bailey brushed her hair back from her forehead and peered down at her. "Now that you *are* safe, do you want to tell me what the heck you were doing crawling into the basement of a crime scene?"

A loud noise smacked the front screen door, and Bailey jumped. Then she heard the familiar whine and the sound of nails scratching as Cooper begged to come in. She peered around the wall in time to see him jump up on the door, hitting it hard enough that it bounced open, just enough for him to get his nose through, then he wiggled the rest of the way in and raced down the hall toward them. His furry butt wiggled with excitement as he tried to lick Bailey and Daisy and squeeze between them.

She looked at Sawyer. "Sorry. I'm sure he's thirsty. Can't we just get him some water, then we'll put him right back out?"

Olive was already opening one of the cabinets and pulling out a disposable bowl. She filled it with water and set it on the floor. Cooper ran over to drink it in big sloppy laps, then ran back to lie at Daisy's feet.

Not letting go of her daughter, Bailey pulled out her phone and called her grandmother. "We found her. She's fine. She was stuck in Werner's basement."

"Oh, thank God," Granny said, letting out a huge breath. "Is she okay? What do you mean *stuck*? Did someone put her down there?"

"No. Apparently, she crawled in herself. I don't know any of the details. We just got her out, but she's okay. Will you let everyone know?"

"Of course. Give her a hug for me."

"I will. We'll be home soon, and we'll tell you everything." She hung up and pushed the phone back into her pocket before peering down at her daughter. "Okay, I'm listening. Why were you in that basement?"

Daisy pointed to Olive. "I was following her."

Olive jerked her head back. "Me?"

The girl nodded. "I was in the bathroom at the gas station when you came in. I heard you on the phone."

"Oh." Olive lowered her eyes, and her shoulders caved inward.

Daisy looked back at her mom and Sawyer. "She was talking to someone, and she sounded scared. Whoever it was wanted her to come over here and steal something. She didn't want to do it. She kept telling them it was a bad idea, and they should just wait. I was in the stall when she came in so I stayed hidden, but I could see her crying through the space between the door and the side. When I heard her say she'd do it now before she lost her nerve, I knew I had to follow her. She banged out of the bathroom so fast I was afraid I'd lose her, so I just opened the door and ran after her. I didn't realize I'd left my backpack, and my phone, until I had ridden halfway into town." She pressed her hands together and peered up at Bailey. "I'm so sorry. I'll pay for a new one. I'll get a job. Or work for you for free for a year."

"You may be doing that anyway as punishment for doing such a dumb thing by following after Olive, but you don't have to buy a new phone. I found yours in your backpack at the gas station."

Daisy's shoulders dropped. "Oh, thank goodness."

"I still don't get how you ended up in the basement," Sawyer said.

"I heard Olive say she was coming to the mayor's house, and I knew he lived by the aunts, so I knew where to go. But there was no way I could catch her on my bike, so I just pedaled as fast as I could, then I cut across the park and ditched my bike in the back yard. I hid in the bushes, but I could see her through the kitchen windows when she came down the back stairs. She had a bright green box in her hands, and she kept putting it down on the kitchen counter then picking it back up again. I figured that's what she was supposed to steal."

They all looked toward Olive, who nodded to the green leather-bound box sitting on the kitchen counter.

"Then someone called her again, and I saw that the basement window in the back was propped open, so I thought I could crawl in there and try to listen to her conversation then sneak back out when she left," Daisy continued. "But the window slammed down behind me, and I couldn't get it back open. I heard her walking down the hall and out the door, so I thought I'd just sneak out through the house, but the basement door was locked. I didn't realize I was totally stuck in there until after she'd left."

"That's quite a story," Sawyer said. "And we'll get to all the ways that was a reckless and foolish thing to do, but first I'd like to hear the rest of it." He pointed to the box. "Ms. Green, do you want to tell us your version?"

Olive let out a sigh. "First of all, I had no idea she was in the bathroom or that she followed me *or* that she was stuck in the basement. I feel terrible for that."

"That's not your fault," he told her. "But I'm more interested in what you came over to take and who wanted you to steal it."

She pointed to the green box. "I didn't steal it. I mean I did. But then I brought it back. That's when I heard someone yelling for help in the basement."

"Why'd you bring it back?" Sawyer asked.

"I just couldn't do it. It didn't feel right," she said. "I mean, don't get me wrong, the mayor was a real bastard, but I'm *not* a thief."

"Who asked you to take it?"

"My boyfriend. Edward. But he's not usually like that. He's been acting crazy all afternoon, ever since he found out that Werner wasn't leaving him any money and that the bank basically owned this house."

"I'll bet," Bailey muttered.

Olive twisted her fingers together. "I know we haven't been together very long, but he said he loved me and that he wanted to marry me. I just had to do this *one thing* for him. He said his aunt had promised him that he could have her engagement ring. I just had to sneak into the house to get it for him. He said it *wasn't* stealing because she'd already told him he could have it. I still had a key from when I worked here, and he told me where to find it. He said it was in a bright green box, but he made me promise not to look in it. He wanted it to be a surprise when he gave it to me."

"Oh, it's gonna be a surprise all right," Bailey said, already recognizing what the bright green box was. She'd come across one when she was researching an earlier book. She nodded to Sawyer. "I can almost guarantee you there's no engagement ring in that box."

"What do you mean, no ring?" Olive looked crestfallen. "Edward told me exactly what to look for, and it was right in the mayor's top dresser drawer, just like he said. I know that's the box he wanted me to take."

Sawyer crossed to the counter and picked up the box. He gingerly lifted the lid and peered inside. "Oh, I'm sure this *is* what he wanted you to take," he said, turning the box toward her. "I'm sorry to tell you, but I don't think it had anything to do with wanting to marry you. He probably just wanted to sell this for the cash."

Olive gasped at the gold Rolex watch nestled inside the box. "That frickin' jerk," she whispered, then buried her face in her hands. "What is wrong with me? I'm such a fool. Why do I always fall for the jerks? Why can't I just find *one* nice guy?"

"You're not the fool. He is," Sawyer said, pointing to the brand name printed on the cream velvet lining inside the box.

Bailey peered into the box and huffed at the obvious fake. "That isn't even a real Rolex. It says it's a Ro-*dex*."

"I never should have trusted him," Olive said. "But now I feel even worse that I fell for a jerk *and* an idiot. And a snake." Tears filled her eyes as she looked up at Sawyer. "But I didn't steal it. I brought it back. You have to believe me."

"I want to," Sawyer told her. "But this isn't the first time you've been accused of stealing from Werner. It makes it a little hard for me to trust you."

"I know. I know this looks bad. But I swear I didn't take anything before. The mayor was so tight with his money, I never even *saw* any cash lying around to take. I think one of his lady friends just accused me because she didn't want a younger woman running around his house wearing a short skirt. Like maybe I was going to try to steal the mayor away. *As if.* That guy was old and gross. How he talked so many women into dating him is beyond me." She shook her head. "Although who am I to talk? I just got duped by his nephew."

"Edward got duped too," Bailey pointed out.

"Yeah, but I don't feel a bit sorry for him. And it's kind of fitting. A phony designer watch for a guy who's got a Dolce and *Banana* shirt and wears knockoff Polo cologne. Next time I see him, I'm gonna tell him you *can* tell the difference."

Knockoff Polo cologne? Something clicked in Bailey's head. "That was it. Imitation Polo. That's what that guy was wearing earlier today—the one who grabbed me."

Chapter
Thirty-Three

"I knew it smelled *almost* familiar," Bailey said. "Like I knew it, but I couldn't quite place it. That must have been why."

Sawyer's fists clenched at his sides. "Edward Humble is the one who shoved you?"

"Shoved you?" Olive looked confused. "What do you mean? I thought you tripped on those chairs in the dark." She pointed to Bailey's eyebrow. "Did someone *do* that to you?" Her face paled. "Did *Edward* do that to you?"

Bailey nodded. "I think so. A man matching his height wearing a dress shirt and smelling like imitation Polo grabbed me from behind when the lights went out and threatened me and my family, then pushed me into the chairs."

"You didn't tell me that," Daisy said, putting an arm around her mom's waist. "No wonder you were freaking out when you couldn't find me today. I'm really sorry, Mom."

Olive sagged against the side of the kitchen counter. "He told me that someone was 'all up in his business' today, but that he took care of them and that they wouldn't be worried about what was going on with him and his uncle's business anymore. But I thought he just meant that he told someone off. I had no idea he hurt you."

"I hope you're dumping this jerk today," Daisy told her. "You can totally do better."

Olive offered her a faint smile. "Thanks. But I don't know. Apparently, I'm not the best at making smart decisions. Up until an hour ago, I thought my life was getting better. I thought I had a boyfriend and a chance at a good job, or at least a better job, one that didn't make me feel like a servant who had to show up wearing a stupid skimpy outfit." Tears filled her eyes as she peered over at Bailey. "I really tried to work hard for Evie and Miss Rosa today. Do you think there's any chance they'll still hire me?"

"I don't know," Bailey answered honestly. "But I'll be glad to talk to them if you'd like."

"Would you?" Olive swiped at her cheeks. "That would be really nice."

Bailey offered her an encouraging smile. She knew what it was like to be offered a second chance after royally screwing up. "Of course. I'm wondering if you can help us with something, though."

Olive's smile turned wary. "Like what? Do you want me to wear a wire and get Edward to admit to asking me to steal that thing?" She pointed to the box. "Or to confess that he's the one who pushed you? Because I will."

"No. But thank you. I appreciate it," Bailey told her. "I was just curious about what you said earlier. When you were talking about having to wear a skimpy outfit."

"What about it?"

"We never found any maid outfits here. Did you take yours home?" Bailey hadn't actually been the one to look for them, but Sawyer had told her that one of the deputies had, and that they couldn't find them.

Olive shuddered. "Gross. No way. He had them dry cleaned and pressed every week. But I'm not surprised you didn't find them. They're in a closet in the pantry, behind one of those weird hidden doors that are all over this house. I'll show you." She led them to the butler's pantry off the kitchen. It was the size of a large walk-in closet and lined with shelves holding dishes for entertaining and large appliances like a blender and slow cooker. She pushed her hand against a square panel above the counter and a door swung open, revealing cleaning supplies and five or six black and white maids' outfits hanging in dry cleaning bags on a rod.

"Cool," Daisy said.

"Yeah, this house is pretty amazing," Olive said. "It was the best part of working here. I liked the house way better than I liked the mayor."

"You said there are hidden doors all over?" Sawyer asked.

"Yeah, there's one in the bathroom upstairs and a couple in the bedrooms. Some of them are just secret doors that let you go from one room to the next, like this one that leads into the dining room." She put her hand against another small panel on the opposite wall and another door swung open into the dining room. "I think servants were supposed to use them or something."

Bailey looked into the room and shuddered as she remembered Werner's body sprawled out on the floor next to the table. She turned away and peered into the other closet, then used one finger on top of the plastic to sift through the maid's outfits.

"See anything weird?" Sawyer said over her shoulder.

She jumped, not realizing he was so close behind her. "Not really. Although I'm not sure exactly what I'm looking for."

"I'm not sure what you're going to find either," he said, reaching up to rifle slowly through them. He paused to look at each one before pushing it forward on the hanging rod. "They look like they've all been dry cleaned."

"Wait, not that one," Bailey said, pointing to where the plastic was stuck to the hem of one of the skirts. "That one's got something on it."

He pulled out his phone and took a photo of the dress, then leaned forward and peered through the plastic. He lifted one corner and sniffed at the fabric. He pulled his head back and cocked an eyebrow at Bailey. "It smells sweet, and a little spicy."

"Like Granny Bee's hot spiced honey?"

He nodded. "Yeah, just like that."

Bailey swallowed as her heart rate quickened. "That means the killer could've been wearing this outfit when they . . . you know . . . did the murder thing." She pulled out her phone and used the flashlight app to get a closer look. Leaning in, she pointed the light at the spot where the plastic was stuck to the skirt. "Look, Sawyer. There's hair stuck in it."

"Like a person's hair?" Daisy asked. Bailey had been so intent on the discovery, she'd almost forgotten she was there. "Can you tell what color it is?"

"If it's white, it could be Werner's," Olive added.

"It is white," Sawyer said. "But it's not Werner's. It's from a cat."

"A white cat?"

"No, not necessarily. But it's from one that has some white in their fur." Sawyer looked at Olive. "Did Werner have a cat?"

Bailey gasped. "Oh my gosh. I hope not. Otherwise, who's been feeding the poor thing this whole time?" She sniffed but didn't catch a whiff of dead cat. *Thank goodness.*

"No way," Olive told Sawyer. "He hated animals. That guy hated just about everything . . . except money . . . and himself. But he was also allergic to pet dander, so he wouldn't even let a dog or a cat in the door." She looked down at Cooper, who had followed them into the pantry and was curled on the floor next to Daisy's feet. "He's probably rolling over in his grave that this cutie is in his house. He got in a huge fight with one of his lady friends about it a few weeks ago. I heard them yelling, and she was super upset."

"About what?"

"About her wanting to bring her cat over here and him telling her no way in heck. He said if she wanted to get married, she'd have to get rid of the cat."

"That's terrible," Daisy said, bending down to give the dog a cuddle. "No way I'd give up Cooper for a boy."

"I'm gonna need to go get an evidence bag for these dresses," Sawyer told them. "So we'd better get out of here."

"Does that mean I'm free to go too?" Olive asked, following them back into the kitchen. "You're not going to arrest me?"

Sawyer shook his head. "No, I'm not. You did bring the watch back, and I'm a firm believer in second chances." He looked over at Bailey as he said the last part and a swirl of butterflies took off in her stomach.

Was he talking about *them*?

"Thanks, Sheriff," Olive said. "I'm just gonna go right now then. And let me know if you change your mind about wearing that wire. I'll totally do it." She swung around to leave and knocked a stack of mail from the side of the kitchen counter.

Envelopes, magazines, and newspapers went flying.

"Oh shoot." She bent down to collect the scattered papers, then held up a copy of the *Humble Herald*, the town's weekly newspaper. "Hey, look," she said, pointing to a color photograph under the fold. "That's *her*. That's the woman I was telling you about. The one who was fighting with the mayor about her cat."

Bailey looked down at the picture and dread filled her previously butterfly-occupied stomach. "Are you sure?"

Olive nodded. "I'm positive."

She couldn't believe it—didn't *want* to believe it.

The date on the paper was from earlier that summer, but the woman was wearing a hideous reddish orange scarf—one that she'd claimed she'd given away years ago.

Chapter Thirty-Four

"Hello?" A familiar voice came from the front of the house, and Evie and Griffin let themselves in. Evie caught sight of Daisy as they came into the kitchen, and she grabbed the girl and pulled her into a tight hug. "I'm so glad you're okay, but you scared the devil out of us."

"I know. I'm sorry." Daisy's voice was muffled as she spoke against Evie's chest.

"You're forgiven if you promise never to do anything like that again."

"I promise."

Evie nodded at her. "Okay, now that we got that out of the way, what the H-E-double hockey sticks is going on? Why were you stuck in the basement?"

Bailey gave them the abbreviated version, but still caught them up on everything they'd missed. Except for the newspaper photo—she was still processing that.

Evie glanced at the green box, then shook her head at Olive. "What an idiot. You deserve better."

"That's what I told her," Daisy said.

"My abuela was really impressed with the work you did this morning," Evie told Olive. "I think she's planning to call you tomorrow to talk about taking some shifts at the café."

Olive looked slightly stunned. "Really?"

"Yeah, really."

"Gosh, thank you. I mean it." She threw her arms around Evie and hugged her tightly before telling them all goodbye. "I'm still in for the wire idea, Sheriff," she called before scooting out the front door.

"Hey, can I ask you guys to run Daisy back to the ranch?" Bailey asked Evie and Griffin.

"Of course," Evie said. "But what are you going to do?" She threw a quick glance at Sawyer then raised an eyebrow questionably.

"Not that." Bailey shook her head and swatted at her friend. She let out a sigh. "We need to have a chat with someone. And it's not going to be fun."

Evie's brow furrowed, and Bailey held up the newspaper and pointed to the photo. Her friend's expression changed from questioning to knowing to despair. "Oh no."

"Oh yes."

"Do you want me to come with you?"

Bailey shook her head. "No, I think I'd better take Sawyer this time."

Evie nodded and squeezed her hand. "We'll keep Daisy with us. Meet us back at the ranch as soon as you can."

"We will."

Evie gave her a hug then wrapped an arm around Daisy's shoulders. "Come on, squirt. You're coming with us."

Sawyer had stayed cool, leaning casually against the counter as they watched Evie and Griffin leave with Daisy and the dog.

He regarded her now with a curious expression. "You ready to tell me what's going on?"

She swallowed. "No. But I'm going to anyway."

*　*　*

Twenty minutes later, Bailey stood on a familiar front porch. Sawyer stood off to the side and nodded for her to knock.

A million feelings raced through her as she pushed the doorbell and heard the chime go off inside. Shock, disbelief, but mainly sadness. This was not a conversation she wanted to have.

The front door opened, and Dot pressed a hand to her chest as she smiled at Bailey. "Oh, honey, you must be so relieved. Bee called me and said you'd found her. I'm so glad she's okay." She stepped forward to give Bailey a hug, then stopped as she caught sight of Sawyer.

Her expression changed from happy to wary as she furrowed her brow. "Sawyer. What are you doing here?"

"Just thought we'd stop by for a chat, Miss Dottie," he said, taking off his hat and holding it in front of him. "Mind if we come in for a bit?"

"No, of course not. I can make tea."

"That won't be necessary."

"What's this about?" Dottie asked as she ushered them into the small sitting room at the front of her house.

Leopold strolled in and wound his way between her legs, and she reached down to pick him up and clutch him to her chest.

"Why don't we sit down?" Sawyer suggested, gesturing toward the small sofa and the two armchairs set up around an antique coffee table. "We just want to visit with you a little bit. About your relationship with Werner Humble."

"Oh," Dottie said, sinking onto the sofa. The cat planted itself on her lap, regarding them both with distrust.

"We think maybe there was more to it than just a few dates," Bailey prompted. "Did Werner propose to you?"

Dottie sighed. "Werner Humble did a lot of things to me. The least of which was propose."

Bailey and Sawyer stayed silent, waiting for her to go on.

"I considered it, you know. I did," she said. "Even though I've been a spinster for my whole life, I thought maybe we could make it work. But that's when I thought he really loved me." Her breath caught, then she swallowed and composed herself again. "Werner Humble was a foul man. I just didn't realize it until it was too late."

"What happened?" Bailey asked softly.

"He wooed me. In the beginning. That man made me feel like I was so special. He was handsome and charming and a good listener. We spent so much time just talking, and I thought he was so interested in me, in my life. He asked me so many questions." She let out a dry laugh. "I realize now that he was just pumping me for information about my financial standings. Which are considerable, I might add."

She thrust her chin up. "You might not think it to look at me, but I'm quite a wealthy woman. I inherited this house from my parents, so I've never had a mortgage, and I've never been one to travel or to spend frivolously. I've always just saved everything. I'm not sure what for. Just because that's what we were taught to do. Save for a rainy day, save for retirement. Save for a wedding, maybe." She looked down at her hands clasped in her lap. "I'd always heard love was blind, but I never knew that it made you stupid too. At least that's what it did to me. Made me stupid and a fool. The first time he asked, I gave him twenty-five thousand dollars. Just like that. He asked, and I wrote him a check."

"Oh no," Bailey whispered. She wondered if that was the one Dot thought she was donating to the rescue shelter. She hadn't mentioned an amount before. She must have thought she was helping a *lot* of animals.

"No wonder he kept me around, right? Silly rich spinster, just pay her a little attention and get her to do whatever you want. I thought for the first time that someone was really seeing me. I thought he really loved me, the way he spoke to me, the gifts he gave me." Her hand fluttered to her bare neck.

Bailey couldn't help but notice the absence of any jewelry on her hand and thought how she must have longed to finally see an engagement or wedding ring there. Poor Dottie. What else had Werner made her believe?

"I look back now, and I can't believe what a fool I was. How he could talk his way out of anything—why he was taking Helen Dobbs to an important event instead of me, how his lunch date with Alice Crawford was really just a business meeting. I didn't even know about Aster until the day you came home and then all the pieces started to fall into place. I went to his house that night to confront him." She glanced over at Sawyer. "I suppose you already know that."

He nodded and pulled the folded newspaper photo from his back pocket and set it on the table in front of him.

She heaved a heavy sigh. "I woke up in the middle of the night the other night in a terror because I'd just remembered this photo and the article that went with it. It wasn't about me. It was about the library, but I was wearing that damned ugly scarf. Leopold *does* hate it. So do I, for that matter. Especially now. But it was in my office the day the reporter was there, and I had a blemish on my chin and thought the scarf might draw the eye away from it. I was still wearing it that night when I went to Werner's, and I must have left it there. That was the first night . . ." She trailed off.

Bailey didn't say anything but laid a comforting hand on her knee.

Dottie looked up, her eyes pleading with Bailey. "You have to understand, for someone like me, who'd been alone for so many years, and I hadn't been with a man in a very long time. He was the first one I trusted to . . . be intimate with . . . then to find out that he had taken a video. Of us. Of our time together. I thought I would die." She buried her face in her hands.

Bailey inhaled a sharp breath, imagining the shock and humiliation that Dottie must have felt. "What did he say? The night you confronted him about Aster and Granny."

Dottie huffed out a shaky breath. "Oh, he did his usual song and dance. He was so charming. He had a way of convincing me to do things, things I would never imagine I would do. At that point, I didn't know about the video he had of us, but he'd alluded to having incriminating evidence on other people, so I got this idea in my head to teach him a lesson, to get some evidence of my own. I just wanted to give him a taste of his own medicine." She pressed her fingers to her lips. Her hands were shaking.

"What did you do?" Bailey asked softly.

"It's humiliating."

"I saw Werner that morning, so I already know some of it." She ignored Sawyer completely as she tried to keep Dot talking, keep her focused on that night. "You can tell me, it's okay."

"I convinced him to play a game. He loved that housekeeper of his to wear one of those maid's outfits, so I put one on and brought out some chocolate-covered strawberries and these little petit fours I'd dropped off the day before. I never considered myself an actress, but that night I gave the performance of a lifetime, persuading him to undress and let me tie him up and blindfold him. He was so vain, he really believed I was into it, but I just wanted to get him into a compromising position and take some incriminating photos, so that I'd have something to hold over him.

"I was just trying to scare him. I wasn't even planning to use the honey, then he started in on the cat again—about how we'd have to get rid of Leopold if we wanted to be together and have more nights like this. I knew it was over between us, had known it all that afternoon, but I just wanted to show him that I wasn't a pushover, wasn't someone he could take advantage of.

"I had a jar of Bee's hot spiced honey in my purse. She'd given it to me to pass on to one of the gals at church who'd had a birthday, but I'd forgotten to do it. He was always going on about how allergic he was, and frankly, I thought he was exaggerating. But apparently he wasn't. I slathered a bunch on a bit of biscuit, but I just touched it to his mouth. That's all it took, just a smidgen, and only seconds for him to start to react. His lips started swelling up and sweat popped out on his forehead, but he could still talk.

"I had the EpiPen in my hand, and I was ready to stab him. I swear I was going to use it, I just wanted him to suffer a little. I know that's terrible, but I was so mad. He'd made such a fool of me. I felt like everyone in town must have been laughing at me, at the poor spinster who thought the mayor was actually in love with her."

She'd been staring into the next room as she spoke, as if lost in the memory of that night. Bailey saw tears brim in Dottie's eyes as she took her hand and squeezed it tightly.

"He was begging me to help him, pleading with me, and God help me, I was relishing the power. For once, I was the one in charge. Then he got angry and started spewing the most vile things, threatening to expose me, expose us and that dirty tape he'd recorded, if I didn't use the pen. That's when I found out he'd recorded us having . . . being . . . together. I was so shocked my hands started shaking, and I dropped the EpiPen. I was going to grab it. I had every intention of picking it up and saving him, but I somehow kicked the thing under the china hutch instead. And then he was yelling again and saying what an idiot I was, and I don't know what came over me, but the next time he opened his mouth to yell, I just pushed the rest of the biscuit into it. He tried to spit it out, but there was more honey that time, and the reaction happened faster. I watched him trying to breathe, kicking and bucking in the chair so hard he knocked it over, and I thought about everything he'd said and everything he'd done to me, and probably to others like me, and I just couldn't pick up the pen.

"All I had to do was wait one more minute and then I wouldn't have to worry at all. No one would. I fretted about what to do, then suddenly it was over, and there was nothing to decide anymore. Oh, I guess I could have called 9-1-1, but I wasn't really thinking clearly. I cleaned up everything I touched and shoved the scarf into my purse. I put the maid's outfit back in the closet. Then I spent hours going through the house, carefully searching for the tape. But I couldn't find it. I couldn't find any of the evidence he'd alluded to having. I started to worry that maybe everything he'd said had just been a big bluff. I actually felt a huge relief when you and Evie told me about Susan and Olive and the cameras. Then I knew I wasn't crazy. But I also knew I had to try again to find the tape."

Bailey gasped. "So it was you who broke into the house the night we were there?"

Dottie nodded. "I wracked my brain for where he could have hidden it, then I remembered all the secret hidden doors he'd shown me on the main level and figured he must have had some upstairs too. I couldn't believe it when I found that room, and all those files. There was information on half the town." Dottie gave her a strange look, like they shared a secret, but it was just for a second, and Bailey wasn't sure she'd even seen anything at all. "I took what was mine and was going to destroy the rest, then I heard something downstairs, voices, and knew someone else was in the house, so I grabbed what I could and ran."

Her shoulders sagged, and she closed her eyes as she leaned back against the sofa. "I'm so tired. Keeping this secret has been awful. But at least prison will have a library, so maybe I'll finally catch up on my reading."

Bailey glanced over at Sawyer, sharing a look and knowing what was going to happen next.

Dottie must have known too because she let out a long breath, then opened her eyes and sat up. She squeezed Bailey's knee. "Honey, I need you to promise me that one of you will take care of Leo. He's the only thing in my life that really matters."

"We will. Absolutely. I promise."

"And I need you to know that I never meant to implicate Bee. I wanted it to look like he ate the honey himself. I never imagined the police would look to her as a suspect. I never would have let her take the blame for me. I hope you believe that."

"I want to. But then why did you put the scarf in her barn?"

"Because I was trying to *help* her. We'd gone out to the ranch to wait for you all to come back from the police station, and that stupid thing was still in my handbag. I wasn't thinking clearly. I was still such a wreck after what I'd done, and I got it in my head to hide the scarf in the barn. I figured either I could come back for it later, or it might not be found at all, or if it was, it would just throw suspicion on Granny's new farm manager instead of her. Or me. And remember, this was *before* we knew she was involved with him. Like I said, my thoughts were all scattered, but I needed to get it out of my bag, and hiding it made the most sense at the time. And if it was found and the police started looking into Lyle, it would give me more time to figure out what to do and how to help Bee." She wrung her hands together in her lap. "I'm so sorry for all the trouble I caused."

"I know you are," Bailey said. "I appreciate you telling us what happened."

"I knew you'd figured it out as soon as I saw Sawyer standing with you on the porch. There was no point denying it. And frankly, it's a relief to get it off my chest and quit having to lie to everyone. You'll explain it to The Hive, though, won't you? Tell them I never meant to hurt anyone." She wrinkled her nose in distaste. "Except for that snake, Werner. Apparently, I did mean to hurt him."

"I'll tell them all exactly the way you told me," Bailey assured her. She knew Dot had killed a man, but her heart still went out to her.

"Thank you." Dottie picked up the cat and squeezed him to her, hugging him tightly then setting him back down and standing up. She nodded to Sawyer. "I'm ready."

He and Bailey stood.

"You know, I'm a very forgiving person, and I can put up with a lot," Dottie said, holding her hands out in front of her as if anticipating the cuffs. "So I might have tried harder to save him, if only he would have liked my cat."

Chapter
Thirty-Five

Bailey poured a healthy swig of honey-apple wine into her teacup. It was the following Friday, and the remaining members of The Hive were in Granny Bee's living room having high tea.

Leopold was curled in her lap, and she absently stroked the cat's furry belly. "Poor Leopold. I think he's depressed."

"He's going to be *fat* and depressed if you keep giving him all those treats," Granny Bee said.

"I just feel bad for him," Bailey said. "He's been uprooted from his home, and I'm sure he misses Dottie."

"She'll be home tomorrow. And with her new ankle jewelry, they'll be able to spend a *lot* of time together," Marigold pointed out.

They weren't sure if Dot would be allowed out on bond since she *had* been accused of murder, but in a surprise turn of events, several women in town had banded together and formed a protest outside the courthouse, waving signs and calling for Dottie to be allowed to be bailed out. Lon Bracken, the new mayor, got involved as well, and the judge agreed to set bail and allow Dottie to return home with an ankle bracelet until her hearing.

Small town life.

Bailey also had to wonder how many of the people involved might have been on Werner's list of blackmail victims and might have benefited from Dottie's actions.

The day after Dottie's arrest, they'd received an anonymous package in the mail containing two sealed envelopes, one addressed to Bailey and the other to Granny Bee. They assumed the other women in The Hive probably received similar packages, but they hadn't talked about it yet.

Bailey had taken hers upstairs to the attic bedroom to open it. Inside, she'd found Daisy's birth certificate, clearly stating who her father was. And another page of information that she didn't think anyone else knew about.

Anyone except Dottie, who had clearly taken the information from the folders and sent it to her friends. She'd wondered what was in Granny's envelope, and if her great-aunts were mailed their secrets as well. With those women, their skeletons could be anything.

"Speaking of spending time together," Evie said, nudging Bailey's knee and bringing her thoughts back to the present. "What's happening with you and the hunky sheriff?"

A smile tugged at the corners of Bailey's lips. "Nothing's *happening*. He just asked me to go to dinner with him tomorrow. I don't even know if it's a date. It could just be two old friends sharing a meal."

"Well, I'll be by tomorrow afternoon to help you pick out a knockout dress for your 'two-old-friends' meal," Evie told her. "Or better yet, I'll bring you one of mine to wear."

"You might have to," Bailey said, touching her eyebrow and glad the purple bruise had almost faded away. "I only brought one dress with me, and I already wore it to the memorial service."

"You should have *all* your clothes up here," Granny Bee said, eyeing her over her mug. It had an animated bee wearing a scowl on it with the words "Bee nice or buzz off" scrolled in yellow and black letters. "When are you going to move yourself and that precious great-granddaughter of mine back to this ranch? You've been gone far too long."

"How does this weekend sound?"

Her grandmother smiled. "That sounds perfect."

Yes, it did to her too.

The end . . .
. . . and just the *bee*-ginning . . .

Recipes

Granny Bee's *Honey I'm Home* Hot Spiced Honey**

From the kitchen of: Blossom Briggs AKA Granny Bee

Ingredients

1 cup honey
3 teaspoons red pepper flakes (more or less to taste)
3 teaspoons Cholula Original hot sauce

Instructions

In a small saucepan, heat honey over low to medium heat.

Once honey is warm, stir in red pepper flakes and hot sauce until combined then simmer on low for ten minutes.

Enjoy warm as a dipping sauce or drizzle for whatever you like . . . chicken, pizza crust, street tacos, fruit, barbeque, chocolate, or our favorite, drizzled over whipped ricotta cheese.

**Note: *Honey I'm Home Hot Spiced Honey* is to be used for edible purposes only . . . so please, for the love of bees, do not use this recipe for nefarious purposes . . . especially not for murder.

Whipped Ricotta Cheese Dip drizzled with Bee's *Honey I'm Home* Hot Spiced Honey

From the kitchen of: Aster Briggs

Ingredients

16 oz carton of whole milk ricotta cheese
2 tablespoons orange juice
2 tablespoons orange zest
3 tablespoons hot spiced honey
Garlic bread to dip

Instructions

In a medium bowl, mix ricotta cheese, orange juice, and zest at medium speed for 2 minutes, until smooth and creamy.

Spoon (or pipe if you want to be fancy) onto a serving plate then drizzle with hot spiced honey and a sprinkle of orange zest.

Slice warm garlic bread into thin slices then dip into the cheese—SO GOOD!

On the off-chance there is any leftover dip, store remainder in the refrigerator.

Granny Bee's Honey Banana Bread

From the kitchen of: Blossom Briggs AKA Granny Bee

Preheat oven to: 325 degrees

Ingredients

⅓ cup unsalted butter, melted

½ cup honey

1 ½ cups banana (2 large or 3 medium), mashed

2 eggs

¼ cup milk

1 tablespoon vanilla extract

¼ teaspoon butter extract

1 ¾ cups all-purpose flour

1 teaspoon baking soda

½ teaspoon salt

Instructions

In a large mixing bowl, whisk together butter and honey, then whisk in mashed banana, eggs, milk, vanilla, and butter extract until well combined.

In a separate bowl, combine flour, baking soda, and salt.

Add wet ingredients to dry then mix lightly, just until combined.

Pour batter into greased 9 x 5 loaf pan.

Bake for 50–55 minutes, or until toothpick comes out clean from the center.

Let cool in pan for 15 minutes, then transfer to wire rack for 30 minutes before slicing.

Optional: mix in chocolate chips or sprinkle crushed nuts onto batter right before baking.

Granny's Honey Poke Cake
With Honey Sauce and Marshmallow Frosting

From the kitchen of: Blossom Briggs AKA Granny Bee

Preheat oven to: 350 degrees

Ingredients

For the cake

2⅔ cups all-purpose flour
1 teaspoon baking powder
¼ teaspoon baking soda
1 teaspoon salt
3 eggs
⅔ cup canola or vegetable oil
1 tablespoon vanilla extract
¼ teaspoon butter extract
1 cup milk
1 cup sugar
½ cup packed light brown sugar
¼ cup honey

For the Honey Glaze

¼ cup brown sugar
¼ cup unsalted butter
½ cup honey

Marshmallow Frosting

1 large jar marshmallow cream
1 cup softened unsalted butter
3 cups powdered sugar
1 teaspoon vanilla extract

Instructions

Grease and flour a 9 x 13 pan and preheat oven to 350 degrees.

Using the electric mixer, combine oil, vanilla, butter extract, eggs, milk, honey, and the sugars. Mix well.

In a separate bowl, combine flour, baking soda, and salt.

Add half the dry ingredients into the sugar mixer then mix until just combined. Add the remaining mixture and mix for about 30 seconds.

Pour into greased and floured pan and bake for 20–25 minutes.

While cake is baking, prepare honey glaze by heating butter, brown sugar, and honey in a small saucepan until melted. Take off burner and let cool slightly.

Take the Honey and Run

Remove cake and let cool 12 minutes then use a wooden skewer to poke holes into the cake about 1 inch apart. Pour warm honey glaze over the cake and spread evenly. Let cake cool completely.

To make frosting, mix softened butter in a mixer then add in marshmallow cream and vanilla. Add in powdered sugar and mix until combined. Frost when cake has completely cooled.

Honey-glazed Quesitos (Cream Cheese Pastries)

From the kitchen of: Rosa Delgado

Preheat oven to: 350 Degrees

Ingredients

1 sheet Pepperidge Farms Puff Pastry, thawed according to package instructions
1 (8 ounce) brick cream cheese, softened
¼ cup sugar
1 teaspoon vanilla extract
1 egg white, beaten slightly
3 tablespoons honey for drizzling

Instructions

Preheat oven to 350 degrees. Line a baking sheet with parchment paper.

On a lightly floured surface, cut puff pastry into 9 equal pieces (should be 4 x 4-inch squares).

In a bowl, mix cream cheese, sugar, and vanilla until soft and creamy. Drop a spoonful of mixture into the center of each puff pastry then fold one corner into the center. Dab a little egg white onto the tip of the opposite corner of pastry then fold it toward the center, just barely overlapping the first corner and using the egg white to stick the dough together. It should look like the quesito is hugging itself with the pastry meeting in the center and the filling showing on the sides.

Repeat with remaining pastries then transfer to the parchment lined baking sheet and brush each pastry lightly with egg white.

Bake for 15–20 minutes, until puffed and golden.

Remove from oven and drizzle pastries with honey.

Enjoy! These are just to die for…but maybe not worth murdering for.

Granny Bee's Crispy Honey Cookies

From the kitchen of: Blossom (Bee) Briggs

Preheat oven to: 375 Degrees

Ingredients

1 cup unsalted butter, softened
1 cup sugar
¼ cup light brown sugar
⅓ cup honey
1 teaspoon vanilla extract
1 teaspoon butter extract
1 large egg
3 cups all-purpose flour
2 teaspoons cornstarch
1 teaspoon baking powder
½ teaspoon baking soda
¾ teaspoon salt
Extra sugar for rolling cookies in

Instructions

Preheat oven to 375 degrees

To electric mixer, add softened butter, sugars, honey, vanilla, and butter extract. Beat until creamy and well-combined. Then add egg and mix again.

In a separate bowl, whisk together flour, cornstarch, baking powder, baking soda, and salt.

Using low speed, gradually add dry ingredients to sugar mixture. Mix until all ingredients are completed combined.

Cover dough with plastic wrap and place in the refrigerator. Chill for 30–60 minutes, or up to 5 days.

Pour a few tablespoons of sugar into a small dish.

Using your palms, roll 1 ½ tablespoon-sized scoops of chilled dough into smooth balls then roll through the sugar. Then place cookies at least 2 inches apart on baking sheet.

Bake for 10–11 minutes or until edges of cookies turn a light golden brown.

Allow cookies to cool at least 5 minutes before moving to a cooling rack.

Then try to eat just one....

Acknowledgments

A s always, my love and thanks go out to my family—Todd, Nick, Tyler, and Paige! Todd, thanks for always believing in me, and for teaching me to love bees. It's no mystery why I love and adore you. You make me laugh every day, and the words it would take to truly thank you would fill a book on their own. I love you. *Always.*

A huge thank you goes out to my mom, Lee Cumba, for all your help with the plotting of this book and the recipes that go with it. I have so much fun talking clues and red herrings with you and plotting fun ways for my characters to get in, and out, of trouble. Thank you for instilling in me a love of mysteries and always believing in my ability to write them.

My dad, Dr. William Bryant, deserves a special thank you as well. Thanks, Dad, for all your help with the farming, ranching, and animal aspects of this book. I can always count on you to offer me guidance and advice.

I can't thank my editor, Faith Ross Black, enough for believing in me and this book, for loving Bailey and Sawyer and Granny Bee, and for making this story so much better with your amazing editing skills. I appreciate everything you do to help make the town of Humble Hills come to life . . . and death. Big thanks to the whole team at Crooked Lane Books for all your efforts and hard work in making this book happen and giving me the most adorable cover ever.

Such a huge thanks goes out to one of my writer besties, Anne Eliot, for your encouragement and support. I will never forget our Salida, mountain, pizza, writing retreat—staying up late, going to the hot springs, eating sooo much pizza (and bad food truck food). You are always willing to listen and talk through my plotting struggles and character crises, and we always have the most fun doing it. Thank you for your steadfast belief in me and for alternately holding my hand and lovingly pushing me to the finish line of this book.

This writing gig is tough, and I wouldn't be able to do it without the support and encouragement of my writing besties who walk this journey with me. Thank you to Michelle Major and Lana Williams for always listening, for all the encouragement, and for the hours and hours of writing sprints and laughter. XO

I have to thank my own dear friend, Evie Beck, for being the inspiration for Bailey's bestie. Your laughter is contagious, you are gorgeous inside and out, and I can totally imagine the two of us getting into hilarious trouble if we ever tried to solve a murder.

I also have to do a special shout-out to my neighbor, Jason Newton, for your advice and guidance with homicide and police procedure. Thanks for always being willing to talk instead of running inside when I wave and holler out, "Hey, I have a question for you."

I want to acknowledge Bear Creek Nature Center for their wonderful bee exhibit and my favorite beekeeper, my husband, Todd. Thanks for sharing your love of bees and teaching me

Acknowledgments

and so many others about all the fascinating things they do. I'm always amazed at how quickly you can always find the queen.

Huge thank you to my agent, Nicole Resciniti at The Seymour Agency, for your advice and your guidance. You are the best, and I'm so thankful you are part of my life.

Big thanks goes out to my street team, Jennie's Page Turners, and for all my readers: the people who have been with me from the start, my loyal readers, my dedicated fans, the ones who have read my stories, who have laughed and cried with me, who have fallen in love with my characters and have clamored for more! Whether you have been with me since the first book or just discovered me with this one, know that I write these stories for you, and I can't thank you enough for reading them. Sending love, laughter, and big Colorado hugs to you all!